Did he leave a no

Everyone seemed ~~_____~~ ____ was a suicide. Maybe I could do some good here after all. "You're assuming that he jumped?" I asked. "Isn't that a little premature?"

Kate's eyes widened in surprise. "No one has suggested anything else. His wife was murdered, then he found out she had been cheating on him and, if that's not enough, they were going broke."

"Well, it's obvious you don't need any help. Although I think you're wrong. I don't believe David committed suicide."

"So what happened? He got careless and toppled over the bridge railing?"

I shook my head stubbornly. "I don't know what happened, but he didn't commit suicide."

Kate's eyes narrowed. "Are you saying somebody pushed him?"

———————— ★ ————————

"If Nancy Drew grew up, got married, ditched her no-good husband, and opened a coffeehouse, she'd be Maggy Thorsen. This is a series I already want a refill on."

—S. J. Rozan, author of *Winter and Night*

Sandra Balzo

Uncommon Grounds

W❖RLDWIDE®

TORONTO • NEW YORK • LONDON
AMSTERDAM • PARIS • SYDNEY • HAMBURG
STOCKHOLM • ATHENS • TOKYO • MILAN
MADRID • WARSAW • BUDAPEST • AUCKLAND

To Bob Hoag,
who took an 18-year-old typist who couldn't type
and taught her how to write instead.

UNCOMMON GROUNDS

A Worldwide Mystery/March 2007

First published by Five Star.

ISBN-13: 978-0-373-26594-7
ISBN-10:   0-373-26594-8

Acknowledgments

Thanks to the owners, both past and present, of my own personal "Uncommon Grounds": That Coffee Place, in Brookfield, Wisconsin. Mary Michalek and Elaine Perez taught me the ropes of coffeedom (sorry about those four broken pots...) and then let me hang out there for hours on end, writing this book. Denise Behrens, who took over the Place, inherited me and *still* didn't throw me out, offering me more encouragement and coffee.

Special thanks to Ted Hertel and Gary Niebuhr, the other two-thirds of my writing group, with whom I share advice, inspiration, and copious amounts of wine as we rip each other apart on a monthly basis.

And to my husband, Tony, and my kids, Mike and Lisa, who have put up with me and my foibles for more years than I care to think about, and still seem to love me.

ONE

I WAS LATE the Monday we were scheduled to open Uncommon Grounds. Patricia would be steamed, I'd thought as I pulled open our front door. Who would have guessed?

Patricia Harper lay in a pool of milk on the floor in front of the espresso machine—face up, blue eyes staring at everything and absolutely nothing. On the floor next to her was the stainless steel frothing pitcher from whence I assumed the spilt milk had come.

I knew I should do something—I just wasn't sure what.

I touched Patricia's arm gingerly. Still warm. So what did that mean? Barely dead? Barely alive? Could you stare like that and still be alive? My other partner, Caron Egan, made a whimpering noise behind me.

Okay, okay, *do* something, Maggy. I slipped my hand under Patricia's blonde hair and repositioned her head to open up the airway. Then I turned toward Caron, who had closed her mouth but hadn't moved much of anything else. "Call 911."

No response. From either of them.

Now I was getting a little ticked. After all, Caron had been there first. She should be the one on the floor, kneeling in milk and something very much worse. The least she could do was contact the EMTs.

"Call 911," I tried again, adding "dammit" for shock effect. The dammit seemed to do it. Slowly Caron came to, like a mime playing at waking up. First, her mouth moved. Then her head waggled from side to side. Then her hands waved. Finally, her feet began to move and walked the rest of her body back into the office to the phone.

Now if only Patricia would get up and do the same.

Fat chance. I leaned down and put my ear next to her mouth to listen for breath sounds.

"Maggy?"

I jumped. The voice calling my name came from the office, though, not from the woman in front of me. Caron's hands were shaking as she came out into the store carrying the phone. "They want to know the address." She put one hand to her forehead. "I can't remember…"

I hated to admit it, but I couldn't remember the number myself right now. "Brookhills is a town of six thousand people," I told her. "They should be able to find us. Tell the county dispatcher we're on Brookhill Road."

But Caron just raised the phone high above her head and gave it one hard shake.

I wasn't sure what that meant. "Why don't you go outside and look above the door for the number," I suggested. Maybe the fresh air would do her some good.

Speaking of fresh air… I pinched Patricia's nose closed, took a deep breath and blew into her mouth three times. Then I sat back on my heels. No go. Okay, so maybe I should try chest compressions.

I thought back to the CPR classes I'd taken fifteen years ago, the year Ted and I bought our Brookhills house. With a three-year-old son, an inground pool was the last thing I'd wanted at the time. But Ted, my about-to-be ex-husband, had assured me everything would be "just fine." Then he patted my hand.

I promptly added a million-dollar umbrella to our homeowners' policy and bought the most expensive pool alarm I could find. Then I enrolled Eric in swimming classes and myself in CPR. I believe in preparing for the worst, and now—just fifteen years later—it was paying off.

Okay, so what was it again? Five chest compressions to one breath? Three to one? Or was that for two-person CPR? Through the window I could see Caron still dancing around outside with the cell phone, trying to read the numbers above the door in the dawn light. I was on my own, I guessed.

I settled for three to one, figuring more was always preferable to less, and got to work, stopping every once in a while to check for a pulse. The muscles in my arms were already starting to burn when I heard the bell on the door tinkle. Caron at last—I'd *make* her help.

But she wasn't alone. Although I couldn't see who it was from my position on the floor behind the counter, I could hear a male voice rumbling. The police, I assumed, and in record time.

"Congratulations, ladies!"

I sat back on my heels.

"I wanted to be your first customer, and I come bearing gifts. Where's Patricia?" The voice was getting nearer now, just on the other side of the counter. "Do you have a vase for these? Let me put them in water for you."

Too late, I identified the speaker: David Harper, Patricia's husband, and from the sound of it, he was rounding the corner and Caron wasn't doing a thing to stop him. I dropped Patricia's head unceremoniously and jumped to my feet to block his view. "Wait—"

He stopped, seeming to realize something was wrong.

"David." I looked at his pleasant face, at the tissue-wrapped bouquet in his hands, and then, miserable coward that I am, I fell back on cop show cliché. "David, there's been an accident. Patricia..." I let it drop there.

David was no fool. He knew his part. "Patricia? Where is she?" He pushed past me and looked down. "Oh Lord, no. How...how?" He dropped the flowers and pulled her to him, sobbing.

I wasn't sure what to do so I picked up the bouquet and took it over to the sink. I was moving carefully now, feeling like time had slowed to a crawl the moment David had arrived. The bright green of the tissue paper, and the purple and yellow of the flowers inside it, seemed intrusive, like an element of color introduced in a black-and-white film.

It was a spring bouquet—daffodils, irises and tulips—that must have come from a florist. It was only April 1st, and our bulbs were still trying to push their way through the frozen ground. Spring flowers, like the first robin, were a sign of hope in Wisconsin. But not this year. Not for David, and not for Patricia's two kids.

The bell on the door tinkled again, and time re-asserted itself. Though I hadn't heard the sirens, Gary Donovan, the Brookhills police chief, had arrived with one of his officers. They looked like they had been rousted out of bed.

Right behind Gary were two EMTs loaded down with red metal boxes. They pushed past the rest of us to get to Patricia. One of them, a sturdy, dark-haired woman, knelt down next to David and asked him to let them examine his wife. Gary pulled out his notebook and turned to me.

"What happened, Maggy?" Gary stands about six-foot-two, has a chest like a bull and a jaw like Jay Leno.

"It's Patricia Harper." I kept my voice low, not wanting

David to overhear for some reason. Like he didn't know it was his wife on the floor.

The female paramedic was shining a penlight in Patricia's open eyes. It made my own hurt just watching.

"Non-responsive," I heard her say.

Gary was waiting. No more explanation of the "who" was necessary, since everyone in Brookhills knew the Harpers. David's father had been a town founder. I turned to the what: "She's dead. I mean, I think she is. I couldn't find a pulse. I did CPR, but…"

Gary moved past me to look at the scene behind the counter. "David just arrived," I explained. "He brought flowers for our…" I gestured toward the bouquet in the sink, and my voice broke, "…grand opening."

Gary grabbed a stack of napkins from the condiment cart behind him and handed them to me. I, in turn, handed some to Caron who was quietly sniffling at a small table to my left.

The EMTs were already packing up their equipment when I turned back, and Gary left me to talk briefly with them. David was next to Patricia again, mumbling something that might have been a prayer. I watched as Gary waited for David to finish and then gently moved him away.

Gary is about the calmest, most reassuring man I know. He headed security for the events I coordinated when I was special events manager at First National Bank, a large financial organization in the city. Gary liked kids and dogs. He talked to plants. But even Gary couldn't make this right.

David's face was stark white under the freckles. "Why? Why?" Gary just shook his head helplessly.

I touched David on the sleeve of what once had been an impeccable Armani suit. "David, come over here and sit down."

I led him to another table and handed him one of my napkins. I almost offered him a cup of coffee, but that would have meant stepping over Patricia's body to reach the pot. I glanced out the window instead.

On the other side of the glass, our papergirl was straining to see in. When our eyes met, she stepped back, dropped the paper on the mat and ran like hell. I would have given anything to follow. I checked my watch—almost 6:30 a.m. Any minute now our first customers might come through that door, expecting a latte or a road cup and find…this.

I moved over to the lanky young cop who had come in with Gary. "Matt, it's almost opening time. Should we lock the door or what?"

Matt glanced at Gary, who was still at Patricia's side. "I'll go out front and keep people out. Let me know if the chief needs me."

I nodded and approached Gary and Patricia, or what used to be Patricia. I couldn't shake the feeling that I was looking at a life-sized mannequin instead. Her color seemed to be fading, the powdered blush on her cheekbones standing out as her face paled.

Willing myself to look away, I studied the counter where Patricia had been standing. She evidently had started to make herself a latte, hence the pitcher on the floor and the gallon of milk sitting on the stainless steel counter next to the sink. The heavy glass mug containing Patricia's double shot of espresso stood next to the milk.

Patricia adored her lattes. I could hear her saying it now, in that slightly Southern accent she'd retained from her childhood. "I ahhdore my *lah*-tays," she'd drawl before taking her first sip.

When Caron and I had decided that Brookhills needed its own coffee house, she had introduced me to Patricia over lattes in hopes she would be the third partner we needed to make the project viable. Patricia had agreed—also over lattes—and now here we were again. But this time it was an ending, not a beginning.

I imagined Patricia coming into the store this morning and making her "lah-tay," probably planning to drink it as she waited for us to arrive. The store would have been quiet and dimly lit by the backlights as she brewed the shots and poured them into the mug for what she called her "plain brown latte": just skim milk and espresso—no sugar, no cinnamon, no nutmeg, no flavoring, no nothing. Not even foam on top.

Pouring the milk into the pitcher, she would have begun to steam it and then…then what? Had she had a heart attack? A stroke? Patricia seemed way too young for either, but maybe I felt that way because she and I were the same age.

Forty-two *was* young, right? Not that I wasn't getting older by the minute. Unlike poor Patricia. When people die, we always look for reasons it happened to them and *won't* happen to us. He smoked and got lung cancer. She drank and drove. But Patricia? What did she do to deserve this, besides being a royal pain in the butt sometimes?

And God knows if that were justification enough, all three of us would be lying there on the floor.

I looked back down at my former partner. Then I looked again. On the palm of her left hand was a bull's-eye, but reversed. White in the center with the outer ring a fiery red. I moved in closer for a better look.

"What's that on her hand?" I asked quietly in Gary's ear.

He jumped—he's not used to me breathing in his ear, it's

not that kind of relationship—and stood up. Then he steered me toward the sink and away from Caron and David. "I think it's a burn." He kept his voice low, too.

A burn? From the milk? It was one heck of a burn to get from steamed milk, which is heated to only about a 160 degrees for lattes. I told Gary so.

"I'm no expert on burns," I went on, reaching out for the frothing wand, "but I wouldn't think that—"

Gary grabbed my arm. "Don't touch anything, Maggy. Something's wrong." He pointed to a dark spot on the otherwise spotless counter. "Was that here before?"

I leaned over to look at the fine black powder. "No, what is it?"

He shook his head. "I can't be sure, but it looks like a scorch mark."

I looked sideways at him as he continued. "I have the medical examiner on the way. We'll know more when he gets here."

I opened my mouth, but Gary kept right on going. "I'll need to talk to you and Caron, but I'd like to do that without David. You go, and I'll call you later."

"Should we drive David home?"

"No," he said firmly. "I need to get some information from him now."

"Gary, what do you think—"

"I don't know what I think yet, Maggy. When I do, I'll let you know."

Right. I tossed my last napkin, which I'd twisted into a frayed rope, in the wastebasket. Only two torn sugar packets sullied the spanking new navy blue basket that Patricia had chosen because of how nicely it tucked below the counter.

On the shelves above the basket stood five cream-colored

bud vases waiting to be filled with fresh flowers and placed on five perfectly-positioned navy tables. The cream pitcher was there, too, where we wouldn't forget to fill it and put it on the condiment cart. Which was also navy.

Cinnamon, nutmeg and cocoa shakers were in their place on the cart, next to small baskets of napkins, stir sticks and individual packets of raw sugar and artificial sweeteners.

We had planned carefully for this first day, so everything would be perfect. So there wouldn't be any surprises.

I sighed, gathered up Caron, and headed out the door.

TWO

OF COURSE, we couldn't just go home. A knot of people stood outside the front door of Uncommon Grounds. The crowd we had prayed for when we planned our opening had arrived. Some for coffee, but most probably drawn by the sirens and flashing lights. And all, unfortunately, standing between us and my car.

Matt was patiently explaining that Uncommon Grounds would be closed until further notice. Rather than achieving his goal of dispersing the crowd, his words only seemed to whet their appetite for news. Small towns were small towns, even places like Brookhills that preferred to think of themselves as "exurbs." Best I could tell, exurbs were where rich people fled when even the suburbs weren't suburban enough.

I spotted a couple of familiar faces in the crowd. Laurel Birmingham was the Brookhills town clerk. A tall redhead, Laurel would have been termed statuesque in more politically incorrect times. At 5'10" she had about six inches and thirty pounds on me, all placed pretty much where they belonged. I liked her anyway.

I wasn't so sure about Laurel's boss, who stood next to her. Rudy Fischer owned the barbershop on the corner of the mall and had just squared off against Patricia in a fiercely contested battle for the part-time office of town chairman. Rudy, the incumbent, had won by a single vote, resulting in a recount that was scheduled for tomorrow. I supposed with Patricia dead it was a moot point, but I wasn't going to tell him that.

Rudy represented the old guard in Brookhills, the original inhabitants who had built sprawling ranch homes of cedar and fieldstone into the hills. Now, twenty-five years later, trendy, extremely pricey houses were springing up all around the gracefully aging original homes.

Property taxes were skyrocketing, forcing some of the now-retired Brookhillians to sell and move. To make matters worse, there were so few vacant lots left in Brookhills that the old homes often were purchased for the land they stood on and summarily bulldozed to make room for yet another white bread mansion.

I had some sympathy for the old guard. My house—actually my former house, where Ted and I had raised our son, Eric—had been one of the originals. Even after twenty years, the neighbors continued to call it the Bernhard house, after the first owners. The Bernhards were long gone. We were gone too, now.

Ted and I had always shaken our heads over friends who had jumped ship during the rocky times of their marriages. How could they break up their families? We swore we would never do that to Eric.

A man of his word, Ted waited until the day our son went off to college to tell me about Rachel, a twenty-four-year-old hygienist working in his dental office. He was sorry, he said as he patted my arm, but he preferred to spend the rest of his life with her.

But this was no time to speculate on how long, or short, I hoped that life might be. I was feeling desperate to get home. Laurel caught sight of us first.

"Maggy, *what* is going on? Matt won't tell us a thing. Is

someone hurt?" Laurel was Brookhills' information pipeline and she required regular feeding.

"It's a fine situation when the police won't inform the town chairman," Rudy muttered, glaring at Matt.

I motioned them over to one side. As we moved, I swear the entire crowd shifted its collective weight and leaned in our direction.

"There's been an accident," I whispered. "Patricia was hurt. I really don't know any more than that."

I turned to Rudy. "I'm sure Chief Donovan will be reporting to you as soon as he—" I stopped as an unmarked, car pulled up, stick-on light flashing. Two men got out.

The man in the passenger seat was Kenneth Williamson, the county medical examiner. The driver of the car was a stranger to me. Probably just under six feet, he had black curly hair and eyes the same dirty gray color as the car he drove. His attitude conveyed authority.

The crowd, still leaning on its collective right foot, suddenly shifted and parted, letting the stranger pass, followed by the doctor. The door closed behind them and all hell broke loose.

"Oh, my God, is she de—" Laurel began.

Rudy started in on Matt, backing him up against the door. "I'm the town chairman, by God, and—"

I didn't wait around to hear the rest. Signaling Laurel that I would call her later, I rescued Caron from her pastor, Langdon Shepherd, and we made for my blue Dodge Caravan.

Nine years old, simulated wood-grain panels, six cupholders—the minivan was one of the last remnants of my former life as wife, mother and PR executive. I wasn't sure what I was anymore, but it sure wasn't that.

On the other hand, I'd probably be driving the Caravan for

ten more years or 200,000 miles—whichever came first—so I should probably shut up about it.

I pulled the van around the corner of the parking lot out of sight of the crowd and stopped at the traffic light leading to Civic Drive. As I waited for our presence to trip the signal, I looked over at Caron. "You okay?"

She nodded.

The light changed and I turned left, ignoring the glare of a morning commuter who would now be exactly two and a half minutes late for work because of me. I tried again with Caron. "Should we go to your house? It's closest."

She nodded wordlessly and I made another turn, this one down Pleasant Street. I had always thought "Pleasant" seemed too pedestrian a name for a street on which Caron's house, at a mere forty-five hundred square f   was one of the smaller homes.

Bernie, Caron's husband, was a successful corporate lawyer, and Caron had been an ad copywriter. That's how I'd met her. We had worked together at First National in the marketing department some twenty years before.

When Caron married Bernie and became pregnant with their oldest, Bernard Jr.(known to everyone, for some reason, as "Nicky"), she decided to stay home. By the time Emma had come along, Caron was happily settled in, as successful at being a full-time wife and mother as she had been a copywriter.

I, on the other hand, had stayed at First National after I married my dentist, Ted, and gave birth to Eric. I scaled back my hours and managed to achieve a fairly good balance between work and home. That didn't stop me from feeling guilty, though. About work, about home—it didn't matter. Guilt is as much a part of my Norwegian heritage as the ice

Ted swore coursed through my veins. Just because I told him to bite me when he said he didn't love me anymore.

I pulled up the driveway and stopped in front of Caron's big Cape Cod. Toby, a pudgy golden retriever, ran up to greet us and I turned off the engine and sat back. Caron was staring fixedly out the front windshield.

She hadn't spoken a word since we left the shop, which was very unCaron-like. She normally chattered when she was upset. Now she wouldn't even look at me.

"Listen, we need to talk about this," I said. "I know you were close to Patricia—"

She turned toward me and started to say something, but then stopped, putting her hands up to her face. "I can't," she mumbled through her fingers, and then started fumbling with the car door. Finally getting it open, she dashed up the sidewalk, Toby at her heels. The front door, when it slammed, nearly took off the dog's nose.

I climbed out of the van and walked up to the door. Toby and I looked at each other and decided to investigate. I rang the doorbell, and Toby sniffed. No answer to the bell, but the dog seemed to be deriving some pleasure from a wad of chewing gum stuck to the mat.

I left him to his fun and headed back to the van. Inside, I folded my arms on the steering wheel and tried to think. One partner dead, another catatonic. This wasn't good.

The crunching of tires on the gravel apron of the driveway interrupted my thoughts, what few there were of them. Caron's husband Bernie was home. He pulled his Navigator up next to me and got out. I watched in my side mirror as he disappeared around the back of my van and then reappeared in my window.

I adored Bernie, all bald, five-foot-six inches of him. He and Ted had been best friends in college. In fact, Bernie had introduced me to Ted. When Ted and I separated, he took the car and the boat, but I got to keep Caron and Bernie. I figured I came out on top.

Bernie was saying something, so I rolled down my window. "…I stopped by the library lobby to pick up a tax form and Mary told me about Patricia. What happened?"

I didn't waste time wondering how Mary, the head librarian at the Brookhills Public Library, had heard the news. Like Laurel, Mary knew everyone and everything in town.

"I'm not sure. She was on the floor when we got there." I frowned. "Caron's the one who found her. She's really upset. I'm worried about her."

Bernie stepped back from the van and looked toward the house. "I'll go talk to her." He started up the driveway, hesitated, and turned back. "Had Patricia been sick?"

"Not that I know of. She…" I hesitated. "Bernie, she had a burn on her hand. There also was a scorch mark on the metal counter."

He looked puzzled. "What are you saying, Maggy?"

I didn't answer.

Then he got it. "Electrocution? You think Patricia was electrocuted? By what? Your coffee machine?" He shook his head. "I find that hard to believe, Maggy. But if it's true, David Harper has one hell of a lawsuit."

Spoken like a lawyer. Still shaking his head, Bernie continued up the driveway to the house, apparently choosing the catatonic wife in the house to the lunatic in the driveway. The lesser of two feebles.

I drove home to wait for Gary's phone call.

MY HOUSE IS UP THE CREEK, and I mean that literally. Poplar Creek runs the length of Brookhills, forming the town's west boundary. Living downstream is fashionable, upstream is *un*fashionable. And the further down or up, the more fashionable or unfashionable you get. Got it?

Down, good.

Up, bad.

I was bad.

In fact, the only thing badder, or further upstream from me in Brookhills, was Christ Christian Church, which I think got special dispensation from God.

But divorce has its privileges, too, and while my tiny ranch wasn't quite the Bernhard house—which was downstream, naturally—it was all mine, from the blue stucco walls in the living room to the lime green toilet in the bathroom.

As I unlocked the door, I heard Frank thunder across the room to greet me. Or he would have thundered, had there been room enough to pick up speed. As it was, he ran three or four steps worth and then plowed blindly into the door, pushing me back into the yard.

Frank belongs to my son. Frank is a sheepdog. Frank is way too big for the house.

Forcing my way back in, I tossed my purse on the bench by the door, scratched Frank hello and headed for the laundry room. There I stripped, dumped my stinky clothes in the washer, and started it.

A hot shower was next. It was only when I stood naked and shivering, a stingy stream of lukewarm water trickling down my back, that I remembered I should have turned on the washer *after* my shower. Not to worry, though, the fill cycle ended before my shower did, sending a last-gasp blast of scalding water through the old pipes just in time to cauterize the goose bumps.

Pulling on a clean "Uncommon Grounds" T-shirt and blue jeans, I returned to the living room feeling, if not quite human, at least fit company for Frank. But then, Frank ate dirt.

I started to flop down on the couch but it was piled high with tax papers. After days of self-inflicted misery, I had admitted defeat yesterday. I needed professional help—. April fifteenth was just two weeks away, and my tax forms were still bare.

Not surprising, I guess. This was the first time I had filed a single return in twenty years. But I'd been sure I could handle it. After all, how hard could it be? Plenty hard, apparently.

So I'd given up and called Mary, who was not only Brookhills' head librarian but also part-time tax accountant, and pleaded for help. She had read me the riot act about being so late and told me to get my buns over to the library pronto with my papers.

I moved the stacks aside carefully now and sank down on the couch. Frank padded over to rub his 110 pounds against my knees like he was a cat. Itch scratched, he simply leaned there until his paws finally slid out from under him and he landed with a satisfied "harrumph" on my feet. I wiggled my bare toes under his fur.

If I was right, Patricia had been electrocuted by the espresso machine. Problem was, the machine had just been installed—by a professional—last Thursday. All of us, including the L'Cafe sales rep, had watched while the technician installed it, then the rep had demonstrated it for us.

And if that weren't proof enough it was working properly, the next day we spent the morning practicing our frothing and tamping, brewing and pouring ad nauseam at Patricia's insistence. Consistency was paramount, she had declared in her dulcet tones. After four hours of this drill, I was ready to strangle her. Electrocution had never entered my mind, honest.

Frank abruptly raised his head a half inch off my foot, listening. I listened, too. Sure enough, a car door slammed in the driveway. I struggled to pull my feet out from under Frank who, having done his part, had gone back to sleep.

By the time I managed to get up, the doorbell was ringing. I moved the curtains and saw Gary standing on the front stoop. Most houses in Brookhills don't have stoops. They have porches, or decks, or even verandas. Mine's a stoop.

I turned the deadbolt and let Gary in. The living room, already overcrowded with tax papers, sheepdog, and furniture purchased for a much bigger—less blue—space, suddenly made me claustrophobic.

"Let's go into the kitchen," I suggested. "I'll make us some coffee." A day without caffeine, after all, is like a day without…well, caffeine.

Gary sat down at the kitchen table and pulled a notebook out of his jacket pocket. "Maggy, I'm afraid I have to ask you some questions. Is Caron here?"

I turned from the cupboard, coffee grinder in hand. "She wasn't feeling well, so I took her home." I put the grinder down. "What did the medical examiner say?"

He rubbed his eyes. "Exactly what I thought he'd say. Cardiac arrest."

"From what?" I set down the grinder.

He pushed back from the table, crossing his left foot over his right knee. "Electrocution, apparently, though we'll know for sure after the autopsy. I think the current either stopped her heart outright or put it into fibrillation. Either way, with no one there to pull her away from the machine or to force her heart into a normal rhythm, she died."

With no one there…

Maybe if I had arrived on time, Patricia would still be alive. "How long had she been there, do you think?"

"At least a half hour. Probably longer. Her pupils were dilated and non-reactive."

I was thinking about the half hour I'd been late. The half hour Patricia had probably been dead.

Gary read my face. "Don't hit yourself over the head with it, Maggy. You likely couldn't have done anything, even if you had found her earlier. Or you could have been electrocuted yourself. She was probably frozen to—" He stopped when he saw my face.

"She was electrocuted by the espresso machine then. But how could that happen?"

He shook his head and picked up the notebook and pen. "You tell me. When did you get it?"

I explained about the installation on Thursday and the practice sessions on Friday. Gary took notes.

"Could it have been an electrical surge or something?" I asked.

He shook his head. "The whole machine was still live when we got there. When I saw Patricia's hand, and the scorch mark on the sink, I suspected electrocution immediately. That's why I wouldn't let you touch it."

I didn't know what to say. Gary shifted in his chair. "Anyway, they threw the breaker and are getting ready to take apart the machine. Do you have a schematic? It would give them something to work from."

"There's one in the office."

"Good." He flipped to a fresh page of the notebook. "Now tell me about this morning."

I gave up on the coffee and sat down at the table across from him. "I was running late. My alarm went off at five-thirty, instead of five. We were supposed to be at the store by five-thirty so we would have plenty of time to brew coffee and set up before we opened at six-thirty. If I had been there—"

Gary gave me a stern look. "Don't start that again. Maybe this was meant to be. Maybe you were meant to oversleep, because it wasn't your time. Now, when did you actually arrive?"

But it was Patricia's time? I answered Gary's question. "It was almost six. I ran in and—"

"Was the door locked?"

I shook my head. "Caron or Patricia must have left it unlocked when they came in."

"So Caron was already there?"

I nodded. "She still had her coat on and was staring at Patricia on the floor. I started CPR, and Caron called 911."

"Is that it?" Gary asked, flipping his notebook closed and starting to stand up.

I nodded, surprised at his abruptness. "Do you want me to come back with you and find the schematic?"

"I have to talk to Caron, then stop at the station." He hesitated. "Actually, maybe you could go to the store and dig out the schematic in the meantime."

He got all the way to the door before he turned around. "One thing you should know, though. When the county medical examiner got the call, he saw who the victim was and called Jake Pavlik, the new county sheriff. The Harpers are important people, and the bureaucrats don't want anything to…slip through the cracks." He seemed to be quoting.

"Slip through the cracks?" I got angry, since Gary was too well-mannered to do it for himself. I like to think of myself as an advocate for those less bitchy. "You've protected presidents for God's sake."

Gary shook his head. "Nobody cares about what I did ten years ago. To them I'm just a retired security guard turned small-town cop."

He was heading for the door. "Anyway, like it or not, Pavlik is at Uncommon Grounds now, and he's in charge. And Maggy, tread carefully. I hear he can be a real prick." He closed the door softly behind him.

THREE

I WASN'T ALL that anxious to get back to Uncommon Grounds, but I couldn't stay holed up in the blue room all day either. Besides, I needed to know what was going on. I filled Frank's food and water bowls, handed him a pig's ear, gathered up the tax papers to drop off with Mary later, and headed out to the van.

Gary's last words were still echoing in my head. Gary Donovan calling somebody a prick, of all things, was totally out of character. It would be like your mom saying it. Gary had been an Eagle Scout, for God's sake. Or still was. I think that's like being an alcoholic, you never completely recover. In the ten years I'd known him, I'd never heard Gary curse. Not once. Pavlik had really gotten to him.

So Pavlik must have been the mysterious dark-haired man with the medical examiner. I hadn't paid much attention to the election, but I knew he'd replaced our former sheriff, an obese man who had died of a heart attack at his desk.

If memory served, the new sheriff in town had been some sort of hotshot in Chicago. His "Take Action" campaign slogan had struck a chord with an electorate who had watched their last sheriff do little but slowly eat himself to death. Pavlik pledged to take an active role in law enforcement in the community. I guessed this was it.

Poor Gary, he didn't need this. He had paid his dues, going from the Milwaukee PD to ATF, and then on to Secret Service.

When he had retired from the government at fifty, Gary took over the security at First National, bringing the albatross of a financial organization into the modern world, security-wise. He irritated the execs by making sure they didn't travel together and endeared himself to me by taking over the security and risk management aspects of two very large events First National sponsored and I managed.

Gary was an enabler in the best sense of the word. For example, when there was a sexual assault in the bank's parking structure, he not only provided security escorts, but also taught self-defense classes so women could feel confident about protecting themselves. Gary figured his job was teaching people *not* to need him.

Which might explain why, four years ago, First National had downsized him. That and the fact that the bank had been robbed of nearly four million dollars a few months earlier.

I'd always suspected that Gary had taken the robbery "on my watch," as he put it, harder than he had the downsizing. But at the time, he'd sworn he was itching to get back into real police work anyway and didn't mind having a nice severance package from First National to finance his search. Not that it had been much of a search. Gary was a Brookhills native and the town had jumped at the chance to bring him in as police chief.

Speaking of the police, as I turned into our parking lot, I saw they had cordoned off the sidewalk in front of the store. At first glance, business around Uncommon Grounds seemed to go on as usual. Until you noticed no one was moving. At the corner, the patrons at Rudy's barbershop looked like they had planted themselves there till the next haircut. Next door, dental patients appeared to be lining up for extractions.

I walked up to the door of my own store and knocked on it.

Inside, I could see a group of suits. One of them moved away from the group and peered through the window. It was Pavlik.

He opened the door. "Yes?"

I had started in, but stopped. I had to, he was blocking the door. "This is my store," I said. "I'm—"

His eyes—yep, dirty gray Chevy—narrowed. *"This,"* he said with emphasis on the "this," "is a sheriff's investigation of a potential crime scene."

Gary's description of Pavlik was proving apt. "Fine. Chief Donovan asked me to give you the schematic for the espresso machine." I stepped back and started to turn away. "But if you'd prefer to find it yourself…"

He held up a booklet. "I already have. You might as well come in, though. I have some questions for you, Mrs…" He let it hang.

God help me, I wanted to stick out my tongue like a five-year-old and say, "You tell *me,* if you're so smart." The idea of him going through our cabinets to find the schematic, which had been in the back of the bottom drawer, next to the box of emergency Tampons, really ticked me off.

I behaved myself, though. "Thorsen, Maggy Thorsen. And it's Ms." I automatically asserted my pending independence and then, just as automatically, felt silly. I stuck out my hand to hide my confusion.

He ignored it and stepped back. "Please come in, Ms. Thorsen, and take a seat. I'll be with you as soon as I'm free."

I sat down to wait. Pavlik returned to the group that was still conferring near the condiment cart and I turned my attention to the spot where we had found Patricia barely three hours ago.

Her body was gone, evidently having been photographed,

poked and prodded sufficiently. The scorch mark remained on the counter just to the left of the sink, along with the puddle of milk on the floor. The pitcher sat on the counter, encased in a giant plastic bag, the gallon of Vitamin D Milk next to it and Patricia's latte mug next to that. All nice and neat. Patricia would have approved.

Pavlik was finishing up, and the group dispersing. A young man who looked like he was wearing his father's suit took the schematic from the sheriff and went over to the espresso machine. A gray-haired woman with a camera and a man who looked like a present-day Ichabod Crane started out the door.

Pavlik called to one of them. "Steve, hang on a second." Ichabod stopped at the door. Pavlik pointed to me. "Get her fingerprints before you leave."

I really hate being called "her"—a carryover from my relationship with Ted's mother, who called me "her," "she," "your wife," or "your mother," depending on whom she was addressing. And all with me in the room.

Steve loped over and fingerprinted me, politely asking my name and recording it before he re-packed his case and left.

Now I read mysteries, I watch TV, I know the police needed my fingerprints to eliminate mine, which belonged there, from others that didn't. It still irritated me. By the time Pavlik finally deigned to speak to me, I was primed:

"I don't know how you treat people in Chicago, but here you'll get a whole lot further with a little common courtesy."

Pavlik raised one black eyebrow at me. "I apologize." He pulled out the chair across the table from me and sat down, flipping open his notebook. "Now, Donovan said there are three partners: Mrs. Harper, you, and…" He checked his notes. "Caron Egan."

He glanced up, his eyes suddenly looking steely blue instead of dirty gray. Weird. "Ms. Egan was with you when you found the body?"

"Yes, Caron was with me." She was there *before* I found the body, too; but if he wanted specifics, he could ask for them.

"Uh-huh. Tell me about the partnership." This time I raised my eyebrows at him. He shifted in his chair. "In other words, how is it set up? If one partner dies, for example, what happens to her share of the business?"

I felt like I had stumbled into a bad movie. "Her interest would go to her next of kin. The remaining partners retain the option to buy that person out at a market value to be determined by an independent audit," I said parroting the partnership agreement. "But since we rent the space and haven't opened yet, we have no market share and no name recognition. The only thing we *do* have is the equipment, which is worth considerably less today than when we bought it two weeks ago."

Pavlik moved on. "Mrs. Harper evidently was here very early. Her husband says he was still asleep when she left home. Do you know what time she was planning to arrive?"

"We all wanted to be in early since this was our grand opening. Five-thirty, latest, so we could be ready to open at six-thirty."

He just nodded.

"I was late," I admitted for the second time that day, "and got here around six. I'm not sure what time Patricia came in, but it was likely before five-thirty."

Pavlik raised the other eyebrow. "Why's that?"

I swallowed. "Patricia is—was—very precise. That's why she handled the books and the scheduling."

"Do you have other employees?"

"No, we're covering all the hours ourselves, at least for now. Patricia mapped it out so two of us works each day. One is the set-up person and starts at five-thirty. The other comes in just before we open at six-thirty, and stays to close. Patricia was supposed to do set-up today and Friday. Caron has Tuesdays and Thursdays, and I have Wednesdays and Saturdays. Each of us has every third day completely off."

Pavlik looked bored.

Not that I cared. "Anyway, my point is that Patricia was the kind of person who wouldn't have wandered in at five-thirty today. I'm sure she came in early to make sure everything was exactly the way she wanted it."

Pavlik shifted gears again. "How long have you known Mrs. Harper and Mrs. Egan?"

"I've known Caron for years, we worked together at First National Bank about twenty years ago. We've been friends ever since. I met Patricia through Caron when we decided to open this place."

"Let's talk about today. What would Mrs. Harper have done when she came in this morning?"

"We have a check-list, it should be taped inside the cabinet door by the sink." I got up to get it and hesitated. "Can I go over there?"

He stood up. "I'll do it." He found the list and brought it over to the table.

A.M. Checklist

☐ Turn on backlights

☐ Plug in and turn on coffee brewers (need 15 minutes to heat)

- [ ] Turn on digital coffee scale
- [ ] Grind coffee for brewed coffees of the day (one regular and one decaf—see schedule) on "regular" grind
- [ ] Grind decaf French Roast for espresso ("fine")
- [ ] Cone grinder filled? Grind first lot
- [ ] Run blinds for espresso
- [ ] Run plain water through both brewers
- [ ] Post names of brewed coffees (better to do the night before)
- [ ] Fill bud vases and put on tables
- [ ] Fill creamer and put on condiment cart
- [ ] Brew coffees of the day
- [ ] Fill baskets in bakery case
- [ ] Put cash in cash register
- [ ] Bring in newspaper (should arrive around 6:15)
- [ ] Turn on front lights, music, flip sign and unlock door at 6:30

Pavlik whistled as he looked the list over. "I see what you mean. She was a little over the top, wasn't she?"

I felt my face flame. "Well, actually, I put together that list."

He sat back and clasped his hands behind his head. "Now, tell me if I'm wrong here, okay?"

I nodded.

"This is a coffee shop, right? You make coffee. You serve some rolls. But you need a seventeen-step checklist to open in the morning? I think NASA uses a shorter countdown for a shuttle launch."

I bristled. "Sixteen, and this is not just 'a coffee shop.' We serve two brewed coffees every day, chosen from the twenty-five types of whole beans we stock. We also do custom brews—customers can pick any of the beans, and we'll make them an individual cup, even if we're not brewing the flavor that day. Then there's espresso, which has to be brewed a shot at a time, and lattes and cappuccinos, both of which can be flavored. And we don't just sell 'rolls,' we serve muffins, scones, Kaisers, croissants and tarts."

I wasn't done. "And as far as the list is concerned. I make lists. That's how I stay on top of things so I'm not the one coming in at four a.m. to make sure everything is okay."

Pavlik leaned forward. "So is that when she got in? Four a.m.?"

I wanted to scream. "How do I know? I wasn't here, I told you that."

"Right. Well, let's start with the list. Can you tell me how far she got?" He spun the sheet around so I could read it.

I didn't bother with the list, I had the thing memorized. I stood up and looked around. First, the backlights. They'd been on when I came in and I told Pavlik so. I continued down the list to the brewers. "Can I step behind the counter?"

He nodded. "Just keep out of Kevin's way." Kevin, the technician, had the top off the espresso machine and seemed to be preparing to dismantle it.

I slipped by, giving the espresso machine and the puddle on the floor wide berth. Reaching the brewers, I found that they were both plugged in and switched on. "She turned on the brewers."

The digital scale was winking at me. "The scale is on, too." I checked the three cans we used for fresh ground coffee—one for the regular coffee of the day, one for decaf and one for decaf French Roast. All full, as was the cone grinder next to the espresso machine.

"She was making a latte," I said, "so she would have run the blinds for the espresso, and she had started brewing coffee," I pointed to the pot sitting on the heating element of the brewer, "so she must have run the clean water through."

"But these other things," Pavlik was looking at the checklist. "The bud vases and the creamers. They're listed before brewing the coffee and they haven't been done."

I just shrugged and Pavlik gave me a smirk. "Good help is hard to find, huh?"

I didn't answer and he got up and came over to where Kevin was still working on the machine. "Tell me how this thing works."

Still smarting from my checklist being violated—and by Patricia of all people, the queen of quality control—I pointed at the cone grinder standing next to the machine. "That's the grinder we use for regular espresso. We keep it filled with beans. Patricia ground some, see?"

I showed him the ground espresso in the dispenser below the whole beans. "When you're making regular espresso, you just put the portafilter under here, pull the lever twice and it dispenses enough ground espresso to brew one shot."

Pavlik was writing this all down. "Porta…what?"

"Portafilter." I spelled it for him and pointed at one. "The portafilter is that small metal coffee filter with the black plastic handle attached. It has a very fine mesh and you fill it with espresso, tamp it down and twist it onto the espresso machine. The steam from the machine is forced through the ground espresso and creates 'essence of coffee,' as Patricia called it." I smiled at the memory.

"So Mrs. Harper was making an espresso?"

I shook my head. "She was brewing espresso, but she was

making a double latte. There was a gallon of milk out and a large mug with two shots of espresso sitting in front of the machine when we found Patricia."

"So a latte is…"

"A third espresso and two thirds steamed milk. Topped with a little froth." I was giving him Coffee 101, but he seemed to find it helpful. Or at least he wasn't sneering.

"Would it be unusual for her to make herself a drink before she finished the checklist?"

"No, not really. If she were here early enough, she would have had plenty of time. Patricia always said she needed a latte to get going in the morning." Unexpectedly, I choked up. The counselor I'd seen after the break-up with Ted had warned me if I continued to suppress my emotions, they might pop out at less appropriate moments. Guess this was what she meant.

Pavlik didn't seem to notice. "She must have gotten here very early in order to have time to make herself a drink."

I nodded, blinking back the tears.

"And you got here very late." His eyes were dark now, probing.

"I think I already said that." Tears, the angry kind I'm more comfortable with at least, pooled in my eyes. I looked down at the table, trying not to let him see he had upset me.

Pavlik excused himself to talk to Kevin, who was gesturing wildly in an effort to communicate something he didn't want me to hear. I stood up to get a napkin. As I wiped my eyes, I surveyed the store.

We had planned the layout of Uncommon Grounds very carefully. The road cups were next to the brewers, the spare filters and pots to the right of them, next to the sink. On the other side of the sink was the dishwasher, with the espresso machine next to that. At a right angle to the espresso machine were the bins of coffee beans. Next to the beans were the grinders.

A place for everything, and everything in its place my mother would say.

But it wasn't.

There was the milk on the floor, of course, but something else was out of place. Only…what?

I moved around the end of the counter to get a better look. Then it hit me. The mat. The rubber mat that was supposed to be in front of the espresso machine, where Patricia had fallen, was now in front of the sink.

I rounded the counter and tapped Pavlik.

He looked over his shoulder. "I'm not through with you, Ms. Thorsen. If you'll just sit…"

"The mat." I pointed. "It's been moved."

He turned all the way around this time. "What?"

I pointed again. "The mat by the sink. It's supposed to be in front of the espresso machine to catch spills."

Patricia had fought us on this seemingly insignificant item. She thought the mat looked tacky, but Caron and I had insisted, since the steam from the frothing wand could make the tile floor slippery.

"It was there when I left on Friday afternoon, although I suppose Patricia could have moved it this morning."

Pavlik was examining the mat. "Or someone else could have," he muttered.

I didn't get it at first. Was Pavlik saying that Patricia's accident had been set up? That someone had moved the rubber mat so she would be electrocuted? But who? And why? Not to mention, when and how?

Pavlik was conferring with Kevin again. I edged closer and

stood on tiptoe to look into the machine from the public side of the counter.

"See," Kevin was saying, "this wire doesn't belong here. It connects the 220-volt current to the frothing wand and makes the whole machine hot. She could have touched any metal surface and zap!"

I jumped and my eyes met Pavlik's above the innards of the machine. "Ms. Thorsen, have a seat," he said flatly. He sent Kevin back to his examination and followed me to the table, where he picked up his pen. "Just one or two more questions, if you don't mind. You said the mat was in front of the espresso machine on Friday when you left. What time was that?"

"Around five-thirty."

"Was anybody else here with you?"

I shifted uneasily in my chair. "Most of the time. In the morning, Patricia, Caron and I practiced on the new machine."

I explained the installation of the machine on Thursday, as well as the trial run. "Patricia and Caron left about two o'clock. Patricia was having us over for dinner and wanted to get ready and Caron had some errands to run. I stayed to wait for the building inspector to do the final inspection at three. It couldn't be done until the espresso machine was wired in."

"And did he come?"

I nodded. "He—"

Pavlik interrupted to ask the inspector's name.

"Roger Karsten." I spelled "Karsten." "Anyway, Roger was late. He showed up around quarter to five."

"Almost two hours late? What did you do all that time?" He was watching me carefully.

Oh nothing. Just kept myself busy re-wiring the espresso machine. Busy hands are happy hands. I tried to answer more calmly than I was feeling. "I cleaned up and retyped the check list you so admire."

He ignored that. "I'm surprised you waited that long for him."

"Well, our building inspector is a bit...difficult." Actually, he was an egotistical young jerk. "We needed him to do the inspection and give us an occupancy permit or we couldn't open. So I thanked him nicely for coming when he finally got here, and then raced out to pick up my dry cleaning before they closed at five."

"Did you make it?"

I shook my head. "No, but they let me in anyway. Then, they couldn't find my dress. When I finally got back to the shop, Roger was gone so I had to go to Town Hall to get the occupancy permit on Saturday morning."

"Everything passed inspection?"

I shrugged. "I assume so. Roger issued the permit."

Pavlik rubbed his head. "So let me make sure I have the timeline straight. You used the machine on Friday morning with your partners. They left at two. You were here alone from two until quarter to five when the inspector arrived."

I nodded warily.

"The inspector, Roger Karsten, came at quarter to five and you left just before five to go to the dry cleaner."

I nodded again.

"You came back to the shop at what time?"

Was it just me, or had we already been over this? "It was at least five-fifteen. The dry cleaner is just around the corner, but it took them a while to make sure they had lost my cleaning."

"And when you came back at five-fifteen, the inspector was gone." I nodded yet again. "Was the door locked?"

I thought back. "Yes, the dead bolt on the front door was

locked. He must have gone out the back door. It locks when you pull it closed behind you."

This time, Pavlik nodded. "That exit leads to the service hallway that connects the rest of the stores in the strip mall." He wrote something down. "What did you do then?"

"Swore because I had missed him, turned off the lights, and left by the front door, locking it behind me." I was tired now. I'd had enough and I wanted to leave. I stood up. "Is that all?"

"Just one more question, Ms. Thorsen." His gray eyes suddenly twinkled. "Don't you think this coffee thing is a fad? I mean how long can you bamboozle people into paying four bucks for a buck-fifty cup of coffee?"

FOUR

BAMBOOZLE?

But despite his quaint choice of words, Pavlik had managed to zero right in on my insecurities.

Were lattes and cappuccinos here to stay? Or would they eventually end up—along with oat bran and sun-dried tomatoes—in the big fondue pot in the sky? The thought was unsettling. Both of mind and stomach.

Putting that aside for the time being, I climbed into the van and tried to give some thought to more pressing matters.

Patricia had been electrocuted. By the espresso machine. And someone had caused it to happen. Did that mean murder? Or some perverted practical joke that had gone awry?

Through the front window of the store, I could see Kevin showing Pavlik the heavy wire that connected the espresso machine to the dedicated 220 circuit.

I hadn't liked the way Pavlik had watched me as I answered his questions. Did he seriously consider me a suspect? I shuddered. No, I didn't want to think about that one either.

I retrieved my tax papers from the back seat and climbed out of the van. The library was just down the block, so I might as well drop the papers off with Mary now. Then on the way home, I'd stop and talk to Caron. Or try to talk to Caron.

IF LAUREL WAS an information pipeline, Mary was the Internet. Between her job as head librarian and part-time CPA work, she knew just about everything there was to know about the denizens of Brookhills.

She was at the reference desk when I entered the Brookhills Public Library, a small, but exceedingly well-stocked one. Mary was small and efficient, too—a tiny woman with the sweet round face that seems to come with being a genuine blonde. In Mary's case, that sweet face was deceptive. She ran a tight ship at the library, and an even tighter one when it came to her accounting clients, the more foolish of whom she referred to as "H&R Blockheads."

Her deep brown eyes were crackling as I approached. I figured I was in for a tax lecture, but Mary had other things on her mind. "Oh God, Maggy, I heard about Patricia."

Since she had been the one who told Bernie, I knew that. What I didn't know was how *she* had found out. I opened my mouth to ask, but Mary was just getting wound up.

"Patricia was just in here on Saturday, you know? Making copies?" She gestured to the row of photocopiers across from her.

Mary's speech pattern turned almost every sentence into a question. I think that's how she gets her information? People just answer her?

Assuming she gives them the chance. "How exactly did she die, Maggy?"

Her hand went to her mouth as a sudden thought seemed to strike. "Oh my God, she didn't commit suicide did she? Maybe she was having money problems, or David was having an affair or something?"

Killed herself with an espresso machine? I doubted it would join pills, guns and wrist-slitting as preferred methods of suicide. I shook my head. "No, I'm sure she didn't kill herself, and you'd certainly know if they were having money problems. Don't you do their taxes?" Mary worked for most of the families in town, so it was a safe assumption.

"David does his own taxes, you know? He does them on his computer, Patricia says…said," she corrected herself with a frown.

Tears were starting to well in Mary's brown eyes and I figured I'd best get out while I could. "Well, you sure don't have to worry about that with me," I said proffering my stack of papers. "Do you think you can figure this out?"

She glanced through, all business again. "Good, you have your deductions itemized. Is everything here on the sale of the house?"

"Yup. I suppose I'm going to get killed on taxes," I ventured.

"Well, we'll see. You know what they say, Uncle Sam wants you—and everything you've got." She was still laughing, freshly buoyed by accountant humor, as I left.

I decided to call Caron instead of stopping. It already had been a long day and I was anxious to get back home.

THE AVERAGE TEMPERATURE in April in Wisconsin is a lot like April in Paris. Funny how it never feels that way.

I was chilled to the bone when I got into the house and decided to build a fire. Unfortunately, when I stepped out of the door to grab the firewood, Frank spotted someone getting out of a car across the street and took off. Naturally, I had to run the dog down, apologize to the terror-stricken man, and drag Frank's big hairy butt back into the house.

He didn't take off on me often; but when he did, it scared the daylights out of me. Our house was right on Poplar Creek

Drive and traffic—especially when Christ Christian had
something going on—could be sporadically heavy.

Both of us safely back in the house, I finally got to my fire.
The fieldstone fireplace took up the entire north wall of the
blue room. Like Frank, it was far too large for the space. But,
also like Frank, it provided me great comfort.

Fire started, and Frank ensconced on the hearth, I
repaired to the kitchen, where I poured myself a glass of fine
red wine and opted for a sleeve of Ritz crackers and a can
of spray cheese to go with it. Major food groups accounted
for (fat and salt, alcohol and aerosol), I settled on the couch
to call Caron. The phone rang four or five times before she
finally answered.

"Hello?" Cautious.

"Caron, it's me, Maggy. Are you okay?"

A sigh came from the other end of the line. "I'm sorry for
being so useless this morning."

Thank God she was sounding more like herself. "I think
you can be excused. You had just found Patricia, after all."

"Can you believe it? She's dead. What should we do? Close?"

My stomach did a flip-flop. What would I do if Caron
wanted to bail out of the store?

"No, of course not," I assured her. "Patricia would have
wanted us to move ahead." In truth, I had no idea what
Patricia would have wanted. I just knew what I wanted. "I'll
call Gary tomorrow and ask him when we can get back into
the store, okay?"

Caron agreed and I hesitated, not knowing if Bernie had
told her what I'd said out on the driveway. "There is something else. It looks like Patricia was electrocuted. On purpose."

"That's ridiculous."

I didn't know if she meant it was ridiculous that Patricia had been electrocuted, or that it had been on purpose. I chose to answer the latter. "The espresso machine was re-wired. It was fine on Friday, so somebody must have messed with it over the weekend."

The other end of the line was silent, but I kept talking. Pavlik's questions about who was where, and when, hadn't been lost on me and I needed to unload. "I was the last one in there on Friday, Caron. I'm afraid they suspect me of tampering with the machine."

"You kill Patricia? Whatever for?"

"Who knows? But the fact remains that I had opportunity, if not motive. You left with Patricia and the only other person who was there alone was Roger." I tailed off speculatively.

"Don't be silly, Maggy," Caron said crisply. "You've been watching too many TV shows. Patricia's death was an accident, pure and simple. Now I have to go." She hung up.

Hello? Had she been listening to anything I said? I sat for a second, then drained my wine glass and got up to go to the kitchen. Time to pull out the Chips Ahoy.

THAT NIGHT I DREAMED about Bruno Hauptmann, the man who died in the electric chair for the murder of the Lindbergh baby—a murder he claimed he didn't commit. Tidy how my subconscious had managed to tie Patricia's method of death and my own fear of being blamed for it, into one neat nightmarish little package.

Contrary to popular belief, things didn't look better in the morning. At least, though, I woke up. And with a plan of sorts.

First, I needed to talk to Gary to see when we could open. Even though Caron and Patricia hadn't needed to take out loans to kick in their shares, I had. To add insult to usury, I'd had to obtain Ted's permission to do so. I wasn't sure which would be more painful, going bankrupt or being humiliated in front of Ted and his hygienist. Not that I'd have to worry about choosing—I'd likely do both.

But money woes aside, maybe Gary could give me an idea of what was going on in Pavlik's twisted little mind. After spending the night trying to convince myself that I couldn't possibly be a serious suspect, I'd given up. Instead of thinking about all the reasons I couldn't have killed Patricia, I needed to figure out who could have. It wouldn't easy. Patricia could be irritating and someone might have wanted to knock her down a few pegs. But kill her?

I thought over what I knew about her. It was all pretty superficial: She and David had been married three or four years now. It was David's first marriage and Patricia's second. Patricia's kids from her first marriage, Courtney and Sam, lived with them in one of the newer subdivisions in town, Brookhills Estates. From what I'd seen, Patricia was devoted to her kids. She also was very involved in her church, Christ Christian and, increasingly, in town politics.

Could her death have something to do with her bid to become town chairman? The election had centered on the battle between Rudy's old coots, as Patricia called them, and the newcomers, represented by Patricia. Surprisingly, it wasn't a question of the older folks wanting to slow down development. It was just the opposite. Rudy and his gang wanted to keep taxes down, so they were encouraging further commercial development along Brookhill Road, the main drag.

A point of contention in the campaign had been Summit

Lawn School, a now-vacant building on Brookhill Road that Rudy wanted torn down to make room for yet another strip mall.

Patricia, on the other hand, wanted to deed the property back to the school district, to allow it to re-open Summit Lawn to alleviate the crowding at Brookhills Elementary. The conditions at Brookhills El had been a subject of debate and referendum for years. Was it really that bad? Could we add on? *Should* we add on? How about building a new school? And on, and on, and on…

While people felt passionate on both sides of the issue— or should I say all sides, because believe me there were more than two—I hardly thought they would kill a person over it. Especially the *loser* in the election.

I decided to stop over at Town Hall before I saw Gary about re-opening the store. I'd forgotten to call Laurel, anyway, and she was probably champing at the bit for information. Maybe I could get some in return.

I found Laurel behind the "Information" counter, appropriately. I pointed at the door to the boardroom. It was closed, but I could hear raised voices from beyond. "What's going on? Sounds like you should be refereeing."

"I had to come out for air, all those over-inflated egos are sucking up the oxygen."

In spite of the circumstances, I laughed. "Who's in there?"

"Well, let's see. Rudy, the rest of the board, Sarah—you know, **Patricia's** campaign manager?—and the town attorney. They're hashing out the details of the recount."

"But Patricia's dead. Why bother with a recount?"

Laurel snorted. "That's what Rudy said. But the bylaws say there has to be a recount. If Patricia actually won instead of Rudy, and can't take office, there will be a special election."

"But Rudy thinks it would be a lot less trouble, if…"

"If we forget the recount, and he stays in office. Then, of course, there's the ballot."

"What ballot?"

Laurel stuck her nose in the air. "One of my poll-workers invalidated a ballot, as she should have, because the voter had marked five supervisors instead of four." We still used paper ballots in Brookhills.

"So…" I prodded.

"So, the question is, should the whole ballot have been in-validated or only the supervisor section? In other words, does the rest of the ballot, including the chairman section, count?"

Shades of Florida and *Gore vs. Bush*. I wondered whether anyone would ever name another kid "Chad." "Who's the vote for?" I asked.

"We don't know. Sophie Daystrom was the poll-worker and she sealed it in an envelope and swears she didn't notice the chairman portion. It's possible the person just skipped that part and instead voted for the extra supervisor. We just don't know."

"So, if the ballot is valid, and if the person voted for a chairman, the results of the election could be affected."

"Right. The ballot will be opened during the recount, which has been rescheduled for tomorrow. It was supposed to be today, but…" She let it go.

After a moment of awkward silence, she cleared her throat. "I have to get back in there. I'm supposed be taking notes." She hesitated again.

It wasn't like Laurel to mince words.

"What?" I demanded.

She cleared her throat again and then blurted. "Did you see

this morning's *CitySentinel?* It says that Patricia's death is suspicious, and you were the last person in the shop."

My heart jumped and crammed itself into my throat. While I had considered the possibility of being a suspect, I hoped I was just being paranoid. Now here I was in the morning paper. I grabbed Laurel's arm. "Does it actually say that I'm a suspect?" I croaked.

Having thrown me into a full-blown panic, Laurel reverted to reassuring. "No, no, of course not. There's just a quote from the sheriff saying they had interviewed you since you were the last one 'on the premises.' Listen, don't worry. Gary will make sure they don't arrest the wrong person."

She disengaged my hand. "I have to go, but I'll talk to you later. Don't worry." She opened the door to the boardroom and dove back into the fray.

As the door closed, I heard Rudy's voice. "I don't understand how we in good conscience can spend taxpayer money—" The door closed, letting out a little whoosh of hot air.

I stood still, letting panic wash over me. I thought about Ted—good, solid Ted. I actually missed him for a second. Then I shook myself. *Please.* Ted and his skills as either a lousy dentist or a philandering husband would have been absolutely no help in this situation.

My skills, though, might be. Hmm. False media allegations. If something like this had happened to one of my events instead of to me, personally, what would I be doing? Simple. First off, I'd get a copy of the story and see for myself what I was dealing with before I went off half-cocked. Maybe Laurel had gotten it wrong.

I barreled out the door heading for the paper box, and

almost collided with Way Benson, a local developer and our landlord at Uncommon Grounds.

"Hello Maggy," he said, a grin on his handsome, weathered face. If Gary was Brookhills' Jay Leno, Way was our Clint Eastwood. "Had some trouble at your place, I hear."

Anxious to see the *CitySentinel,* I just nodded and ducked under the arm holding open the door. Way was tall, about six-four, and had the muscular build and complexion of a man who had spent a lot of his life working outside. He had been a contractor before he moved into development and had been extremely successful at both. Much as I tried, especially now that we were leasing from him, I had never quite trusted Way. There was a hard edge to him.

He was still talking. "Too bad about Patricia Harper. You and Caron still going to try to make a go of it?"

I turned to face him and he let the door close. "Of course. I'm going to see Gary now to find out when we can open."

Way nodded. "I just came from Donovan's office myself. Had to correct some misinformation I read in the paper." He patted me on the shoulder and ducked into the building.

Misinformation, huh? I had to see that paper. There was one copy left in the *CitySentinel* paper box. I fought to pull it out of the front window of the box and—ignoring the first page headlines shouting "Cuts in public schools," "STDs, pregnancy rates up in suburban youth," and "Violent tax day protests possible in Chicago"—turned to the suburban news page:

"Brookhills woman electrocuted by coffeepot." The subhead, "Foul play suspected." Patricia would hate that. No class at all.

But at least the story was buried inside, not on the front page, and it really didn't say much more than Laurel had already told me. On the other hand, Brookhills' weekly newspaper, *The Observer,* would undoubtedly lead with the story and be looking for more information. *The Observer* came out on Thursdays and today was Tuesday. That meant the deadline was tonight. I'd have to stay out of Editor Kate McNamara's way until then.

I crossed the gravel parking lot to the Police Department. Town Hall shared space with the Fire Department in a new building that had been erected after the old Fire Department had burned down. Don't ask.

The new Town Hall/Fire Department made the single-story concrete block Police Department across the way look like a squatter in contrast. Two of the town's four black-and-red squad cars were parked in the drive out front. No one was at the counter when I walked in, but Gary popped his head out of his office in response to the jangle of the bell and waved me in.

I settled into his side chair, one of those vinyl jobs that lets out a whoosh when you sit down. I always felt like I was in Mayberry when I sat in Gary's office. Any second, Opie would trot in with his fishin' pole.

Gary studied my face. "You okay?"

I waved the paper at him. "I'm not sure. Does Pavlik seriously think I had something to do with Patricia's death?"

Gary leaned back in his chair, a worn, wheeled version of mine, and stretched. "I don't know, Maggy. He's leaving me pretty much out of this—having me do more housekeeping than investigating. Speaking of housekeeping, they've taken the espresso machine for evidence, but should be done with your shop this afternoon. You can open tomorrow if you want."

"Wanting has nothing to do with it, I'm afraid. We *have* to open. We have rent due at the end of the month, and I have a loan to pay." I pulled out my calendar and made a note. "I'll call and see if we can lease a machine for a while. Do you have any idea how long ours will be gone?"

Gary shrugged. "Could be months. Would it be cheaper to buy a new one rather than rent?"

"A new one? Do you have any idea how much those puppies go for?" I tapped my pen on the calendar. "I wonder if we can get an extension on our rent in a pinch." That reminded me. "Way said he was just in here 'correcting some misinformation.' What did he want?"

"Now, Maggy," Gary said, his wide face reddening, "you know I can't talk to you about that."

"Gary, there are people out there wondering if I electrocuted my business partner. You can't blame me for wanting to know what's going on."

He put his hand over mine. "Listen to me." His eyes were golden brown and very serious. "I'm not going to let Pavlik railroad you. You have to believe that."

The fact that Gary actually thought Pavlik might try to, scared the heck out of me in and of itself. "Then tell me what Way wanted."

He was fiddling with his pen, not looking at me. "Way came here to tell me that the newspaper was wrong. That someone else was at the shop after you."

I jumped up. "But that's great! That means somebody else could have done it." I stopped. Gary still wasn't looking at me. "What's wrong?"

He finally set the pen aside and looked up. "I'm sorry, Maggy, but this muddies the waters even more. Way saw somebody leaving Uncommon Grounds by the back door on Saturday afternoon. It was Caron."

FIVE

I SAT BACK DOWN. "Caron? He has to be wrong. Caron didn't say anything about being at the shop this weekend, even when I told her I was the last one there. She wouldn't—"

Gary was shaking his head. "I know, I know. She didn't say a word to me either. And I asked her point blank, when was the last time she was in Uncommon Grounds. If Way is right, she lied to me."

"But I've known Caron for twenty years," I said flatly. "She doesn't lie."

Gary leaned forward, and the chair squealed under his weight. "Well, I'll tell you one thing. If she did, she's in big trouble. Not only with me, but with Pavlik."

Pavlik. My mind was racing. If Caron lied, there had to be a good reason. "Gary, did you tell him about this?"

"Pavlik? Not yet."

I let out a sigh of relief.

"Don't get too comfortable," Gary warned. "You know I have to."

I had a bright idea. "Let me talk to her first. I'll let you know what she says, then we can decide what to do. Maybe there's a perfectly innocent explanation."

Which would still leave *me* hanging out to dry, of course. Talk about your Catch-22.

Gary stood up. "There's no 'we,' here, Maggy, and no

'deciding what to do.' I have to go to Pavlik on this no matter what I think of him."

I stood up, too, and grabbed his arm. "Just wait half an hour. I'll go see her right now."

Gary looked me in the eye, then looked away. "Tell you what I'll do. I'll leave a message on Pavlik's voice mail for him to call. When he does, I'll tell him what Way told me."

"So…" I wasn't sure how this would buy me time.

Gary rolled his eyes. "Pavlik's not very prompt about returning phone calls. It should buy you that half an hour, at least."

Ohhhh. Good thinking. This way Gary would have fulfilled his professional obligation and I'd still have time to fulfill my personal one. I hugged him and grabbed the newspaper I'd balanced on the corner of the desk. "You are a gem, thank you." I swung around and headed out the door.

Gary's voice followed me. "Call me with what you find out, Maggy, but remember this isn't my case. Anything I know goes straight to Pavlik."

Back in the parking lot, I checked my watch: 10:14 a.m. Caron had better be home. I was getting angrier at her by the second. How could she sit there last night and listen to me whine, knowing full well that I hadn't been the last one in Uncommon Grounds?

As I walked to my car, I allowed myself another thought. Maybe *Way* had lied. But why?

Preoccupied, I realized too late that the woman bearing down on me from the Town Hall side of the parking lot was Kate McNamara, ace reporter. Between us stood my minivan. I increased my pace, trying to reach the van first. She did likewise. By the time we got to the Caravan, we were both practically at a dead run.

"Maggy!" she demanded, puffing. Everything Kate said was either a demand or a command.

I countered with "breezy." "Hi, Kate, I'd love to chat, but I have an appointment." I flashed her a smile and swung open the door of the van.

She managed to avoid the door as it swung open and wedge herself between the now open door and the driver's seat, so I couldn't get in myself. Slick. I considered slamming the door on her, but balked at outright personal injury. Besides, I'd spent twenty years in PR and Marketing, I could handle one small-town reporter.

I stepped back and, reassured I wasn't going to bolt, Kate moved out from behind the door. "I understand that you're a suspect in Patricia Harper's murder. Do you have a comment?"

I nodded at the *CitySentinel* in Kate's hand. "Researching your story, Kate?"

She looked down at the newspaper and tucked it under her arm. "I'm on my way to see Chief Donovan and thought I should give you a chance to comment. That's more than this rag did."

I just looked at her. Never rush to fill silences when you're talking to a reporter. Make them ask the questions.

She tried again. "So what happened, Maggy? I understand you were the last one to have access to the murder weapon."

I wondered if a frothing wand had ever been entered into evidence before. "Caron and I are both terribly upset by Patricia's death," I said evenly, "and we will do whatever we can to assist the police in their investigation. Our thoughts are with David Harper and with Patricia's two children, and we would hate for anyone to exploit the sad situation for the sake of a story."

Taking advantage of the fact that Kate was scribbling down the quote, I stepped around the door and into the driver's seat.

Then I drove off, leaving her in the dust, I hoped both literally and figuratively.

IT WAS ALREADY ten forty-five when I got to Caron's house. "You lied to me and you lied to Gary," I blasted her with when she opened the door. "Why?"

Caron's face crumpled, but she tried to cover. "What in the world are you—"

I interrupted. "You told Gary you weren't in Uncommon Grounds after you left on Friday." I was moving toward her into the foyer as I spoke and she was giving ground. "Last night, you let me go on and on about my being the last one there. How *could* you?"

By this time, I was in the foyer and she was practically backed into the antique table across from the door. Tears began to roll down her cheeks and I stopped, ashamed of myself. After all, Caron was not only my partner, but she was my friend. I owed her the chance to explain. "Can we sit down?"

She nodded, the freckles standing out starkly against her pale face. Her good manners, even now, took over as she led me toward the living room. I steered her into the kitchen instead. This was not a living room conversation. We needed a table between us.

Caron kept glancing at me, a question in her brown eyes.

I answered it. "Way saw you leaving Uncommon Grounds on Saturday afternoon."

She nodded and sat down heavily at the table. I took the chair across from her and waited. Finally, she looked up to meet my eyes. She reminded me of a deer trapped in the middle of traffic. Run and be killed, or stay and be killed. The proverbial rock and the hard place.

I decided to put her out of her misery. Reaching across the table, I took her hand. "Tell me," I said.

"I've done something horrible, Maggy. Oh God." She put her hands to her face.

My heart stood still. She had really done it. Caron had killed Patricia.

"—got married in college," Caron was saying. "He's the only man I'd ever dated. Then we got married and had the kids—"

Had the woman lost her mind? "What in the world are you talking about?" I demanded.

She stopped and looked at me. "I'm having—had—an affair. It's over."

My jaw dropped. Here I was thinking that my best friend had murdered someone by hot-wiring an espresso machine, and she was admitting to an affair. "You're fooling around?"

Caron watched her fingers trace the planks of the oak table. "That's why I was at Uncommon Grounds on Saturday. I was meeting Roger."

Roger? Roger Karsten? The building inspector? "Aww, geez, Caron. He's what? Twenty-eight?"

She nodded miserably. "I know, I know. I've been a fool. Bernie is a wonderful man. But I just wanted some excitement, I guess."

She was pleading for my understanding. I wasn't sure if I could give it to her, at least right now.

"You see," she continued, "I've always done what was expected of me. Went to the right school, met the right guy, got married, had kids; bought a house. The whole load."

Yeah, I thought, the whole load—successful career, nice husband, good kids, big house in the country and more money than she could spend. Any thinking person's nightmare.

Caron was still talking. "Now that the kids are practically gone, I have time to think about what *I* want."

"And you want *Roger Karsten?*" I asked dryly.

Her eyes dropped again. "Well, no, but he seemed to want me, and that made me feel—"

"Like an idiot apparently. Does Bernie know?"

She shook her head, seeming horrified at the thought. "Of course not. I ended it with Roger and hoped…"

The dam broke again. I handed her a tissue and waited.

"Maggy, what am I going to do? If I tell the police, Bernie will find out. If I don't, they'll think I had something to do with Patricia's death."

Back to the rock and the hard place. "But you don't have a choice. Way told Gary he saw you leaving by the back door. Gary left a message for the sheriff." I checked my watch. It was a little after eleven. "He probably has it by now."

Caron looked as sick as I felt. "Maybe I can just say I stopped by to get something."

"And forgot to mention it? And who's to say that nobody saw Roger?"

Caron was thinking furiously. "I know. I'll say there was a problem with the inspection and Roger had to come back Saturday afternoon and finish up." She was getting up. "I'll call Roger and tell him to say—"

For a moment, hope burned bright. I was sorry to lift my leg on it. "Won't work. I picked up the Occupancy Permit Saturday morning. It wouldn't have been issued if he hadn't finished the inspection."

Caron sat back down. "Maybe Roger forgot something…" She trailed off.

A tool perhaps. "That might work," I said carefully. "The only thing anyone could prove was that you were there together. Who's to say, except for the two of you, what you were doing there?" And where exactly you were doing it. The counter? The desk? I hoped she'd disinfected.

Caron started for the phone on the planning desk. "I have to get hold of Roger."

"Will he lie for you?" I asked, wondering if I would, if it came right down to it.

"He'd better," she said grimly as she picked up the phone. "He owes me." Just then the doorbell rang.

"I'll get that," I said hastily and hurried out. I didn't want to hear this particular conversation.

My mind was racing as I went to the door. So Caron was having an affair. I tried to force myself to look at it objectively, to not put my personal experience into play. After all, plenty of women had affairs. For every cheating man, there was a cheating woman, right?

Right. Dirtballs, all.

I peeked out the etched glass sidelight of the door. As I'd feared, there was a county sheriff's car in the driveway and a Pavlik at the door.

I took a deep breath, released it, and opened the door. "Sheriff, how nice to see you." Too late, I realized it was an unlikely way to greet someone who suspected you of murder.

To his credit, Pavlik didn't remark on the welcome. "Thank you, Ms. Thorsen." He stepped in, wearing a well-tailored gray cashmere topcoat. "Am I interrupting a business meeting?"

"Oh, no…well, yes. I came over to talk to Caron about re-opening the store. I understand we can get back in later today?"

Pavlik nodded. "We'll be done by one or two this afternoon, but I'm afraid you'll have a bit of a mess. Fingerprint powder, body fluids. We try to clean up the best we can, but…" He shrugged, smiling pleasantly.

My stomach was churning. "I know it seems heartless," I explained, "but we just can't afford to stay closed long. There are loans and rent that have to be paid no matter what."

"Of course, business is business. Your partner dying couldn't come at a more inopportune time." He moved in just close enough to make me feel uncomfortable, his eyes dark and watching me. "You know, Mrs. Harper was electrocuted."

I nodded.

"The whole espresso machine was live. Somebody had re-wired it. But I don't have to tell you that, do I? You were there."

"There?" The word caught in my throat.

"At the store, when Kevin took apart the machine. You were there." He was watching me closely.

I nodded again.

He wasn't done. "You shouldn't have left so soon. You didn't see the most interesting part."

He pulled a thick black electrical wire from his coat pocket. It was in another plastic bag. He pointed to a small green wire. "See that? It's the ground wire." He put it up to my face. "If you look real closely, you can see it's been cut. Between that, the rubber mat being moved, and the skim milk we found on the floor…"

He shrugged and put the bag back into his coat pocket, his eyes never leaving mine. "She was able to start making her drink because the handles on those portafilters of yours are plastic. And so are the buttons she had to push to brew the espresso. She probably didn't even realize anything was wrong. Not until the moment she pulled out that frothing wand with her left hand, while picking up the metal pitcher from the stainless steel counter with her right."

His eyes were so dark now I couldn't see the pupils, his body so close I could feel him breathe. "You see, the electricity entered her left hand, shot right across her body through the heart and then exited her right hand."

He traced the path up my left arm, across my shoulders and down my right, matching his words. His hand lingered on mine. "It probably blew the pitcher right off the counter."

His face was no further than three inches from mine now. He turned and his cheek, rough with stubble, brushed me. His mouth was close to my ear. His voice, low.

"Just how long do you suppose she hung there, Ms. Thorsen, before her heart finally stopped? Before she finally died, and her muscles released so she could fall? What do you think? A minute? Five minutes? Ten?" His breath was hot against my ear.

I jerked back, nearly knocking the silk flower arrangement off the hall table.

Just then, Caron breezed into the foyer. She looked like a different woman. Hair brushed, makeup repaired. "I'm sorry, I was on the phone. I'm Caron Egan." She offered Pavlik her hand.

He smiled and took it as if we had been making polite small talk while we waited for her. "Mrs. Egan, I'm Jake Pavlik, the county sheriff. Might I have a moment of your time?"

Caron nodded and smiled back. "I recognize you from your campaign literature, Sheriff." Before my very eyes, Caron had gone from trapped animal to coquette.

As for myself, I needed to get out. And now. I flung open the door and started down the walk, talking to Caron over my shoulder as I went. "I'll call L'Cafe to see if we can get a loaner installed this afternoon. The sheriff says we can get back into the shop around two."

I was at the van, fumbling to get my keys out of my purse when Pavlik called my name. I had to force myself to turn and look back. He and Caron still stood in the doorway. Caron had a puzzled look on her face.

Pavlik smiled politely, a different man than the one who had mentally assaulted me just now. "Ms. Thorsen, where will I find you later?"

I struggled to control my voice, show a little bravado even. "L'Cafe or Uncommon Grounds maybe. You'll just have to find me."

Pavlik raised his eyebrows. "Oh, believe me, Ms. Thorsen, if I want you, I will."

SIX

AFTER CARON AND PAVLIK closed the door, I sat in my van trying to get the shaking under control. I must have sat there for twenty minutes before I finally reached for the ignition, and then only because I didn't want to still be there when Pavlik came out.

I put the van into reverse. My foot was trembling so badly on the accelerator that the Caravan bucked all the way down the driveway. Stopping at the end, I waited for traffic on Pleasant to pass.

Damn Pavlik. And damn me. I'd fed him just the reaction he'd probably been after. But did he really believe I'd killed Patricia? The whole idea was ridiculous.

Melodramatic.

Scary as hell.

So what did he expect me to do now? Run?

I stepped on the gas and the van shot backwards out onto the street right in front of a Lexus. The Lexus' horn blared and the driver swerved around me, taking the time to throw me the finger as he did.

I waved back and drove myself to the police station. Gary took one look at my face and led me back to his office, where I sat as he poured us each a cup of coffee.

"Milk?" Gary asked, handing me a mug.

Having experienced Gary's idea of coffee, I nodded. At

Uncommon Grounds, our policy was to dump any pot that sat on the heating element longer than thirty minutes. Gary, on the other hand, preferred his coffee "aged," like fine wine. But who was I to look a caffeinated gift horse in the mouth?

Gary went to his fridge and pulled out a red and white half-pint of whole milk that looked suspiciously like he'd filched it from Brookhills Elementary the last time he did his "Stranger Danger" talk. I wondered how long ago that had been.

Apparently so did Gary. He dumped half the carton into his own mug and peered into its depths before declaring the milk "okay" and sliding it over to me.

It was sort of like having a royal taster in times of yore. Or a canary in the mines. I used the rest of the carton in my coffee, transforming it from black sludge to gray sludge, and took a sip.

"Better?" Gary asked, watching me.

"Much, thank you," I said hoarsely.

"I take it Pavlik made an appearance at Caron's?"

He smiled and I cracked a little one back at him. "You could say that. The man certainly knows how to hold an audience."

I told Gary what Pavlik had said and how he'd said it.

He listened, his face stony. "He's just trying to scare you, Maggy. That kind of stuff probably works in Chicago."

"But why *me?*" Shades of Nancy Kerrigan.

Gary shrugged. "He's probably not interested in you any more than he's interested in David or Caron. Just somebody who'll give him a quick solution and make him look like a big shot."

"So you don't think—"

Gary stood up. "You didn't do anything, Maggy. So there's no way he can prove you did."

I opened my mouth and he raised his hand. "Forget it. If

he gives you more problems, you let me know and I'll take care of him."

I smiled. "My hero."

Gary laughed and pulled his hat off the file cabinet. "You bet, and your hero's hungry. Let's go to Goddard's for butter burgers."

Leave it to Gary to realize I needed comfort food. Goddard's Pharmacy boasted an old-fashioned lunch counter specializing in The Better Butter Burger: A quarter-pound hamburger on a toasted Kaiser roll topped with a slab of melting butter. Thick malts and shakes were served up in old-fashioned metal cups that got all frosty on the outside. A veritable feast of cholesterol and fat. How could I say no to that?

But first, I had to make a call. I used Gary's phone to call L'Cafe. The woman who answered had heard what had happened to the *last* espresso machine, and efficiently arranged for a tech to pick up a loaner and meet me at the store with it at three.

That arranged, Gary and I headed over to Goddard's, which was on the opposite end of the strip mall from Uncommon Grounds. I'd heard that Mrs. Goddard had been worried when Way announced that we were moving into the mall. She probably felt we would give them a run for the coffee dollar. She needn't have worried. Goddard's was where the seniors in town met daily and, personally, I didn't think they could be blasted out of their booths.

Sure enough, the stragglers from breakfast were still there at nearly noon, nursing their bottomless cups of coffee. Rudy was in the "power booth" in the corner, talking animatedly to someone I couldn't see. In the next booth over, Pastor Shepherd sat with Henry Wested, a resident of Brookhills Senior Manor. The senior living facility backed up to Poplar

Creek and served as the dividing line between upstream and downstream. Neutral territory, like Switzerland.

People were staring at Gary and me, and why not? Here was the number one murder suspect dining with the police chief. Who knew what could happen? There might even be an arrest. What a bitter Butter Burger *that* would be to swallow.

Gary and I waved to the assembly and took a booth in the back, careful to avoid the seats that were invisibly, yet indelibly earmarked for the regulars. I had once seen four-foot ten-inch Sophie Daystrom and the rest of her octogenarian posse run a tourist who had innocently settled into "their booth" clean out of the lunchroom.

Safely seated, I ordered a Better Butter Burger with extra fried onions (just let Pavlik try to get near me again) and a chocolate shake. Gary had the Better Butter Burger Biggie plate with fries and a pineapple shake.

"I assume you had a chance to talk to Caron before Pavlik arrived?" Gary asked.

"Yes, and thank you for that," I said.

He wasn't going to let me off that easily. "So what did she have to say for herself?"

Eh, a moral dilemma. I hated to lie to Gary, but even if Caron had done something stupid—adultery, not murder—Bernie shouldn't have to suffer public humiliation because of it. Normally, I'd trust Gary with this secret, but I knew his professional ethics would take precedence over friendship. Gary took his moral obligations very seriously.

Me, less so. "She said Roger left something there on Friday and she let him in on Saturday to get it." And she had said it. It just happened to be a lie.

"Roger was there Saturday, too?" Gary's voice rose and

then fell, as heads turned. "Why in the world didn't she say anything?" he whispered.

"I guess she didn't think it was important. She's pretty upset, you know." I leaned across the table. "Gary, we both know Caron didn't kill Patricia. And certainly not with an espresso machine, for God's sake."

Our food came then and Gary didn't answer as our waitress slapped the heavy white plates onto the table. Reaching into her apron pocket, she thumbed carefully through a stack of grease-stained checks before finding the right ones and dropping them on the table.

We salted, ketchuped and mustarded our burgers in silence. Gary picked his up, flipped it upside down and took a bite. I took a long, fruitless pull on the straw of my chocolate shake and waited. The quiet was thicker than the shake.

Finally he spoke. "Maggy, let's face it, *any*body killing someone this way is unbelievable. But somebody did do it."

"But not Caron," I said stubbornly. "I know Caron."

We went back to eating in silence. There really wasn't much else to say anyway, I guess. Finally, Gary wiped his mouth with the paper napkin and picked up his check. "I have to get back." He pulled two singles out of his pocket and tossed them on the table.

As he started to slide out of the booth, he hesitated. "Did you hear about the robbery attempt at First National's main office?"

"They left a pipe bomb, didn't they?" I asked. "Just like the other one."

The "other one" I referred to was the robbery four years ago, the one that had likely cost Gary his job. In that case, the pipe bomb had exploded, demolishing half of the front lobby and killing two people. One was a sixty-two-year-old female bank teller. The other was a man, but there wasn't enough left of him to identify. Gary had hypothesized that the unidentified male had been holding the bomb when it exploded and was one of the perpetrators.

"They were luckier than we were," Gary was saying. "Pastorini says the pipe bomb was bigger than ours. If it had gone off…" He shook his head.

Ours. We had our own bomb, Gary and I did. And it had been haunting him for years.

Louis Pastorini had been Gary's assistant and was now head of First National security. "You did everything you could, Gary." I touched his sleeve and he looked at me. "You know that, I know that and Pastorini knows that."

"It wasn't enough, though, was it? Two people died and the bank lost four million dollars."

And you lost your job, I thought. "The funds were insured," I said, instead. "No one lost any money."

Gary just shrugged and stood up, his face reverting to his "police chief" personae. "I know there's something you're not telling me, Maggy. If you're going to nose around in Patricia's death, and I know you are," he held up his hand to silence my protest, "be careful. I'll help you as much as I can, but I'm not sure what good that will do you with Pavlik."

After he left, I took another hard pull on my shake. Gary was right. I *was* hiding Caron's affair from him and I *was* going to nose around. It was either that or let Pavlik persecute, and potentially prosecute, Caron and/or me. Gary seemed powerless to help us under the circumstances—a fact I sure didn't want to remind him of. He had enough on his plate. I looked over at the remains of his burger and copped a fry.

As I nibbled the fry, I eyed the people around me, trying

to spot someone who knew Patricia well. Of course. Langdon.
The spindly gray-haired pastor seemed to be preparing to
leave. I dropped the fry, grabbed the check and pretended to
head for the cash register.

Langdon and Henry's table was en route. I stopped at the
end of Langdon's bench, trapping him in the booth.

"Langdon, Henry, how are you?" Langdon, ever the gentleman, tried to rise. The result was sort of a bent knee bow.
I backed off so he could shuffle out of the booth sideways.

He took my hand. "Maggy, Maggy, we've suffered a
terrible loss." He patted my hand. "God has a reason for everything, my dear, we mustn't question His wisdom. All
things work together for good to them that love God."

I nodded, refraining from pointing out that if God really
wanted someone to get frothed to death, he had a very strange
sense of humor.

"I'm sure you're right, Langdon." I gave in and patted back.
"But the fact remains that Patricia has been taken far too soon."

He patted. "It's a reminder to us all, Maggy, that we must
love each other while there's still time."

Judging by Ted, Caron and Roger, that idea was taking root
in Brookhills. "I understand Patricia was very active at Christ
Christian," I said. "I'm sure you'll miss her terribly."

"She's been a tireless worker for God. We've been so lucky
to have her—organizing fund-raisers, teaching Sunday
School, chairing the Education Committee. Though in the
last few months, she had resigned a number of her posts with
the church, she remained faithful in her attendance."

"I suppose with the store and the town election, something
had to give."

I had said it a little off-handedly for Langdon's taste. Behind his thick glasses, he winced. "Perhaps. Blessedly, though, David has always been a tower of strength. He's financial secretary for the congregation, as well as head of our Men's Bible Study. I only wish he would let us provide comfort to him now in his time of grief." He shook his head dejectedly. "He seems to be avoiding me."

I pictured Langdon, Bible in hand, chasing down poor David in order to comfort him.

"We all find solace in our own way, Pastor." 1 Maggy, Verse Trite.

Langdon raised a bony finger as a thought struck. "I must remember to call Sarah Kingston. Sarah doesn't speak about her emotions, but she must be suffering greatly."

Sarah, Patricia's campaign manager.

Sarah was a no-nonsense type. So much so, that I'd wondered at the friendship between the two women: Patricia, the consummate suburban matron. Sarah—blunt, outspoken and, if you could believe it in Brookhills, having absolutely no fashion sense.

A thought struck *me* now. Maybe Sarah would give me the lowdown on Patricia. Why hadn't I thought of her myself?

But first I had to deflect Langdon, so I could get to her first. "I'm not sure if it's my place to tell you, Langdon," I started, "but Kate McNamara was very agitated the last time I saw her." It was true. She'd nearly tackled me in the Town Hall parking lot.

"Really?" Langdon said thoughtfully. "Kate isn't a member of our congregation, but perhaps I should stop by *The Observer* when we're done here."

"I think that's a wonderful idea," I said. "Good to see you, Langdon. Henry." I smiled at both of them and then smiled my way right through the cash register line and all the way out the door.

I *love* helping people.

SEVEN

SARAH KINGSTON'S OFFICE was across the street from Town Hall. She was on the phone and waved me to the visitor's chair. "No, I won't present an offer like that, Evan. My client won't entertain it, that house is worth three-fifty if it's worth a dime. Don't waste my time with this lowball shit." Slam.

She turned to me. "Can you believe that? Beautiful house on Cardinal Lane, priced right, and they offer twenty-five percent below asking. It's a goddamn insult."

Sarah was a real estate agent. With her baggy jackets, pleated trousers, sensible shoes and blunt manner, she neither looked nor acted like a member of the Whatever-Million Dollar Sales Club, at least in a town like Brookhills. But she had been, for more years than I could remember.

"By law, don't you have to present any offer you receive?" I asked.

She snickered. "Yes, and when I *do* receive that offer from Evan, it will be $20,000 higher than if we hadn't talked. Now what do you want?"

Like I said, blunt. I decided to be equally blunt and to appeal to the business instincts of a woman who had made it on her own.

"Listen, I know Patricia was your friend and I'm sure you want to find out how she died as much as we do."

"The morning paper suggests that you had something to do with it," she said, pursing her lips.

"I didn't," I said flatly. "And neither did Caron."

"Then what happened?"

"I don't know, and neither does the sheriff obviously. Gary, who might have a chance at figuring it out since he at least knows the people around here, has been taken off the case."

"So that leaves you? The defender of truth and justice?" She was laughing at me.

I squirmed. "I need to defend myself," I admitted. "And I need to defend Caron. I don't want to sound mercenary, but if this whole thing isn't settled soon, we could lose the business—or worse."

Sarah pushed back her chair and peered at me through glasses that rode low on her nose. "Mercenary, shmercenary. If you were a man, no one would be giving you shit about wanting to re-open your business."

She had a point.

"Does Pavlik think you and Caron zapped Patricia to get the business?" she asked.

I got a sick feeling in the bottom of my stomach when she mentioned Pavlik's name. "I think he realizes neither of us has much to gain, but he may be looking for the easiest solution. At this point that's us, either separately or together."

"What about Roger Karsten?"

I nearly choked. How did Sarah know about Caron and Roger? "What about Roger Karsten?" I echoed.

Sarah looked speculative. "Ah, so they don't know about the affair. That's interesting. I assumed it was common knowledge—to everyone but her husband, of course."

And her best friend. "I don't know how common it is, I just heard this morning. How did you find out?"

"I guess she had to tell someone."

I felt a twinge of jealousy, like in the fourth grade, when Debbie Spence told everyone Cindy Kuchenbacher was her best friend. But what about *me??* Did all those years of sitting in alphabetical order mean *nothing?* "I didn't realize you two were that close," I sniffed.

Sarah shrugged. "We got fairly close during the campaign. She really didn't have a lot of female friends."

Waaait a second. "Campaign? Are you talking about Patricia or Caron?"

"Patricia."

We looked at each other aghast.

"Now let me get this straight," I said. "Patricia and Roger Karsten were having an affair?"

"Had. Patricia ended it about two weeks ago." Sarah was too quick, though, to let my reference to Caron pass. "And I take it, Roger was also screwing Caron. Now that's a fine kettle of fish, isn't it?"

I was practically speechless. Practically. "First Ted, then Caron, and now Patricia. What is this? 'One Flew Over the Cuckold's Nest'?"

Sarah laughed uproariously and lighted a cigarette. Virginia Slims Menthol. I didn't even know they still made them. But Sarah *was* a 70s' kind of woman. "Grow up, Maggy. It happens all the time."

Like I didn't know it.

"Anyway, it seems to me you're missing the point," she continued. "If Roger was fooling around with Patricia and Caron, maybe Caron found out and—"

I interrupted. "No," I said decisively. "Caron told me she ended the affair."

"And you believe her."

"Yes, I believe her. And Roger would make a much better suspect anyway."

"How so?" Sarah asked, blowing a smoke ring.

I watched, fascinated, as it billowed up toward the ceiling. Cool. But I could be cool, too. I quirked one eyebrow. "You said that Patricia ended things. Maybe Roger didn't like it. Maybe Roger killed her. He not only had access to the espresso machine, but with his background he had the capability to rewire it." I was perfectly willing to throw Roger to the dogs, the slimeball.

Sarah wagged her cigarette at me. "Hmm. Roger isn't such a bad idea." She smiled widely, exposing huge front teeth. Combined with her abnormally long face, the teeth gave her an equine look. "Maybe we can pin it on him."

Sounded good to me. Sarah pulled a pad of paper toward her. "Let's list the suspects and possible motives. First we have Roger." She tapped her pen on the desk. "I suppose Patricia could have given him trouble, without exposing herself, so to speak." Her laugh sounded suspiciously like a neigh to me. "Maybe he was taking kick-backs and Patricia found out."

I was surprised that a woman as practical as Sarah was prone to flights of fantasy, but I was happy to fuel them, if it would take her mind off Caron. "And what about Rudy? Maybe he was so worried about the possibility of losing the election he killed her. And," I pointed out with a flourish, "his barbershop backs onto the same hallway as Uncommon Grounds. It wouldn't have been a problem for him to get in and out without being seen."

Sarah looked skeptical, but wrote it down anyway. "I can't see Rudy with an espresso machine. A straight razor maybe, but—"

"Who knows what people are capable of," I said eagerly. "And what about David, don't they always suspect the…" I stopped, ashamed of myself for treating this like a game when the sight of David's face when he saw Patricia was still so fresh in my memory.

Sarah shook her head, voicing what I was thinking. "I know David Harper. He did not kill his wife."

"Then there's Way," I suggested, trying to get us past the awkwardness. "He was awfully eager to tell Gary he'd seen Caron at the shop on Saturday."

Sarah hadn't heard about that, so I filled her in. She listened and then sighed, her long face regretful. "I know you don't want to hear this, Maggy, but Caron had both motive and opportunity."

"Motive, what motive? Roger dumped Patricia for Caron, so why would Caron kill her? Besides, I don't think Caron knows about Patricia and Roger even now." I checked my watch. It was nearly two.

Sarah pushed a strand of hair off her face and grinned. "Are you sure there was nothing going on between you and Roger? You're the only one left."

"For God's sake, I'm ten years older than he is," I said as I got up to leave. "And I'm—"

"More like fifteen years, by my calculations," she corrected, following me to the door. "But not for long and, unlike Caron and Patricia, you'll have every right to play around. Heck, you don't even have to worry about getting pregnant anymore."

I stopped. Geez, it seemed like you couldn't do anything involving your reproductive organs in Brookhills these days without someone knowing about it. Leave it to Sarah to call a spayed, a spayed.

I turned on her. "Here's a pregnant thought for you, Sarah. Starbucks has like six thousand stores right this second. I say 'right this second' because they've probably added a couple since we started talking."

I held up a finger. "I have one store. And that one hasn't opened yet. You want to give me advice?" Sarah just stared at me and I moved closer, happy to have her or anyone else on the defensive for once. "Tell me how I'm going to get the store open and profitable before I lose everything I've worked for over the last twenty years."

"I'm sorry, Maggy, but…." She stopped and backed off. I waited for the apology.

But Sarah just sniffed and backed off some more. "Whoa. Better Butter Burger? Extra onions?"

Arggh. I left. And I didn't regret the onions—not one iota.

As I PULLED AWAY from the curb in front of Kingston Realty, I saw Kate McNamara come tearing out of Town Hall. I thought perhaps Langdon was giving chase, but no such luck. Kate merely crossed the parking lot and slammed her way into the police station. I wondered what had set her off?

Then again, Kate was the type of person who always acted like she had something important to do. Even if that something was covering a Tiny Tot's dance recital in the high school gym. Of course, TT dance recitals *were* big events in Brookhills, where doting parents presented their four-year-olds with roses after the performances.

Maybe I was just jealous. It had been a long time since anybody had given me roses.

I drove the short distance down Civic Drive to the side parking lot of Uncommon Grounds. The store was situated in

Benson Plaza on the Corner of Civic and Brookhill Road, the main east/west drag in Brookhills.

We had chosen that location because there was easy access from both Civic and Brookhill. In the coffee business, those morning commuters picking up their road cups were your bread and butter. You had to get them in and out fast.

I turned into the Civic Drive entrance and pulled up next to the building, intending to use the service entrance by the trash dumpsters. It was the door Way had seen Caron using on Saturday.

As I got out of my van, I saw Tony Bruno, the dentist who leased the space next to us. He was talking to someone standing just inside the door. Much as I liked Tony, I veered to the front, not wanting to see to anyone just now. I had enough to think about.

Both Caron and Patricia had been fooling around with Roger Karsten. I knew my reaction to the news probably had more to do with Ted and me, than with Caron and Roger or Patricia and Roger, but geez…

As I rounded the corner to the front entrance of the store, I was relieved to see the police cars gone. The only remnant of Monday's awful events was the torn end of the yellow police tape still tied to the light pole. I pulled at it, but the plastic only stretched, fixing the knot even tighter. I'd have to come out with a scissors later.

Inside the scene wasn't quite as normal. There was black powder everywhere. Fingerprint powder, I assumed, and the mess had been made worse by someone wiping at it with a wet paper towel. The towel, now black, still lay on the counter.

I picked it up by one corner and gingerly dropped it into the basket under the counter. I wondered whether the fingerprint stuff was toxic. Not wanting to take any chances, I donned rubber gloves and got out the hand vacuum to get up the loose stuff.

The floor had been cleaned up fairly well, despite Pavlik's talk of body fluids. I looked at the now vacant spot where the espresso machine had stood, and then at the counter still scorched black. The picture Pavlik had painted for me popped into my head, and the room threatened to start spinning. I grabbed at the counter to let things settle down a bit, to try to think of anything besides the way Patricia had died.

Like Sarah and her crack about not having to worry about getting pregnant. And Little Ms. Tooth DeLay, who Ted said wanted to have "lots" of kids. He seemed delighted. Ted, the guy who didn't want more kids. Who had talked me into getting my tubes tied last year, instead of getting a vasectomy himself.

Yup, that did it. I was back to my usual self: angry and bitter. Which for me, also meant efficient.

I vacuumed first, then got out the buckets and disinfectant and cleaned the counter and floor. When I was done, I threw the rags into the wastebasket and followed them with the filter bag from the vacuum and, finally, my rubber gloves. Wanting it all hermetically sealed, I pulled the plastic liner out of the basket and tied it up tight.

I checked the clock. It was just past two-thirty. I still had a little time before the L'Cafe man arrived. Grabbing the trash bag, I headed to the back door.

I pulled it open and let out a scream.

EIGHT

As MY EYES adjusted to the dimness of the service hall, I realized the dark figure at the door was Pavlik.

I wanted to scream again.

Instead, I stepped back.

"Ms. Thorsen," he said, smiling as he came through the door. "I didn't mean to startle you."

Like hell he didn't. But I could take the high road, too. "That's all right. I was just cleaning up."

He looked around. "Good job, you would never know that a woman had died here."

So much for the high road. "Sheriff, if you have something to say to me, just say it. I'm not independently wealthy. I need this place. Everything I have is invested in it. If you think that's hard-headed or heartless or whatever, that's just too damn bad."

Pavlik's jaw dropped. I shook my garbage bag at him. "Does this look like fun? Believe me, I'm not some socialite, playing at this. I'm separated. I have a son in college, a mortgage and a loan for this place that I used what little equity I have in my house to secure. If I lose this business, I lose everything." Including what little self-respect I had left, apparently.

Pavlik started to speak, but I was on a roll. "And as far as your little performance earlier, thanks for leaving me with an image of Patricia's death that I'll never forget. But I didn't have anything to do with it. If you think otherwise, then arrest me. Otherwise stay the hell away from me."

For a second, Pavlik looked like he was thinking about that arrest part, then he shrugged. "I probably owe you an apology."

Talk about taking the wind out of one's sails. I didn't know what to say.

"I was looking to stir things up." He met my eyes. "At least from you I get some honest emotion, even if you're a little…" He seemed to be searching for the right word. "…manic."

It appeared he'd found it.

He held up his hand like he was going to ward off my protest, but there wasn't much I could say to the charge. I *was* a little nuts these days.

"Everyone here seems to be hiding behind these walls of propriety," he went on. "Even Harper. His wife is dead and he's inviting me in for cookies. Your friend Mrs. Egan is acting like I'm a gentleman caller, for God's sake. It's just plain spooky. What is this? Stepford?"

"They can't help it," I said, thinking maybe this guy was human after all. He watched movies. Read books. Saw plays. "People here care about appearances. They're interested in their children, their homes, their schools and their churches. Sometimes, I have to admit, I think that's *all* they're interested in."

That must have reminded Pavlik of something, because he flipped open his notebook and waved me over to a table. "Speaking of churches, Mr. and Mrs. Harper belong to Christ Christian, right? The priest over there—"

"Langdon Shepherd," I supplied. "He's called a minister or a pastor. I think priests are mainly Catholic, and maybe Episcopalian, too. I'm not sure." I was bubbling over with information, possibly because the subject wasn't *me*, for once.

"Sorry. I was brought up Jewish, so I don't know the lingo." His smile backlit his eyes, making them blue again. I had a sudden unholy thought and suppressed it. Go figure. Only a few minutes ago, I'd thought he was the devil incarnate.

But Pavlik was getting down to business. "Anyway, Pastor Shepherd told me he'd seen Mr. and Mrs. Harper on Sunday and everything seemed fine. He also said Mr. and Mrs. Egan belong to his church."

I nodded.

"Now when I spoke with Mrs. Egan, she said your building inspector left something behind on Friday." His eyes darkened again. "Do you know anything about that?"

The talk about church had been a diversion, but his eyes had tipped me off that the real question was coming. I shrugged. "I don't know. I told you, I wasn't re when he left. I suppose he could have. What did he forget?" It seemed a logical off-hand kind of question.

Maybe not. The eyes got even muddier. "Didn't you see it?"

"No, I didn't." I left it at that. Embroidering the story without knowing what Caron herself had said could only get me in deeper.

He studied me and then wrote something down. "I understand all of you were at the Harper house on Friday night."

I nodded, glad to get back into safer territory. "I told you—that's why I had to get my dress from the dry cleaner. Patricia and David invited Bernie, Caron and me over to celebrate our opening."

Pavlik raised his eyebrows. "Just the five of you? You didn't bring anyone?"

Weird question coming from him, and one that was none of his business. So why did it make me feel like I was back in high school with no date for the junior prom? Then, I had burst into tears and hidden in the Girls' Room. That seemed inadvisable now. Instead I just shook my head and said, "No."

Pavlik started to smile, but apparently thought better of it. "Tell me about the party."

I thought back to Friday night. Patricia had done it up right, of course. Canapés, grilled swordfish steaks with lemon and capers, three kinds of wine—all with corks—and a wonderful fresh fruit and cream, or was it crème, thing for dessert.

As perfect as the meal was, somewhere between the canapés and the swordfish, tension had crept in. Patricia seemed irritated with David; and David, for his part, was hustling all evening to try to smooth things over.

Conversation had revolved around the opening of Uncommon Grounds. Bernie and David, bless their hearts, had even tried to appear interested as we talked coffee endlessly. We also discussed the election and the scheduled recount. Patricia had been shocked to discover from Caron, who always had bits of miscellany at her fingertips, that a tie vote would be resolved by a flip of the coin.

At the time, I didn't know why it had upset her so much. I'd assumed that the thought of something so important being determined by mere chance, upset her nicely ordered view of the world. Now I realized that if the disputed ballot were a vote for Patricia, it could throw the election into a tie. A tie that would be resolved by a flip of the coin. It really did seem awfully…well, flippant.

We also talked about April fifteenth coming up fast. I'd admitted that I hadn't done my taxes yet and Patricia had taken the opportunity to needle David, who apparently hadn't filed yet either.

I filled Pavlik in on the evening, but left out any suggestion of an argument between Patricia and David. I didn't think my vague impressions amounted to much. Maybe I'd ask Caron what she thought.

I did pitch the election angle to Pavlik, though, outlining the invalidated ballot and the tie-breaking procedure. It was my turn to divert him from what I saw as his main targets: Caron and me.

He was decidedly skeptical, though. "So you think this Rudy Fischer killed her to ensure a win in an election that he had already won?"

"Well, it may not be that simple. Maybe he knows somehow that the invalidated ballot was a vote for Patricia."

"But from what you've told me that would only mean a tie vote. He still has a fifty-fifty chance of winning. Wouldn't he wait until he knew the results of the coin toss before committing murder over it?"

Ah, but it was all becoming clear to me now. "If he waited until after the recount and the coin toss and *then* killed Patricia, there would be a new election. He wouldn't just be given the office by default."

"Uh-huh, and this Rudy is what, seventy-five years old?"

"Seventy-two," I mumbled. Patricia had made an issue of Rudy's age in her campaign literature.

"Do you suppose he even knows what an espresso machine looks like, much less how to re-wire one?"

"Well—" I started.

His point made, Pavlik moved on. "Now about Friday night. How did Mrs. Harper and Mrs. Egan seem to be getting along?"

I'd been thinking instead of listening, a bad habit of mine, so at first I thought he was asking about Patricia and David, not Patricia and Caron. I opened my mouth, closed it, and then started all over again. "Fine. We were all excited about opening the store."

"Interesting." That thud was the sound of the other shoe dropping. "Because from what I hear, they had plenty of reason to dislike each other." He was watching me carefully.

"Really?" I croaked.

"You need to practice that. You're not a very good liar. I find it hard to believe that you didn't know that both of your partners were seeing the same man—unbeknownst to their husbands, of course."

Unbeknownst—good word. "Nobody told me, not until today." I met his eyes. I might be bad at lying, but I was really good at telling the truth. "And to be honest, I don't believe that either of them was aware of the other one. If they were, they were awfully good actors."

"Maybe one of them had reason to be."

"Right. Caron killed Patricia because Roger had broken up with Patricia and moved on to Caron. That makes a lot of sense," I said sarcastically.

But Pavlik was following the same train of thought Sarah had earlier. He got off at a different station. "Unless Mrs. Harper threatened to expose them. You said people here care about appearances. Maybe Mrs. Harper wanted Karsten back and threatened to go to Mrs. Egan's husband."

Me and my big mouth. "So Caron killed her because it would be much better if Bernie found out she was a murderer, rather than an adulteress?"

"It's happened before, more times than you would want to know."

"Not here. Not Caron. I would stake my life on it."

"Maybe you are." He seemed to be sizing me up. "If the saboteur wasn't you, Mrs. Egan, or Mr. Karsten, then that leaves us with a random crime. That means you or Mrs. Egan could have gotten it just as easily."

There was a knock on the door. Through the window I could see a red truck backed up to the curb. Outside the door was a stocky man in his early fifties with a dark beard and a loaner espresso machine on a hand truck. It was Ed, the same technician who had installed the first machine, so I let him in.

He went right to work and I went back to Pavlik. Not that I wanted to. I figured Ed was listening avidly from below the counter where he was unpacking the machine, so I kept my voice down. "You don't really believe that, do you?" I asked Pavlik.

"Why not?" he whispered back. "And there's another point you might consider. Electrocution is an inexact art. If Mrs. Harper hadn't been touching the countertop, or if the countertop and pitcher hadn't been metal, it's possible she only would have been injured."

"So you're saying that it wasn't necessarily a murder attempt? Then what was it?"

Pavlik shrugged. "I don't know. A warning maybe? It just seems an inefficient way to kill someone, if that's what you're trying to do."

"So…"

"So, I'm still investigating." He put away his notebook and stood up. "And in the meantime, it wouldn't hurt for you and Mrs. Egan to be careful."

He pulled out his card and handed it to me. "Just in case." He was out the front door before I could say anything.

I was looking down at the card in my hand, when he stuck

his head back in. "Hey!" Both Ed and I jumped. He was talking to Ed, though. "You'd better get new plates for this truck or you're going to be pulled over." Once a Chicago cop, always a Chicago cop.

As Pavlik slid into his car, I saw Caron's Volvo pull into the lot. Pavlik did, too, and he got back out to talk to her. The conversation didn't take long and Caron was white-faced when she came in. I led her to a table away from Ed's ears.

"He told you, I assume?"

Caron knew what I was asking. "Roger, that little creep," she hissed back. "First Patricia, then me. I bet the whole town knows. You probably would have been next."

Ugh. Not in this lifetime. "Did Pavlik tell you how he found out?"

She ran a hand through her short brown hair. "From two or three different sources he said."

"Listen, Pavlik thinks this gives you a motive. I've been trying to come up with someone else who wanted Patricia dead." Caron shot daggers at me. "Okay, okay, let me rephrase that: I'm trying to think of *anyone* who may have wanted her dead."

Caron looked miserable. "Like who?"

"I don't know. Rudy, or Roger, or even Way? He seemed awfully eager to tell the police he saw you there on Saturday."

Caron was considering. "You know, the sheriff asked me about Patricia's party on Friday night."

"I know, he asked me, too. I told him about Rudy and the election and the coin flip, but he didn't seem to think that Rudy was capable of this."

Caron sighed, and I went on hurriedly. "I didn't tell him about the argument Patricia and David seemed to be having. Or was I imagining the tension in the air?"

"No, it was there all right. We got to their house before you did and Patricia was all put out about the television being on. You know how guys are, you invite people over and they think it's perfectly acceptable for everybody to sit down and watch TV."

"Excuse me." It was Ed. "I've got the machine hooked up, but it's different than your other one, so you'd better take a look."

We went over to the espresso machine, which looked to be an older model than ours. Ed confirmed it. "This machine isn't fully programmable like your other baby."

Ed had been enamored of our first machine, which could be programmed like a computer for different-sized shots and strengths. "Push this button for a full shot, this one for a half. You can do double shots, using this double portafilter, but that means you've got to change the amount of espresso you're using."

I nodded and tried to cut to the chase. "So if we're doing single shots, we just use these." I pointed to the buttons that had drawings of tiny coffee cups on them. "And if we want two shots we can use both sides of the machine." Each side had its own espresso brewer and steaming wand.

Ed nodded, conceding my apparent inability to understand anything more complex. "Yeah, that should get you through. Did the police take the other machine?"

He looked fascinated. I decided I didn't like Ed much. "If that's all, let me give you a check."

"I'll take a check for the rental on the machine, but I'm an independent contractor and I'd prefer cash for the labor portion."

Of course he would. I wrote the check to L'Cafe and had to go into my wallet to come up with the two twenties and a ten for Ed. Pavlik's card was on the counter, so I stuck it in my handbag.

As Ed packed up his tools, Tony Bruno came in. Tony was a nice man and a good dentist. I also suspected that he didn't like Ted—his fellow dentist and my former fellow—much. That earned him bonus points with me these days.

Tony was one of the group that hung out at Goddard's, so I was surprised to see him stop by. "Hi Tony, I'm sorry, we're not set up yet. We'll be opening tomorrow."

He stepped aside to let Ed pass with a pleasant, "Back again, huh? These girls really keep you hopping." Then he nodded. "I know. I just wanted to say how sorry I am about Mrs. Harper. She seemed like a nice woman. I feel so badly for the Harper kids."

He looked around the shop. "This is very nice, very nice. You say you'll be open tomorrow?"

Caron answered him, since I was distracted by the red Probe that had just pulled into the spot Ed had vacated. Kate McNamara. Was there still time to hide? I decided I could probably get away, but that would mean leaving Caron to the dogs. I sighed and pulled open the door. "Come on in, Kate."

I was braced for retaliation for my setting Langdon on her, but this time I wasn't Kate's target. She stormed in and looked around. "Where's that bastard, Pavlik?" she demanded.

Tony quickly excused himself, promising to return in the morning. At the same time, Caron snuck out the back way, leaving me alone with Kate. So much for loyalty.

Kate, unaware that the *new* prime suspect was escaping, continued, her face just this side of crimson. "His office said he was here, now where is he?"

"Kate! Calm down before you pop a gasket. Pavlik left half an hour ago. What do you want him for?"

"He's trying to block the press from the recount tomorrow.

He can't do that! Has he ever heard of freedom of the press? Public meeting laws? The Constitution, for God's sake?"

I have to say I was relieved to hear that Pavlik must think there was more to the political angle than he had let on. I decided to play dumb in hope of finding out how much Kate knew. "Why would Pavlik be interested in the recount?"

Kate was disdainful. "Well, obviously, he thinks the election might have something to do with Patricia's death. You know small town politics is a hot bed of graft and corruption."

Uh-huh. I played along. "Really? In Brookhills?"

"Of course," Kate snapped. "Why else would…" Suddenly she seemed to realize she was in danger of providing me with information I hadn't stuck two quarters in a paper box for. She shut her mouth abruptly. "I'm afraid you'll just have to wait for this week's edition of *The Observer,* Maggy. Or maybe, just maybe, you show me yours, I'll show you mine."

She slammed out the door.

THAT NIGHT I WENT to bed early. Before I did, though, I tried to reach David again. Caron and I had both called repeatedly throughout the day and had failed to connect with anything but the answer machine. Sure enough, I got the machine again. I pulled aside the curtains and looked out the window as I waited for the beep. There was a car across the street again. Andrea next door must have a new boyfriend. Or maybe I was being stalked. *Beep, beep, beeeep.*

I followed the advice on the recording and left a detailed message. "David, this is Maggy. I'm sure you don't feel like talking to a lot of people right now, but Caron and I wanted to see how you and the kids are. We, uh, we're planning to open the shop tomorrow, and wanted to make sure that was all right with you. Also, we wondered if a date had been set for Patricia's funeral."

Finishing up with a hurried, "So call us when you feel up to it," I hung up. I felt awful for talking about business and funeral arrangements in the same breath.

I called Frank in from the yard and confided that I felt like a real shit. He licked my face and we went to bed. Not together. Unlike some people, I had standards.

NINE

THE NEXT MORNING, Caron and I met in the parking lot at 5:30 a.m. so we could enter the store together. I'm not sure what we expected. We didn't have any more partners to find dead.

Once inside with the coast—and the floor—clear, we put on a CD to bolster our courage and swung into action.

By 6:00, the brewers were plugged in and switched on and the brewed coffees of the day, Breakfast Blend and Viennese Cinnamon Decaf, were ground. Caron ran plain water through the brewers to clear out the water that had been sitting in the lines, while I filled the creamers.

"Dang," I said, putting the remainder of the quart of cream in the fridge. "We don't have any whole milk." The police must have taken the gallon that had been sitting out on the counter. Not that we would have used it anyway.

"We'll just have to use two percent," Caron said, posting the names of Today's Brews on the menu board.

"I could go get some," I volunteered, checking my watch. "The QuickieMart—"

"Don't you dare leave me here alone," Caron said, hanging the menu on the wall and turning to face me.

She looked nervous and why not? She had plenty to be nervous about these days: The affair. Bernie's reaction if he found out about the affair. The question of whether Roger would keep his mouth shut about the affair. The question of whether *I* would keep my mouth shut about the affair. Oh, and then there was Pavlik, of course, and Patricia's death itself.

"It's going to be okay, Caron," I said, going over to give her a hug.

She pulled back and looked at me. "I hope so," was all she said, and we went back to work in silence.

BY THE TIME 6:20 rolled around, we had filled the bud vases with daisies and put them out, a pot of each coffee was brewed and waiting, and another of each was in progress. By 6:25, the bakery truck had arrived and the pastry was in baskets in the display counter.

At 6:30, I turned on the front lights, flipped the sign to "Open," and unlocked the door to...no one. I stepped out and looked around. No one. I picked up the newspaper and walked back in, dropping it on the reading shelf.

"No one," I said to Caron.

She was less concerned. "Nobody knows we're opening today. We'll just look at this as a dry run."

"Not too dry, I hope," I muttered.

Caron was looking towards the window. "Maybe you'll get your wish."

I turned around. Sure enough, cars were pulling into the parking lot. One, then two, then three, then four. Since nothing else was open on this side of the shopping center, they had to be heading to Uncommon Grounds.

Now I'm no fool, I know they were coming partially—who am I kidding—*mostly* from curiosity. I'm not proud, though. Come for the crime, stay for the coffee.

I manned the espresso machine and Caron poured the brewed coffees and handled the pastry. As we had planned with Patricia, we tried to greet everyone by name. We knew about half the people and would be working on memorizing the names of the other half, assuming they came back, over the next week or two.

Among the first arrivals was Henry Wested, who walked over from the senior home. He ordered a double cappuccino and settled into the corner stool at the counter.

Laurel came, too, (large decaf, steamed milk, to go) as well as Way (large breakfast blend, black) and Rudy (small breakfast blend—a token purchase before he headed over to Goddard's for his real coffee).

Gary, coffee purist that he was, wouldn't let me talk him into something as exotic as a cappuccino or a latte. He did ask for a cup of Breakfast Blend to go, though. As I was pouring it, Laurel passed by on her way to the condiment cart. Gary sniffed. "Do you call that coffee or is there a cinnamon bun stuffed in there?" He gestured to her road cup.

Laurel laughed. "It's 'Viennese Cinnamon,' you cretin." She turned to me and winked. "If it doesn't look and smell like motor oil, he doesn't consider it coffee."

It was true. I could picture Gary sneaking back to his office and dumping the fresh coffee into his old pot to stiffen it up a bit over the burner before he doctored it up and drank it.

I handed Gary his coffee and he toasted Laurel with the cup. "See you at the recount at nine, I assume?"

"Wouldn't miss it for the world," Laurel muttered darkly as she left. Gary gave me a wave and a wink and followed.

The next man in line was grousing about something to the woman behind him. When he turned, I recognized him. His name was Pete-something-or-other and he was one of the movers who had moved me out of my old house and into the new.

I could see Pete trying to figure out where he knew me from, and his eyes turned speculative as he got it. First, he had moved me from a nice big house into a shack, and now here I was waitressing. He probably figured I'd been dumped and left destitute. He was at least half right.

"Yeah," he said, sidling up to the counter, "you might want to tell your bosses here that some working men need to get moving early. Maybe they should think about opening earlier."

I didn't illuminate him about my ownership status, since God knows I might be waitressing at Goddard's next week. "Oh, really? What time do you start?"

Pete looked like he played football in high school—itsy bitsy head set on a tree trunk neck. The salt and pepper beard helped even him out some, making his head look bigger and hiding part of his neck. He propped his arms on the counter and I feared for the glass-topped bakery case. "Me? I'm off to work by five, five-thirty, at the latest. I'm running late today. Had to take my kid to school."

He looked around to see if anyone was listening and said, in what he seemed to think was a quiet voice, "You know, I seen lights in here early the day your boss-lady was killed, when I was sitting at the stoplight on Civic. But I didn't see nothing when I drove past. Wish I would of known, maybe I could have helped." He handed me a bill and I pulled his change out the cash register.

As I put it in his hand, I asked, "So you went by at about five?"

He rocked back on his heels and considered. "No, not that early, probably more like quarter after."

"Could you see into the store? Were all the lights on?"

He folded up his bills and put them in his pocket. "The lights were real dim, you know, like emergency lights? I could

just see shapes, like the counter and the tables, but no people."
He dropped his loose change in the tip jar and went out.

As I made a mocha for the woman Pete had been talking
to, I wondered whether his information meant anything. The
lights he was talking about had to be the backlights. If they
were on at five-fifteen, that meant that Patricia was already
here. The fact that he hadn't seen her meant that either she was
in the back room, or that she was already on the floor. Dead.

I pumped chocolate into the mocha. Well, if nothing else,
the information might help Pavlik pin down the time of death.
I'd tell him the next time he materialized.

The queue in front of the cash register was long, out the
door at times, but most people seemed to relish the chance to
stand and talk. Some spoke openly about the murder, even
asking questions. Others whispered, glancing at Caron and me
furtively. I think I preferred the people who went ahead and
stuck their foot in it.

By 9:00 a.m., the time the recount was scheduled to begin at
Town Hall, the rush had ended. The cash register tape told us we
had sold sixty-three cups of coffee, twenty-two specialty drinks
and thirty pieces of pastry. Not bad in two and a half hours.

The "To-Go" crowd had pretty much gone, but the little
tables were nearly filled. A couple of them contained moms,
happy for adult conversation after the rigors of getting their
kids off to school. At another, an older man and a woman in
suits were discussing business. At the counter, a young guy
in khakis and a golf shirt was doing some paperwork.

Henry still sat in the corner watching the world go by with
an empty cappuccino cup. I went over to clear the table next
to him and took along the coffee pot.

"It was good seeing you yesterday, Henry," I said in an

effort to make up for the fact that I'd been so focused on Langdon at Goddard's, that I'd barely nodded to Henry. "Can I give you some coffee in there?"

I stood poised with the pot over his cup, and he nodded. "How did you like the cappuccino?" I asked, as I poured.

"Very good," Henry mumbled. "Used to drink them when I was in Europe during the war."

"Ah, that explains it. I don't think a lot of the older people around here have ever had a cappuccino. Maybe you'll convert them for us." Was I a marketing whiz, or what?

Henry nodded and turned his attention to his coffee. I took the hint and retreated behind the counter.

Laurel had promised to call with the results of the recount. I figured it would take at least two hours, so I was surprised when the phone rang at nine-thirty. "Uncommon Grounds. Can I help you?"

"It's gone," the voice on the other end of the line said.

"Laurel? What's gone?" My only contact with her this morning had been over a large Viennese Cinnamon and I doubted the loss of that could have caused the tremor in her voice.

"The ballot. It's vanished."

"But how could that be?"

"You're asking me?" She seemed to be verging on hysteria. "How would I know? I'm only the town clerk. The ballot was only locked in *my* cabinet, by *my* volunteer. How should I know? All I know is that it's gone. I've got to go, here comes that bitch Kate McNamara." Slam.

The moms were leaving and shouting goodbye. I waved back distractedly. The disputed ballot was gone. Meaning what? I didn't know and I didn't have time to think about it at the moment. A group of seniors came in and I spent the next half hour explaining cappuccinos vs. lattes vs. mochas.

By the time 11:00 a.m. rolled around, things had quieted way down again. Henry had left around nine-thirty and only one table was currently occupied, by a pair of women in tennis whites. I'd told Caron about the missing ballot and though she still hadn't been very talkative, we'd agreed that it pointed toward Rudy, since he remained the clear winner if the ballot wasn't found.

That was assuming the results hadn't changed in the recount itself, something Laurel hadn't mentioned in her truncated phone call. I tried to call her back, but kept getting disconnected. An early lunch break seemed in order. Caron agreed, as long as I brought her back a cheeseburger from Goddard's.

Waiting for the light to change so I could turn left out of the parking lot onto Civic, I saw Kate McNamara's Probe heading the opposite direction toward her office. She looked intent, like a woman who had gotten her story. I hesitated, almost turning right to follow her, but then saw someone was already following her. Langdon Shepherd in his Christ Christian Chevy Suburban.

I turned left.

When I got to Town Hall, Jeannie, Laurel's young assistant, told me Laurel had just left "for lunch, I suppose." I stuck my head into some of the other offices, but no one else was around either.

I decided to give Jeannie a try. "So, what happened this morning with the recount?"

She glared at me from under her pouffy brown bangs. "What happened? Who knows? I was out here trying to keep up with these phones. There was this big commotion, then it got quiet, then more people yelling and then, about ten minutes ago, everybody just walked out, just like that, and left me here." The phone rang. Jeannie picked it up and slammed it back down again.

With nothing to be gained from Jeannie except, perhaps, a bloody nose, I left. Sitting in my car, I tried to decide what to do next. Gary's squad wasn't outside the police station, so I assumed he wasn't there either.

I gave in and decided to go see Kate. I knew she was at her office and I didn't have time to track down anyone else. I just hoped Langdon had either been heading elsewhere or had already come and gone. I checked my watch. I'd better get moving, I had to get back to Uncommon Grounds with Caron's cheeseburger. I didn't want to add low blood sugar to her problems.

Happily, Kate was in and Langdon was nowhere in sight. The receptionist, who doubled as the paper's circulation manager and photographer, led me back. Kate was hanging up the phone when I came in.

"Well," she said, "does this mean you're willing to talk to the press, Maggy?"

I'd been thinking about how to deal with Kate. I sat down and leaned forward, planting my elbows on her desk. "I'm willing to talk with you, Kate, but there are some conditions." Maggy's my name, hardball's my game.

"Off the record doesn't do anything for me," she warned.

"That's not one of them. You and I both know you're past your deadline. *The Observer* is being printed as we speak. So here's the deal: I'll talk to you for next week's edition. In return, I want you to tell me what you know. You said it: You show me yours, I'll show you mine."

Kate nodded and sat back in her chair. "That's fair."

I wasn't done. "Two other conditions. What I tell you stays

confidential until you go to press next Wednesday. That's to
your advantage as well as mine. You don't want the *CitySen-*
tinel to get a jump on you." I was acting like I had a whole
lot more information than I did, but it was working. I had Kate
practically salivating.

I continued. "Finally, I know an honorable newswoman
like yourself would never do this, but I'll say it anyway. No
special editions. The paper is printed on Wednesday next
week and goes out on Thursday. Agreed?"

The expression on Kate's face told me that the thought of
a special edition had crossed this honorable newswoman's
mind. She agreed anyway.

I dove right in. "So, what happened at this morning's
recount?"

Kate grinned, suddenly all dark hair and rosy cheeks. She
might be a pleasant person to have around when she wasn't
playing newspaper mogul. Without the scowl, you even
noticed her snub nose and freckles.

"What didn't happen?" She referred to her steno pad.
"Let's see, present were Rudy Fischer, his campaign man-
ager—what's his name, Paul Lukas?—and Chief Donovan,
Laurel Birmingham, Sheriff Pavlik, Way Benson, Sarah
Kingston and Gene Diaz."

The last name caught my attention. "The town attorney?"

"Yeah, to make sure everything was on the up and up.
Interesting thing is, though, he let it slip that Patricia Harper
had made an appointment with him for yesterday afternoon."

Yesterday, the day on which the recount had originally
been scheduled. "You think she was preparing some sort of
objection, in case the recount went against her?"

Kate looked speculative. "Or, maybe she was going to

charge the town or Rudy with election fraud." She nearly clapped her hands in journalistic glee.

"But that's fairly standard isn't it? Someone loses an election and they say the other guy broke the rules? Remember last year, when one of the supervisors complained about Georgia Armstrong forgetting that 'Paid by' line on the bottom of her flyer? They don't overturn elections for that kind of thing, do they?"

Kate shook her head. "No, not usually, unless it has a material effect on the outcome of the election. Sometimes they just kick up a fuss to set themselves up for the next election." I had to admit Kate knew her stuff when it came to the town's inner workings.

"Well, I know Patricia was upset about this coin toss thing in case of a tie," I said. "Did Gene say when she set up the appointment?" Since Patricia hadn't known about the coin toss until Friday night, she would have had to call Diaz over the weekend to set up a meeting on that subject.

"No, why?"

I didn't see any reason why I shouldn't tell her, so I filled her in and then shifted the subject a bit. "I know about the ballot and that it disappeared. Did they do the rest of the recount?"

"Uh-huh. They did the recount first and that came out the same. Rudy by one vote."

And what did that do to my theory? "Then what?"

"Then Gary gets up and goes to the file cabinet in the corner." Kate was enjoying parceling out the information.

"Was it locked? Did Gary have a key?" I asked.

"Laurel Birmingham had given him the key the minute she found out the ballot was contested. Covering her butt, I assume." There was no love lost between Laurel and Kate.

"Were there any other keys?"

"Laurel says no, but it was a file cabinet for crying out loud, not a safe. Who knows how many keys there might have been?"

I had to agree. In my old office, the file cabinets could be opened by just about any key you found laying around. Or by hitting it three times with your shoe. "So Gary goes to open the file cabinet and there's nothing there?"

"Yup, he opens the top drawer, then the next, then the next. Nothing, except old stationery and paperclips. So Laurel gets on the phone to Sophie, her senile old ballot counter, to make sure she locked it in there. Of course, the old lady is absolutely positive it was in the top drawer in the front, but she probably can't remember what day it is."

"Oh I don't know, Sophie Daystrom seems pretty sharp." Not to mention a little scary.

Kate flushed. "Okay, maybe I'm exaggerating. But here's a ballot that nobody except her saw and now it's gone. Maybe she put it somewhere else or maybe it doesn't exist."

"Have you talked to Sophie?"

"No, I tried to call her, but there was no answer."

She probably had caller ID. "So what happened then?" I asked Kate.

"All hell broke out." She smiled at the memory. "Rudy yelling there was never a ballot in the first place. Sarah saying that one of his cronies must have stolen it. Way arguing—"

I interrupted. "Wait a second, what was Way doing there?"

Kate shrugged. "I told you he was there. It was an open meeting."

"So what was he saying?" I was nursing my newly born distrust of Way Benson.

"Just that it really didn't matter since Patricia was dead."

I decided to plant a seed and hoped it would flourish in Kate's fertile imagination. "Interesting, if he felt that way, why was he there in the first place?"

She hesitated. "Are you saying maybe Way had something to do with the ballot?"

I stood up. "I'm saying it's awfully convenient that Patricia died when she did—for Rudy and who knows who else."

Kate stood up, too. "Way Benson is a powerful man around here, Maggy."

I laughed. "And a big advertiser, I suppose. Are you going to let that keep you from doing a thorough investigation, Kate?" The seed watered, I started to leave the garden.

Kate's voice stopped me. "Oh, Maggy?"

I turned. Kate pointed at a purple leaflet on her desk. "I *will* get you back for siccing Langdon Shepherd on me. You know that, don't you?"

She laughed and a shiver ran up my spine.

Funny how frightening a snub-nosed, freckled-face brunette can be when she puts her mind to it.

TEN

As I WALKED AROUND the corner to Uncommon Grounds with the greasy bag from Goddard's, I gave some consideration to the election and the missing ballot. Unlike Rudy, Way probably had the skill to re-wire the machine and electrocute Patricia. He also had access to Uncommon Grounds, since he owned the mall. But how could he know that Patricia would use the machine first and be killed?

Pavlik was right, it could have been any of us dead on that floor. Would Way—or Rudy—benefit from either Caron's death or mine? I couldn't see how. And what about the missing ballot? The only way it could pose a problem for Rudy was if it were a vote for Patricia. But who could have known that other than Sophie?

And then there was the point that Pavlik had brought up. How could the killer be sure that the espresso machine would kill its victim? Unless scaring us would serve the same end.

A blue Mercedes was in the parking lot and when I entered the store, David was talking to Caron. I gave him a quick hug. "How are you doing?" I asked.

He looked like he was doing terrible. He wore a suit and tie, but the white dress shirt looked like it had spent the night on the floor. "I'm sorry I didn't return your messages. I just haven't been functioning very well without Patricia. I just don't understand..."

David grimaced and ran a freckled hand over his face.

"The service will be at Christ Christian tomorrow at ten a.m. No visitation, I didn't think I—we—could deal with that."

"How are the kids, David?" Caron asked.

"All right, I guess. I just thank God that they're in private school. They're more insulated there than they would be at a public school. They're not hearing all the…talk," he finished.

I hoped David hadn't heard quite all the talk either. I exchanged looks with Caron, who was crimson. "We'll close the store tomorrow in Patricia's memory," I told David.

He shook his head. "No. Please. Close so you can attend the funeral if you want, but you really should be open the rest of the day. This is a business, you can't just close up."

I have to admit I'd been concerned about opening one day and being closed the next, but I'd have done it nonetheless. "Maybe we'll close nine-thirty to noon," I compromised. "Does that sound reasonable?"

Caron nodded, seeming eager to move the subject away from the treacherous ground it had tread earlier. "That way we won't disappoint the early crowd. It's quiet around noon anyway."

But David wasn't paying attention to Caron, he was looking at the espresso machine. "Is this the machine?" he asked.

"No!" I was horrified. "They took the old one away for evidence. We wouldn't, we couldn't…"

David raised his hand. "It's all right, Maggy." He looked like a beaten man. "I have to go home and do some work. Can you make me a large skim latte to go?"

Making a latte with David watching was the last thing I wanted to do. But I did it.

I knew he was reliving what must have been Patricia's last moments as I brewed the shots and poured them into a road cup. "Uh, any flavor in here, David?" I asked to break the silence.

"No," he said. "Just plain." I added fresh milk to the pitcher and pulled out the frothing wand. The same thing Patricia had done before…

Caron made an inadvertent sound, almost a groan, but David remained silent. I wasn't sure why he was doing this. Maybe he thought it would be cleansing somehow. He waited as I brought the milk up to one hundred and sixty degrees and poured it into the cup, topping it with a bit of foam. Then he took the cup, thanked me and left, pausing to grab a couple of sugars from the condiment cart on the way out.

As the door closed behind him, Caron picked up her cheeseburger and walked into the office, leaving me alone.

THE REST OF THE DAY was fairly uneventful. Business picked up again around two in the afternoon. To our surprise, the afternoon customers were much younger, like around fifteen. Teenagers seemed to have found in coffee something that not only made them feel like adults, but also was legal and couldn't get them pregnant.

By four-thirty, the after-school crowd had thinned and we began our preparations for closing. By five-thirty, the machines were cleaned and the floor mopped and Caron and I had departed, clutching white bags of leftover pastry. We had over-ordered on muffins and under-ordered on scones and Kaiser rolls. That, unlike some things, could be fixed.

When I got home, I fed Frank a blueberry muffin. I pulled out the pumpkin chocolate chip for myself and put a call into Sophie, the ballot lady. She didn't answer her phone—probably still hiding from Kate or out terrorizing clueless tourists at Goddard's.

Taking a bite of muffin, I dialed Laurel, who actually

answered and gave me a synopsis of today's events at Town Hall, which pretty much paralleled Kate's version. Then I asked the big question. "Is Sophie absolutely sure she put the ballot in the file cabinet?"

"Yes!"

I guess she had heard the big question before. "Okay, okay. So who else had a key?"

"Sophie gave the key to me. I gave it to Gary. Was there another key? I don't think so, but who knows? Any other questions you want to ask me that I've already heard from both Gary and the sheriff? Not to mention that McNamara woman. She's hounding poor Sophie, so Sophie went to Miami for the rest of the week. That'll drive McNamara crazy."

I was all for that. "Did anyone else see the ballot, Laurel? Was anyone else there?" I shoved Frank, who was sniffing around my lap for crumbs, back with my bare foot.

Laurel was quiet for a moment. "I'm not sure. Sophie didn't mention anyone else, but I suppose there were other poll-workers around."

"So it's possible someone knows what was on the ballot, even if Sophie doesn't?"

"It's possible," she admitted.

"Okay, Laurel, thanks. Did you know that Patricia's funeral is tomorrow?"

She did. The notice was in the *CitySentinel*. We said goodbye and hung up.

I mopped up the pool of drool Frank had left on the corner of the coffee table as he watched me eat my muffin. Then I went into the bathroom to run a nice hot bath. My feet and back hurt from the long hours of standing and my head hurt from the long hours of thinking. This stuff was harder than it looked.

As the tub filled, I left the bathroom to grab my pajamas. By the time I got back, Frank was lying on the towel next to the tub. I climbed awkwardly over him and sank gratefully, if not gracefully, into the tub, sliding down so the water was up to my chin.

Way, with or without Rudy, was now my chief suspect. Motive? I'd have to work on that, but I was pretty sure it had to do with Way's development projects. Way Benson was used to getting what he wanted from Rudy and the town board.

Maybe Patricia would have caused him trouble if she had been elected. Maybe Rudy was on the take. Maybe Patricia had found out about it.

That would explain her appointment with the town attorney, too. And if Patricia hadn't been killed outright? Then maybe the killer figured a bad shock would be enough to warn her off.

I shook my head and the bathwater swish-swashed around me. Maybe this and maybe that. A call to Gene Diaz and another to Sarah to get the scoop on the real estate development dirt in town, were definitely in order for tomorrow.

But tonight, bed. Morning comes much too quickly when work starts at 6:00 a.m.

CARON APPARENTLY HAD gotten a second wind. By the time I arrived at 6:00, she had half the checklist complete. I put up a notice that we would be closed 9:30 a.m. to noon and got to work, too. Business was brisk, although not as brisk as it had been the day before.

Henry was in again and was practically garrulous, for Henry. He requested a half decaf, half regular cappuccino, saying he'd had trouble sleeping the night before. "I never sleep good anymore," he grumbled.

"No? Why not?" I asked as I frothed the milk for his cappuccino. Already, I'd learned that someone's health, especially if they were elderly, was a great conversation starter.

"Don't know. Just know the older I get, less sleep I need. Taken to going out for a walk after the news, try to tire myself out; but even so, sometimes I don't fall asleep until one, maybe two in the morning."

Personally, I thought a walk in the night air at eleven might have the same effect on me. "Maybe the walk wakes you up, instead of tires you out," I suggested.

Henry shrugged. "Most times it's quiet and I walk down along the creek. Relaxes me. Though I can't tonight. Thursday nights them hooligans are always down there making a racket. Barging around with flashlights, playing 'Cowboys and Indians' or something."

I rang up his drink and handed him the change. "The kids around here like to play 'Bloody Murder.' I wonder if their parents know they're out."

The truth was half the kids in Brookhills weren't as well supervised as their parents liked to think they were. Poplar Creek, which ran right behind the senior complex, was one of their favorite hangouts and, despite what I'd just told Henry, I didn't think the teens were playing either 'Cowboys and Indians' or 'Bloody Murder.' More likely 'Roll the Condom,' though given the teen pregnancy and STD rates the *CitySentinel* had reported, maybe they weren't playing by those rules either.

Taking his cup, Henry shuffled over to his corner, apparently socially spent.

Sarah Kingston was next in line.

"Sarah, I'm glad you stopped by," I said. She'd saved me a phone call.

"Why?" Sarah demanded suspiciously.

"Because we want you to spend lots of money here. What did you think? Your sparkling personality?"

Sarah grinned. "That's what I like, an honest business woman." She glanced at the customer behind her and leaned in. "Did you hear about the ballot?"

I nodded and gestured for her to meet me at the end of the counter, leaving Caron to take care of the next person in line. "So what do you think?" I asked. "Rudy? Way? Both of them?"

"Could be, although I don't think it's their style. Fact is, though, Way Benson stands to make a lot of money if Rudy and the board decide to tear down Summit Lawn School."

"Why?" If I'd been Frank, my ears would have perked up. Then again, if I were Frank, I'd be home sleeping now.

"Because, my dear, Way owns the land adjacent to the school. Whether he buys the school and develops the land, or someone else does, he'll win. They'll need his parcel in order to go retail there." She raised her eyebrows, wiggled her fingers at me and exited stage right.

I wondered how much Sarah meant by a bundle. Enough to kill for? I guessed that depended on the person. Summit Lawn was on Brookhill Road, the most valuable strip of real estate around. What's more, the road was completely developed, with the exception of the school property itself. Speculation was that the land would be worth millions.

So which of the surrounding properties did Way own? On one side was a gas station, on the other, a tavern. Either or both could be torn down and replaced with new development with no tears shed by town officials.

CARON AND I TOOK TURNS changing in the back room and left the store at nine forty-five for Patricia's funeral. Christ Christian's lot was full when we got there, and we had to park three blocks away. We barely made it in by ten.

Standing in the back of the crowded church, the chances of finding two seats together seemed remote until we saw Bernie waving to us. We made our way down the side aisle and excused ourselves all the way to our seats just as the music changed and David and the family were escorted to the front pews.

David was pale, but composed. Courtney, a pretty blonde child, walked with him, holding his hand. Sam followed alone. The three filed into the front pew and remained standing. Langdon gestured for the congregation to rise to sing the opening hymn.

The service lasted about an hour. Langdon spoke about Patricia's faith and dedication to the church, her family and her community. Patricia's son, Sam, managed to make it through a scripture reading before breaking down. That was followed by the song, "On Eagles' Wings," which always does me in even if has become to funerals what "Proud Mary" is to wedding receptions.

As the casket was carried out, there was an undertone of sniffling accompanying the organ music. A life cut short, a mother leaving her children too soon.

And why? Someone here might know the answer. I glanced around the church as we waited in our pew to be dismissed by the ushers. Everyone seemed to be there, including law enforcement. Gary was keeping a watchful eye from his position behind David, where the receiving line—or whatever it's called at a funeral—had formed. Pavlik was standing at the door and seemed to be looking in my direction, but at someone just beyond me.

I turned around to look, but the pew in front of us had just been dismissed and people were streaming past. Laurel and Mary came by, then Rudy. Up ahead I could see Way, and in front of him, Roger Karsten. Roger was good-looking, I supposed, in a pretty-boy way. Curly blonde hair, blue eyes.

As I watched, Roger shook hands with David. David nodded woodenly, accepting Roger's condolences, but didn't seem to react any differently to him than to anyone else. Sam, to David's left, was another story.

I nudged Caron. "Look, Sam won't shake hands with Roger." Sam looked right through Karsten, moving on to shake the hand of the next person in line. It was very well done, considering the kid was only fifteen. I have adult friends who have worked years to be able to snub someone as effectively as Sam had just done.

"So Sam knows," Caron said softly next to me.

Startled, I glanced at Bernie. He smiled, albeit painfully, and put his arm around Caron's shoulder. "It's all right Maggy. Caron told me about her and Roger, and Patricia."

"And you're…"

He sighed and pulled Caron a little closer. "Okay, or we will be. We just need some time." Caron was crying.

I hoped she realized what she had in Bernie. He was giving her the chance I had denied Ted. Then again, Ted hadn't dumped his hygienist, like Caron had dumped Roger. Instead, she would be promoted to trophy wife shortly after the divorce became final. So much for parallels…

By the time we slid out of our pew, most of the crowd had moved into Fellowship Hall for coffee and cake. Langdon was next to David, who looked pale and exhausted. He thanked Langdon and assured him that he would see him on Sunday before he turned to me. I hugged him and said all the appropriate things, which, of course, never are.

We had to get back to the store, but I wanted to see who else was in Fellowship Hall. The person I was looking for was Roger Karsten, though I figured it was unlikely he would hang out to chat at his former mistress's funeral, especially after the reception Sam had given him.

But as luck would have it, Roger was made of sterner stuff—or perhaps just totally insensitive stuff. I caught a glimpse of him just coming out of the men's room. He straightened his tie, looked around and made a quick right out the side door. I dashed across Fellowship Hall and followed.

"Roger!" I yelled, chasing him down the sidewalk.

He kept right on walking.

I took a short cut across the church lawn, trying to cut him off and sinking up to my sensible two-inch heels in the process. "Roger," I called again, as I dodged around the church sign and caught up to him in the parking lot.

He turned abruptly and I pulled up short, a glob of lawn clinging to each shoe. Roger looked down at my shoes and then up my body until he finally reached my face.

"I want to talk to you about Patricia," I said.

"I didn't know Mrs. Harper very well. I just came to pay my respects." He turned away.

I grabbed his arm and whispered, "I want to talk to you about Patricia *and* Caron."

That got his attention. His mouth opened but nothing came out, so he slammed it shut. Running a hand through his curly blonde locks, he must have decided to bluff. "Mrs. Harper and Mrs. Egan are—were—your partners. What would I know about them?"

I decided to play hardball with the chump, since it had worked so well with Kate. Taking a step backward, I took the volume up a couple of decibels. "That's not the question. The question is, what do I know about them—and you…" A group of people walked past us on their way to their cars.

This time Roger grabbed my arm. Ouch. Sarah could have this hard-boiled P.I. stuff. I pulled away and rubbed my elbow. "Hey, that hurt."

He had the grace to look embarrassed, but only for a moment. "What do you mean, about them and me?" he whispered.

"Let's cut the crap." I managed to keep my voice low but, I hoped, menacing. "I know you were fooling around with Patricia and Caron. Don't bother to deny it."

"Okay, okay."

Hey, this wasn't so hard after all.

Karsten rubbed at his chin, like an old man putting on Aqua Velva. He looked around. "All right. I had…a relationship with Patricia and one with Caron. But not at the same time."

And that made it all right.

He was shaking his head. "I suppose the whole town knows about it by now. Patricia's kid sure knows. That damn sheriff said he wouldn't say anything unless he had to."

I exploded. "You little shit. You're worried about your reputation. I can't believe you had the nerve to show up here today. For God's sake, think of someone beside yourself. Like David, for example. Or Sam. Or Bernie Egan. Or Caron."

"Now wait a second. I wasn't alone in this. It takes—"

Honest to God, if he said "it takes two to tango," I was going to smack him one. I waved my hands to cut him off. "Just tell me, was it over with Patricia before you hopped in bed with Caron?"

He nodded. "I told you that."

Yeah, like I believed anything he said. "And it's over with Caron?"

"Yeah, she—"

I waved him down again. "I'm not interested in the details. Who ended it, you or Patricia?" It couldn't hurt to confirm what Sarah had told me.

But Roger surprised me. "I did. She said she couldn't divorce David." He lifted his shoulders. "I didn't understand. I thought she loved me."

Now I was confused. "You're saying that you ended the affair? That Patricia didn't?"

He had been looking down at the sidewalk, but now he looked up. There were tears in his eyes. "You asked me why I came here?"

I nodded.

"I came here because I loved her. I just wanted to say goodbye." He turned and walked away.

ELEVEN

OKAY, LET'S LAY this out. Roger and Patricia had an affair. Patricia wouldn't leave her husband, so Roger broke it off. And immediately jumped in bed with Caron. But still loved Patricia.

The strange thing was, I thought Roger actually meant it. I guess he had his own personal code of ethics. Honor among sleaze. I shook my head and started back toward Uncommon Grounds.

As I crossed the sidewalk to the store, I saw Tony Bruno in his dental office window. I waved and he came out, white coat flapping. "Just back from the funeral?" he asked.

I told him I was.

"Such a shame. So young for a lady to die." He shook his head sadly and pointed to Uncommon Grounds. "A couple of people stopped by, not too many."

I wasn't sure if that was good news or bad. "Do you want to come in for a cup?" I said, trying to get my keys out of my purse. "I'll buy."

But Tony was buttoning his white coat. "Thank you, no. This time of year, my family and I, we go up to our cabin in Door County on Friday morning and come back in time for mass on Sunday. That means Thursday is always a very busy day for me."

I shivered in the April air. "Isn't it awfully cool up there this early in the year?" If you picture Wisconsin as a mitten,

Door County is the thumb, with Lake Michigan on the east and Green Bay—the body of water, not the city or the team—on the west.

Tony shrugged. "It's cold—but there's plenty of work to be done. Painting, planting, putting in the pier. We all work together and it gets done. Then in the summer, we can relax."

I wished him a nice weekend and ducked in the door. We all work together, Tony said, and it gets done. I looked around the store. With Patricia gone and Caron acting so distant, it was not only harder to get the work done, but it was getting downright lonely.

I hoped now that Caron had told Bernie, she would be more herself. I was worried about her. While I was fairly certain that Pavlik didn't consider me a serious suspect any longer, I thought Caron still was. It was a good sign, though, that the sheriff had taken the time to go to the recount. It meant he hadn't ruled anything out. Yet.

As I flipped the "closed" sign in the window to "open," I saw Bernie drop Caron off at the curb. She leaned back in and kissed him before turning toward the door. Caron was my friend. I would do what I could to help her, and if that meant ratting on Way Benson or Roger Karsten, even better.

THE REST OF THE AFTERNOON sped by, a mad blur of lattes and biscottis. It was my turn to close since Caron had opened. By the time I finished vacuuming, I'd made up my mind to call Pavlik the next morning.

He saved me the trouble. He was leaning against my van in the parking lot when I walked out of the store. He still wore the dark suit he'd had on at the funeral.

As I approached the van, he straightened up and I noticed

that the Caravan had left powdery white traces on the back of his suit coat. I started to tell him, but he interrupted.

"Ms. Thorsen, I need to talk to you." He looked grim. "We can do it at your home or at my office."

Now what did this mean? I wiggled my fingers vaguely toward the store. "Couldn't we talk here?"

He nodded toward the assorted people in the parking lot and storefronts who were casually, or so they thought, watching us. "No."

Well, I sure didn't want to go downtown, so I might as well show the copper what great digs I had. Besides, Frank was there and I had a sudden vision of sheepdog drool streaming down one of Pavlik's well-pressed pants legs. I told him to follow me home.

Unfortunately for me and fortunately for Pavlik, Frank was a perfect gentleman. He did snuffle a bit on Pavlik's pants, but the sheriff didn't seem to mind. "Don't worry, I have a dog at home."

He knelt down to give Frank a good rub on his belly. Yes, belly. Frank, upon seeing a strange man enter my home, immediately rolled over on his back, his pink tongue lolling out one side of his mouth.

"You're pathetic," I told him.

Pavlik finished the scratch and stood up, a smile on his face. "How old is he?" Dog people ask the same questions about dogs that kid people ask about kids. Except kid people usually don't ask which breeder you use.

"About two," I said, leading him into the kitchen. "He's my son's. He left him with me when he went off to college."

Now, a kid person would have asked which college, Pavlik was concerned about the dog. "He's a big guy. A dog like this needs plenty of exercise." He looked around my tiny house, ready to slap me with a dog abuse citation, no doubt.

I sank down at the table and waved him to do likewise. "I know, I know. A neighbor boy comes over after school and walks him when I can't. He really is too big for this place, but there was no choice. Me or the pound."

Pavlik nodded. He was looking positively congenial. It must cut down on headcount in the office to be able to play "good cop/bad cop" all by himself. "Same with my dog. She's not perfect, but I couldn't let them put her down."

"What kind of dog do you have?" I pictured a German Shepherd or a Doberman. I wasn't disappointed.

"A pit bull."

My God, a pit bull? "You're a police officer, how can you own a pit bull?" I sputtered.

He rose in defense of his dog. "You know, a pit bull, or any other kind of dog for that matter, is not intrinsically evil. It's the people who train them to rip each other apart who are evil."

"Rip each other *and* people apart," I pointed out. "You can't tell me they aren't aggressive dogs to start out with." I pointed to Frank, who was lying with his hairy chin on my shoe. "You could never get a dog like Frank to fight."

Pavlik looked weary all of a sudden, but his eyes met mine head on. "You could if you starved him and made him fight other dogs for scraps of food. You could if you alternated beatings with praise to keep him off balance. Gave him food one time, and beat him with a two-by-four the next. Any dog can be made vicious."

Pavlik stood up and paced to the counter. "We busted a pit bull ring in Chicago. God, you should have seen those dogs. Scared, hungry. Absolutely berserk. The lame ones they used as bait for the healthy ones. Give them a taste of blood."

"And your dog?" I asked, feeling sick.

"I found her in a filthy cage. No food. No water. She was so weak she couldn't stand. She was little more than a puppy herself and they had been using her for breeding. Litter after litter." Pavlik leaned against the kitchen counter. "The only people she had ever known had abused her. And you know what?"

I shook my head.

"When I opened the cage she came to me. Slid on her stomach, her tail—what was left of it—wagging this tentative wag. Like she expected to be hit, but hadn't quite given up hope of better from me." Pavlik smiled sadly. "When I scratched her behind the ears, she flipped over on her back, just like Frank did before."

He shook his head. "Even with all the abuse she suffered at human hands, she still had to try."

Okay, so I'm a sucker for dog and kid stories. By this time, I was blinking back tears. "So how long have you had her?"

"About three years now. But enough about dogs." He sat back down, getting all official again. "I need some information from you."

Talk about a change of subjects. And personalities. But if Pavlik wanted information, I was happy to give it to him. I filled him in on Summit Lawn School and told him what Sarah had said about Way's involvement. "So, you see? Way Benson could have implicated Caron to cover his own tail." I looked to Pavlik for agreement.

And got none, of course. "Why would he have killed her now? It's no different than when you theorized that Rudy Fischer did it. Mrs. Harper lost the election. *If* the ballot was legal and *if* it was for Mrs. Harper, it only meant a tie. Why would Benson kill her before the coin toss, even before the ballot was opened?"

"Maybe he knew who it was for. It is missing after all. Why would somebody steal it if it wasn't important?" I was dancing around his point and we both knew it.

Pavlik folded his arms. "We're taking the word of an eighty-year old woman there even was a ballot."

"Because she's eighty, she's automatically unreliable? You know, much like pit bulls, old people should be judged on an individual basis. Sophie Daystrom is *not* senile." But she was a bit of a pit bull, I had to admit.

He raised his hands to ward me off. "Okay, okay, but I don't think this town board thing has any bearing on the case. It's just clouding the issue. Right now, I'm more interested in Mrs. Harper's affair with Karsten."

Maybe I would have more luck pitching Roger as the prime suspect. "Sarah Kingston, Patricia's campaign manager, told me that Patricia had kissed Karsten off." I leaned forward in my seat and waved my finger to make my point. "Not Karsten, though. No, he says he stopped seeing her because she wouldn't divorce David. Now there's a motive for you. The spurned lover. It all fits." I sat back in my seat and crossed my arms, satisfied.

Pavlik was staring at me, fascinated. "Why do you do that?"

I looked around uncertainly. "Do what?"

"Start acting like some kind of bad TV private eye all of a sudden. It's like talking to someone with multiple personalities."

"Oh, please, that's like *Sybil* calling *Eve* schizophrenic."

He thought about that for a second, then opened his mouth and closed it again. I wasn't sure if he'd gotten the allusion, but at least it had shut him up.

"All I'm trying to do is help," I added.

Pavlik rubbed his chin. "Okay, so if you want to help, tell me everything you know about David Harper."

"David? You think David did this?" I leapt to David's defense, ignoring the fact that even I had entertained the notion he might be involved.

"Listen," I protested, "you didn't see David when he came into the shop and found Patricia dead. He was devastated, I would swear to it."

"I know, I heard all about it from Donovan."

I didn't like the way Pavlik said Gary's name. "You know, Gary Donovan has more experience than you'll ever have. Police force, Secret Service, corporate security and now police chief. You owe him some respect."

Pavlik's eyes narrowed. "I show people respect when they earn that respect. Donovan did a lousy job at the crime scene."

"We didn't know it was a crime scene," I pointed out.

"Any intelligent adult could have seen there was something wrong. It should have bit him in the ass."

I shook my head and bit my tongue. I was afraid I was doing Gary more harm than good here.

Pavlik switched subjects. Now there was a surprise. "If Mrs. Harper was the target, and since there haven't been any attempts on you or Mrs. Egan, I think we can be fairly sure of that—"

"Attempts on us?" He was being pretty matter-of-fact about something he had never even mentioned before. Especially when that something involved my life and Caron's. "Were you doing anything to prevent these possible attempts?"

Pavlik smiled. "We've been keeping an eye on both of you."

I remembered the car out in front of my house Monday and Tuesday nights. Protection or surveillance? It amounted to the same thing in this case. The car hadn't been there last night. "You gave up pretty easily, didn't you?"

"It was unlikely that either of you were the target for the

same reasons it's difficult to believe that Mrs. Harper was: How could the killer know who would use the machine first?"

It seemed like we were going in circles. Nobody could have done it, because no one would have done it. "But Patricia *was* killed."

"So maybe it was sabotage gone wrong."

"You think we have our competitors worried?"

He glared at me and continued. "Or someone knew Mrs. Harper well enough to be sure she would go in early *and* make herself a latte. Now you and Mrs. Egan, arguably, knew her well enough, and her husband knew her well enough. Maybe even Sarah Kingston."

I thought that was a stretch. Actually, all of it was a stretch and I told him so. Then I asked him pointedly what he wanted to know about David.

"Everything. I can't find anything on him."

"I'm not surprised, David is about as white bread as they come. He owns his own consulting firm. I think he's in market research, Patricia said. Consumer goods. David couldn't—"

"How long have they lived here?" Pavlik interrupted.

"Let's see. David's been in Brookhills forever, but Patricia and the kids moved here three or four years ago when she and David got married."

"Mrs. Harper was divorced?" Pavlik perked right up and even I got excited at the thought of a bitter ex-husband running around out there.

Then I remembered. "I'm pretty sure Patricia is a widow," I said. "Caron would know for sure."

"Mrs. Egan doesn't seem to want to talk to me anymore," Pavlik said, making a note. "Her husband's an attorney?"

I nodded. Bernie's specialty was patent law. Pavlik had

better watch out or Bernie might slap him with a trademark. I didn't tell Pavlik that, of course, I was still steamed at his crack about Gary.

"I assume Mr. Egan knows about the affair between his wife and Mr. Karsten by now."

I nodded. "Caron told him."

"But from the civil way they spoke at the funeral, I don't think that Mr. Harper knows about *his* wife's affair with Karsten." He was watching me carefully.

"I don't think so either," I said slowly.

"But," he continued, still watching me, "the son, Sam, certainly doesn't care for Karsten."

So Pavlik had seen the exchange, or the lack of exchange, between Sam and Karsten, too. But he couldn't seriously suspect Sam. He was just a kid. "You don't think Sam killed his mother, do you?" I asked incredulously.

"If it was Karsten who was dead, I might look at the kid. But not his mother. Not like this."

I nodded in agreement and we sat in what might have been mistaken for companionable silence for a moment. Then I stood up. "If you don't have any other questions, Sheriff, I have some things to get done tonight."

Pavlik stood as well. "I think that's all for now." He hesitated. "I was going to stop for a sandwich on the way home. Would you like to maybe go…" He let it trail off.

It had been a long time, but I was fairly certain Pavlik had just asked me out. My mouth fell open. "Umm, thanks, but I don't…"

"Eat?" Pavlik grinned. "Okay, I guess I'll just have to go it alone."

After I'd seen him out, I leaned against the door until I

heard the engine start and then pulled aside the curtain to watch the car pull away.

I don't eat?

Swift.

Admittedly, not my finest moment. But, still, wasn't this a teensy bit odd? I mean, in three separate conversations, the man had accused me of being, in turn, manic, schizophrenic, and a murderer. And then he wants to do dinner?

Why?

Well, regardless of his motives, I wasn't ready for interspecies dating—and I was quite certain Pavlik was a whole different kind of animal than I was used to.

The animal I *was* used to gave me a nudge with his nose.

I let the curtain drop. "Want to watch a little TV?" I asked.

Frank barked.

He was right. First we needed to order a pizza.

BY THE TIME THE NEWS and Letterman's monologue was over, Frank was snoring and the pizza box was empty. Hey, it was a medium and Frank loves sausage and green olives.

I went to throw the box away and stopped with my hand hovering over the kitchen trash.

The wastebasket.

Patricia drank her lattes without sugar, so why were there two empty sugar packets in the wastebasket at the shop the morning she died?

I set the pizza box on top of the basket and wandered out to the front window. In my mind's eye, I could see David picking up the two sugars yesterday as he left the store carrying an identical drink to the one Patricia usually drank. Identical, that is, except that David took sugar in his.

So maybe, I thought, Patricia wasn't making a latte for herself. Maybe she was making one for someone who was with her. Someone who used sugar. Like David. It would be so easy to ask her to make him a latte, just like he'd ask me to do yesterday, and then...

Then what? David just stood back and watched Patricia die? But even if you bought that, why would he kill her? She was having an affair, but he didn't seem to know about it. And even if he did, would he kill her for it? He was a stalwart Christian, after all. But what did that mean under these circumstances? An "eye for an eye"? Or divine forgiveness? Depended on which part of the Bible David read, I supposed.

The sound of multiple car engines turning over nearby heralded the exodus of a stream of cars from Christ Christian. Must be big doings downstream, I thought, as the parade passed me by, David's car among them. Could he have been at the church all this time?

So what did I do now? Call Pavlik? He'd laugh at my playing...what did he call it? Bad TV private eye?

And, granted, two small pieces of paper in the trash weren't much to go on. But combined with a motive, like if David *had* suspected Patricia was having an affair...

I watched as the last taillights disappeared down Poplar Creek Drive.

Well then, that was something altogether different.

TWELVE

THE NEXT MORNING while I was brewing coffee, I decided I needed to find a Watson.

Even Sherlock Holmes, in his opium-induced stupor enjoyed talking to someone beside himself. Like Holmes, I needed a sounding board, a sidekick—an Archie to my Nero Wolfe, a Pancho to my Cisco.

Caron, who would have been the logical choice just a week ago, was tuning in and out like a car radio trying to pick up a weak signal on a country road. At the moment, having refused my help with a five-pound bag of Guatemalan, she was strewing beans all over the floor as she struggled to pour it into one of the Lucite display bins.

The cover of the bin flipped down and I moved to lift it, getting a snarl for my efforts. No, Caron wouldn't do.

Continuing down the hierarchy of friendship, we came to Gary, who, being the police chief and all, would have obvious ethical problems with getting involved. Then there was Frank, who was a dog.

Laurel, I hated to say, was too much of a talker, much as I loved that about her. Mary, same thing.

That left Sarah. The problem with Sarah, though, was that she was a bulldozer. I wasn't sure I could control her.

The only other person who came to mind was Kate McNamara. Hmm. No, that was ludicrous. Not only wasn't she a friend, but she was pushy, conniving, smart-mouthed and…coming in the door.

"Morning, Kate," I called. Just call me perky.

Kate stomped up to the counter and slapped her notebook on the bakery case.

"Well?" she demanded.

"Latte?" I hazarded a guess.

"Information. It's your turn. What was the sheriff doing at your house last night?"

There weren't a lot of people in the store, but the ones who were—Henry and two women in jogging suits—turned to look at me. Caron kept spilling the beans. I motioned for Kate to meet me in the office and crunched my way across the floor to get there.

Our office is so tiny the desk and a single chair nearly fills it. I perched on the edge of the desk, while Kate loomed in the doorway.

"So what's the deal, Maggy? What did Pavlik want?" Her expression turned wily. "Or was this a personal call?"

Did Pancho ever ask, "Hey, Cisco, you gettin' any?" I didn't think so.

"No, it wasn't a personal call. He had some questions—nothing that you don't already know." Okay, so I lied. And I was getting better at it. "Have you found out why Patricia was going to see Diaz?"

Kate rubbed her nose and reflected, eventually deciding to answer my question. She was way too easy. "All he would say was that Patricia called him on Saturday to set up an appointment. She didn't say why."

"On Saturday, hmm? So she called him at home? Or was he at the office?"

"Home. I understand they're personal friends."

"So if they were friends, why didn't she tell him what she wanted?"

Kate eyed me. "I know what you're up to. Just like last time, you're going to pump me for information and then take off before I get a chance to ask *you* anything."

"But this is my store," I said, reasonably, "I can't take off this time."

She gave that some thought, too. I had never realized how gullible the woman was. "He said she didn't seem to be able to talk. She was very business-like, simply asked for an appointment on Tuesday afternoon and that was it. She could have been making a doctor's appointment for as personal as it was, he says."

Maybe she wanted anyone who overheard to think she was making a doctor's appointment. Like David? I nodded to show Kate I had heard, and tried to find a tidbit of information I could feed back to prime the pump. I certainly couldn't tell her about Patricia and Roger.

"You know, Way Benson has plans to develop the property where Summit Lawn School stands," I offered feebly. "Maybe the missing ballot—"

Kate snorted. "Are you still obsessing about that? There was no vote for chairman on it. Neither name had been checked. It means nothing." She started back into the store. "You are absolutely useless as a source."

I followed her out front. "Wait. How could you know that? Did they find it?"

She shook her head. "I asked the other poll workers. One of them saw it before Sophie Daystrom locked it up."

"Who?"

"Him." Kate pointed across the store at Henry, who was working on a cup of Mocha Java and a piece of coffee cake, and flounced out the door.

DAMN. HERE HENRY WAS sitting in my own store every morning and I had to find this out from Kate.

The two women in jogging suits had gone—presumably to jog, though you couldn't be sure of that. Shopping was considered exercise in Brookhills, too.

I picked up my coffee pot and slithered over to Henry. "Henry," I said to get his attention. "I understand you saw the ballot that Sophie locked up."

He nodded. "Much ado about nothing. Top part was blank. Told the sheriff that yesterday."

Double damn. Pavlik had known and he hadn't told me either. "You're absolutely sure?"

Henry looked affronted. "Course I'm sure. Don't think I can see with my own eyes? Voted for five supervisors, the fool. Clear enough. People just don't read."

I filled his cup and retreated.

I was ticked. Pavlik expected information from me, had even asked for my help. Heck, he even asked me out to dinner! But he had known the entire time that the missing ballot had nothing to do with the case and hadn't said a word. But…if the ballot were meaningless, why had someone taken it?

Is a puzzlement. I needed to talk this over with someone, and it sure wasn't going to be Kate.

I looked over at Caron, who was now trying to dig out the coffee scoop she'd left in the bottom of the bin before she poured in the beans.

Sarah it was.

I WAS AFRAID TO LEAVE Caron in the store alone while she was still getting transmissions from another planet, so I called and asked Sarah to dinner. She countered by inviting me to her house. Being a lousy cook, I accepted gratefully.

After closing, I ran home to let Frank out and then headed straight over to Sarah's house.

Sarah Kingston lived in the same neighborhood as Patricia and David, just a few blocks over. I parked on the street and strolled up the sidewalk, enjoying the nighttime view of the house. It was a Painted Lady, a beautiful Victorian-style home dressed in shades of cream and rose. It was gorgeous, a truly genteel lady.

Which was why it was such a shock to be received by Sarah in her baggy jacket and trousers rather than a Victorian lady, or even a Brookhills Barbie. The contrast between Sarah and her house intensified as she showed me into the parlor, painted a clear shade of yellow and decorated in multiple floral patterns.

"Did you—" I started.

"Of course not. Do I look like Martha Stewart?" She looked around. "Have to admit, though, I like what the decorator did."

I must have looked surprised.

"You dress a house like you do a person, Maggy," the lady of the manor said. "Appropriately. Putting contemporary furnishings in a house like this would look as ridiculous as putting a frilly dress on an old horse like me."

I choked back a laugh, then realized Sarah already was laughing. She asked if I wanted a drink. I took a glass of wine and she made herself a rum and Coke. Then she lit a Virginia Slim.

Rum and Coke? Virginia Slims? I was caught in a time warp. I couldn't help but like Sarah's disregard for the fashion of the day, though, whether it was in clothes, drink or smokes. It was refreshing. Especially in Brookhills, where people were entirely too full of themselves. Myself included, sometimes.

I relaxed for what seemed like the first time in days—four days in fact. "I need to talk," I said.

She didn't ask about what. She just nodded and I went ahead and spilled everything. As I went, Sarah asked questions, seeming to organize the facts in her head as I spoke.

When I was done, she recapped. "Okay, so we have the same five suspects. Rudy, Way, Roger, David and Caron." She waved down my objection at Caron's inclusion. "Shush. Just be glad you're not on the list."

"I would trust Caron with my life." Or I would have, before she went crazy, I thought.

"Nice dramatic sweeping statement," Sarah said, stubbing out her cigarette in an antique ashtray. "But don't ever do that."

"Do what?" I'd missed the segue somewhere.

"Don't ever trust anyone with your life."

Oh, that, I thought.

Sarah was still talking. And stubbing out that damn cigarette like it was a bug that wouldn't quite die. "*You* are the only one you can count on, haven't you figured that out by now, Maggy? You trusted Ted with your life, didn't you? And see where it got you?"

Geez, and I thought I was a cynic. Compared with Sarah, I was *Pollyanna* meets *Rebecca of Sunnybrook Farm.*

I took the ashtray away from her. "It got me a good kid."

Her face changed. "There is that, isn't there?"

"I guess we need to look at each of our suspects for motive

and opportunity, don't we?" I ventured in the uncomfortable silence that followed.

Sarah stood up. "It will be easier on the computer."

She whisked me into her office, which was dominated by an antique cherry desk and the gorgeous matching gun cabinet behind it. "You shoot?" I asked.

"My father taught me," she said shortly, pulling a black laptop computer out of her briefcase and firing it up. "Those were his guns."

I wondered if she had trusted *him*.

Before long, Sarah had a page set up for each suspect with space for motive and opportunity.

"Wow," I said, as I watched her from the side chair, "I feel so…"

"Useless? You should." She tabbed over to "Motive" next to Rudy's name. "What's Rudy's motive?"

"Patricia's election would have meant an end to his position as town chairman. And possibly any kickbacks that go with the job," I supplied.

Sarah sat back in her chair. "But Patricia didn't win. And we don't know if there were any kickbacks."

"Just put it down," I said crossly.

"Fine. Opportunity?"

"His barber shop is right down the hall from Uncommon Grounds. He could have snuck in over the weekend."

"With all that fornicating going on?" Sarah snickered and typed it in anyway. "Okay," she continued, "for Way, we have pretty much the same stuff, for what it's worth." She typed furiously.

"Except that Way owns the strip mall and has a key to the store," I pointed out.

"True. I'll put a plus sign next to 'Opportunity.' Now we come to Roger. You said he said he broke up with Patricia because she wouldn't leave David. Right?"

I agreed.

"So maybe he killed her because of that. If he couldn't have her, no one would."

A romantic. Who would have thought it of Sarah? "Do people really do that?" I asked.

"Sure, all the time." She was busy filling in the "Motive" blank. "Now, opportunity."

"Simple. He was alone there on Friday afternoon when I went to the cleaners."

"Would he have had enough time?"

I considered. "It was about fifteen minutes or so. Maybe." I was questioning myself now. "Or I suppose he could have done it on Saturday."

"And what was Caron doing, watching or writhing in ecstasy?"

I ignored her. "Maybe she gave him a key. Maybe he got there early on Monday."

"Maybe you should ask Caron. Maybe she'll tell you."

I gave her a dirty look, but she was on to the next suspect, Caron herself.

"Okay. Caron's motive is obvious. She was pissed because her boyfriend had been screwing Patricia. We only have the two lovebirds' word that Patricia was last week's meat. Maybe he was screwing them both."

Forget that thing about Sarah being a romantic. "No, no, no. If Roger was cheating on Caron" (who was cheating on Bernie) "with Patricia" (who was cheating on David), "then Caron would have killed Roger, not Patricia."

Sarah was typing away. "Not if she loved him. She'd kill her rival to keep him."

"But she dumped him. She went back to Bernie and confessed for God's sake." Maybe bringing Sarah into this was a lousy idea after all.

"Sure. Covering her butt. Okay, opportunity we got, too. She could have done it anytime on the weekend. Or even come in early on Monday."

"No, she—"

"Okay, okay. On to our last suspect, David. What's his motive?"

"Maybe he found out about Roger and Patricia."

Sarah looked thoughtful. "It didn't look like he knew at the funeral."

"How can we find out for sure?"

"If he doesn't know now, he's probably the only one in town. Maybe we should talk to Sam."

"Sam? I don't think that's a good idea."

But Sarah was nodding decisively. "Sam's working on my car. I'll talk to him."

"Sam's working on your car?" I didn't let Eric touch my car—at least not the innards—and he was three years older than Sam.

"Sure. He and David take care of Patricia's Jag and David's Mercedes. Those cars are at nearly twenty years old and they run better than the new ones you buy today." She entered David's possible motive on the spreadsheet. "Opportunity?"

I'd filled her in on my sugar packet theory. "I guess he could have used Patricia's key on the weekend and tampered with the machine. Then maybe he came into the store with her on Monday morning, asked for a latte and…"

"Zap." Sarah finished typing and sat back. She ran her hand through her hair, looking old suddenly. "You know, Patricia wasn't perfect, but she considered me a friend. One of the few she had. I'll do whatever I can to find out who killed her."

With that, she printed out a copy for each of us and we went in to have dinner and to talk about something—anything—else.

AFTER DINNER, we went back to the computer, but to explore this time. I didn't have high-speed access yet and was still using a dial-up modem for my already outdated three-year-old computer. A bunch of options were available in Brook-hills, offered by everyone from the telephone company, cable TV people and cell phone folks, to a car dealer down the street. Sarah was going to show me the ropes so I'd know what to look for.

Her laptop had all the bells and acronyms: CD-ROM, CD-RW, DVD, LAN, and, I was happy to see, the same e-mail program I had. At least I'd make one choice that met with her approval.

We hopped on the Internet, so I could see how she performed on the highway. Sarah logged on using her e-mail address, RealNag. Now here was a woman who had no delusions about herself. She typed in her password, and a "Welcome RealNag!" board came up.

"Look at this garbage," Sarah said, as she scrolled through her list of mail. "'Get rich, surfing the Internet.' 'They're here! Aliens reach earth.' 'Hot, hot, hot! Free live sex!'" She deleted each without reading it and we were off and surfing. Sarah's prowess with her high-speed access was impressive. For fun, I had her do a search on a new kind of South American coffee Caron and I were considering. She found the information I needed in probably a tenth of the time it would have taken me.

"Great, can you forward that to my e-mail?" I asked.

"Sure." She copied and pasted the page we were looking at into a document and started to type "maggyt." The rest, "horsen," filled in as if by magic.

"Whoa," I said, "that's my old e-mail address, where did that come from?"

Sarah backspaced, deleting the address. "You're on my mailing list for the agency. Once I send you an e-mail, the program auto-adds you to my address book. Isn't that how yours works?" She looked sideways at me.

Darned if I knew. "I guess I haven't really paid much attention. I have an address book?"

Sarah groaned. "Never mind, that's for another lesson. What's your new address?"

"Noted—n…o…t…e…d."

"No Ted, huh? Cute," Sarah said, typing it in. "Was that your e-mail declaration of independence?"

"Uh-huh. I was sick of getting his Viagra and porno ads, so I opened a new account."

"Everybody gets that stuff," Sara said, clicking "Send." "There, it's gone. When you get my e-mail, just respond to it and you'll automatically add me to your address book."

Wherever that was.

Sarah did another coffee search and somehow we landed on a chat board. Mostly English was being spoken, sprinkled with other languages I couldn't readily identify. Some of the speakers seemed to be inside the countries they discussed. The talk centered on rebellion, retaliation and death.

"My God." I sat back and watched the scrolling messages.

"Can they say those things? Aren't they afraid of being tracked? Especially now?"

Sarah shrugged. "They're probably using remailers. Remailers are services that strip the return addresses off messages and then send them on to their destinations. That way people can write freely without fear of reprisal. We used to think that was a good thing. After 9/11, we're not so sure anymore."

I had a sudden thought. "But we didn't use a remailer. Couldn't we get in trouble for being here?"

Sarah shrugged. "Last time I checked, the Bill of Rights still protected free speech or, in this case, free surfing."

I shivered. "Let's get out of here anyway."

Sarah looked at me, "You think that's scary? Watch this." She typed in the address of another website. "This is a people locator. See what happens when I type in your name?"

She did, and clicked on "Find." Within seconds, screen after screen opened. Some said, "Sorry, try search again," but others listed my name, address and phone number. Some were my old address, but most were up-to-date. One even gave my old e-mail address and offered to find out what high school I went to.

"That's amazing," I said. "You could find anyone, anywhere."

"Pretty much," Sarah agreed. "A Big Brother of our very own making." She was busy typing again. "Here—here's Ted."

Sure enough. Again, both the old information and the new came up.

"Let's invade someone else's privacy," I said. "Try Pavlik." So I was curious. Sue me.

A few seconds and there it was. Pavlik's old address and phone number in Chicago. And some new information, to me, at least: A *Susan* Pavlik at the same address. Maybe he hadn't been asking me out, after all. Maybe he had just been hungry.

It was an ego-bruising thought, especially for an ego that already had been stomped on by four-inch stiletto heels.

"Ah," said Sarah, "wife or ex-wife, do you think?"

Well, there was that, I supposed.

Another window opened. Pavlik's new address. Sans Susan. My self-worth perked right up. Then I took a look at the address. "Springwood Village—that's the complex where Ted lived when I met him. Bunch of single guys looking for action." Or at least that's the way it was a quarter of a century ago. "And, he lives in the same building Ted did, practically next door."

"Small world, huh?" Sarah said, knocking an ash off her omni-present cigarette.

Way too small for my money and, thanks to the Internet, getting smaller every day.

THIRTEEN

THE NEXT DAY was Saturday, our first Saturday at Uncommon Grounds, and we had no idea what business was going to be like.

It turned out to be brisk. We were scheduled to open at eight, but people were already waiting outside when we arrived at seven-thirty. Make a note: Open at seven-thirty on Saturdays. Of course, then they'll be waiting at seven. I filed that under "Good Problems" and went to work.

The store was packed with coffee drinkers when Gary came in about ten. He looked tired. Since there wasn't a seat to be had in the place, I pulled him back to the office and made him sit down.

Setting his coffee cup on the desk, he rolled the chair back a couple of feet until he literally had his back against the wall and then stretched. I watched, hoping the chair wouldn't flip over on him. Not that there was room.

"Hear about the Midwest robbery?" he asked.

"Midwest Bank? They were robbed, too?" I guess I'd been a little preoccupied lately.

"Yup, but no explosives this time. It still may be the same guy, though."

"Is the video helping at all?" I had been catching glimpses of the surveillance tape from the First National robbery on the news, but hadn't been able to get a good look.

Gary shook his head. "It's pretty grainy. It could be

anybody—medium height, medium build, beard, maybe real, maybe not. And to top it off, Pastorini says they managed to skirt Midwest's surveillance cameras."

"Witnesses?" I asked.

"You know witnesses." Gary shrugged. "The guy had a stocking cap on so they couldn't see his hair, he was medium height and had loose clothes on so they couldn't see his build. One thing, though, he didn't have a beard."

"But you said the beard in the first robbery might have been fake."

"Yeah." Gary looked down into his coffee for a moment. Then he looked up and smiled sheepishly. "Funny, even now I can't quite let go. Pastorini must think I'm an awful pest."

"Are you thinking these robberies might be connected with ours? But you figured our dead guy, the one who was blown up, was the…"

I couldn't think of any word but "perp," and that sounded too much like a TV show. I'd already been accused of that. "…bad guy," I finished lamely.

Gary grinned at me in the little boy way he had sometimes. Like when he asked me to water his plants while he was away and "forgot" to mention that there were fifty-eight of them, give or take a seedling. He'd been smiling for weeks after that, and he had a great smile. I just hadn't seen much of it lately.

"Bad guy, huh?" He laughed out loud and then sobered all too quickly. "There was more than one person involved in our robbery, I'm sure, but in answer to your question: No, I guess I don't seriously think it's the same people, it's just…"

He shifted in his chair and shifted subjects at the same time. "So how are things going with you?"

Boy, was that the wrong question to ask. Despite my best intentions to leave him out of all this, I unloaded with everything I knew, or even thought I knew, including my suspicions of David.

"I feel terrible even thinking this," I finished up with. "You saw David with Patricia Monday morning. Was that an act?"

Gary took a swig of coffee and thought for a moment. "I didn't think so. But you know, Maggy, the spouse is always suspected in a case like this. Pavlik's already looking at David, I'm sure. It probably wouldn't take much for him to bring him in for questioning."

And that would be a nightmare. For David and for Sam and Courtney.

"Over a couple of sugar packets?" I protested. "I'm probably making way too big a deal of this."

"Probably." Gary stood up and drained his cup. "But so might Pavlik."

I took the cup from him. "Listen, I have no intention of saying anything to Pavlik about this. You won't either, will you?"

Gary hesitated, then shook his head. The sheepish expression was back. "Truthfully, Maggy, if I bring Pavlik something like this, he'll think I'm nuts. I already have enough problems with him.

"But," he held up a finger, "if you come up with anything else that supports this, you need to tell me and I need to tell him."

I promised and followed Gary out into the store where the line was out the door and Caron was looking panicky. I was already pouring coffee as Gary slid past the crowd and out the door with a wave.

I went back to work, wishing I'd kept my big mouth shut.

AFTER WE CLOSED, I went over to the library to check with Mary about my taxes. April fifteenth was a little more than a week away. She assured me that she would have them done, but said she couldn't talk right now. She had to fill in for the children's librarian and was about to do four-year-old story hour. Better her than me.

I moved on to Sarah's office. I was feeling badly about my conversation with Gary. I never should have told him something I didn't want him to pass on. It put him in an awkward position. But what made me feel worse was that Gary didn't even want to pass it on, afraid that Pavlik would embarrass him.

That wasn't Gary.

Not *my* Gary.

Someone was in the office with Sarah when I got there. That someone was Sam Harper, and he was crying. I slid to a stop at her door and tried to back out discreetly.

Sarah stood up behind her desk and practically whistled me down. "Maggy! Come in here!"

I couldn't believe she could be this insensitive. Figuring Sam would feel even worse if I turned and ran out the door, I came in and gave him a hug. "How are you, Sam?"

"I'm okay, Mrs. Thorsen." A well-brought-up child.

Sarah stepped in. "Sam and I were talking about Roger Karsten."

My stomach tied in knots. I said nothing.

Sam spoke, bravado showing through the tears now. "I'm glad you're looking into my mother's murder, Mrs. Thorsen. That stupid sheriff won't listen to anything I say. I told him that Karsten killed my mother."

"Why do you say that, Sam?" I asked gently, shooting Sarah a dirty look.

"Because I saw them together," he burst out. "I told my mother I saw them together and that she was sinning. I told her to stop." He was crying in earnest again.

"What did she say?" I tried to imagine this young man, a kid really, confronting his mother.

Sam was hunched over in his chair, pulling at his knuckles which already were raw. He looked up and met my eyes. "She said she had ended it. She said he hadn't liked it, but she had told him it was over. She cried." His voice broke, but he pushed on. "She begged me not to tell Dad. I told her I wouldn't."

I hadn't realized Sam called David "Dad." "So your dad doesn't know?" I asked, following his lead.

"He does now. This morning…" He was crying so hard he could barely speak. "I…I didn't mean to…but, he didn't… didn't…"

I put my arms around him again and he put his head on my shoulder and sobbed. I looked helplessly at Sarah over his head.

Sam's tears finally subsided into huge gulps. Sarah got him a Coke, and then asked, "Did your father have any idea?"

Sam shook his head miserably. "It was like I'd hit him in the gut with my fist. He'd been talking about forgiving Mom's killer and forgiveness being divine and all that bullshit. I couldn't stand it any more. I said it. I told him."

"Where is your dad now?" I asked him.

"Praying." He spat out the word. "He told me he needed to think. Needed to pray. That's his answer for everything. He's not like…"

He stopped and stood up, trying to play man. "Okay, Mrs. Kingston. I'll have your car finished tonight. You want me to bring it by?"

Sarah, to her credit, went along. She stood up, too, and

shook his hand. "Thank you, Sam. I'd appreciate that." Then he was gone.

My sidekick dropped her head on the desk. I got up to get us each some caffeine, which I needed like a hole in the head.

Sarah lifted her head as I put the can of Coke on her desk. She picked it up, wiped the wet ring off the desk with her hand, and placed the can on a coaster. "God, that was awful. I am so sorry."

I sank into a chair. "I don't know—maybe he needed to talk to someone."

"Maybe. But with kids these days you never know if they're going to go off afterwards and blow their brains out."

"Sarah!"

"Well, look at the papers, for God's sake. Some kid gets bad grades and he hangs himself. God, I feel awful." She took a swig of Coke from the can and promptly got the hiccups. "I hate that," she muttered.

"Do you think we should go find him?"

"I'll go to the house when we're done here. You can drop me off."

I nodded. "So…what does this do to our suspects? We know that David didn't know about the affair."

"It still leaves us with that mysterious call to the town attorney, though."

"Who was a personal friend," I added. Our eyes met. "You don't think that she and Diaz…"

"I can't believe she'd do that after Sam gave her holy hell," Sarah said.

"Maybe she called Diaz to end it."

Sarah shrugged, but didn't answer. I knew what she was thinking: Nothing seemed impossible at this point.

"So where does this leave us?" I asked again.

"Nowhere." She stood up. "I can't concentrate. I have to check on that kid. Can you drop me off now?"

I said I could, and I did. Then I picked up a bottle of wine and went home to Frank. Sometimes a drink with a good friend fixes you right up. That my good friend was a dog, didn't escape me.

BEFORE OPENING the bottle of wine, I sat down at the desk in the kitchen, undid the phone line and plugged it into the side of the computer. The dial-up modem took forever compared with Sarah's high-speed access, but eventually I was on e-mail.

I clicked open the e-mail from Sarah and printed the coffee information to show Caron. Then I hit "Reply" and sent back a "Thanks."

Sarah had said her e-mail address would automatically be added to my address book when I replied. But she'd forgotten to tell me where the address book was. I clicked on "Write Mail" and typed "R…e…", intending to send her another message asking that question, and the "a-l-n-a-g" filled itself in. Well, wherever the address book was, it was working the way Sarah had said it would.

I had typed in the message and sent it off to her, when an instant message popped up. "hi ma."

Eric, bless his heart. I had planned to instant message him myself tonight. Even if he was out, his "away message"—designed to let his friends know where to find him—was a *great* way for me to keep tabs on him. For example, "movie brb" meant that he was at a movie and would be right back. Sometimes he even said *what* movie.

Cool, huh? I thought of the "away message" as Mother's

Little Helper—though perhaps not as effective at calming nerves as the Rolling Stones' version. But still…

I typed back: "I'm surprised you're home on a Saturday night. Everything okay?"

"its 2 early yet"

Eric's generation seemed to have abandoned spelling, capitalization and punctuation altogether. But they did write, and you had to give them points for that.

I pumped him for information about school, and then: "Do you remember Sam Harper?"

"eh, he went 2 bc 2 or 3 years younger than me"

"Bc" being Brookhills Christian. "What's he like?" I was starting to feel silly typing full sentences.

"quiet got caught with girl at pc but who hasnt"

"Pc"—Poplar Creek. I didn't bother asking whether Eric had ever been caught at Brookhills' version of Lovers Lane. I'd just get an answer I couldn't decipher anyway.

"Do you think Sam has a good head on his shoulders?" What I was really asking was whether we needed to worry about the kid blowing *off* that head.

"Is he stable?" I clarified.

"is any kid that age stable"

Spoken—or written—as a mature man of eighteen. I told Eric to be good and wished him a good night.

He told me the two were "mutually xclusive" and signed off.

Higher education, wider vocabulary, worse spelling, but the message still translated to, "Butt out, Mom."

Spirits buoyed without the help of spirits, I put the bottle of wine away and went to bed.

FOURTEEN

THE NEXT MORNING I slept in. Sunday, we had decided, was going to be a day of rest, damn it. The store was closed.

At 8:00 a.m. I padded out to the kitchen to make coffee—a busman's holiday, but a holiday nonetheless. I opened the cabinet, looking for beans—a Scandinavian, perhaps, or a Mexican Altura. Nothing. The gastronomic equivalent of the shoemaker's children going without shoes.

Sighing, I dug to the furthermost reaches of the freezer, moving aside single hot dogs and matching freezer-burned buns. Finally I reached my dirty little secret. A small red can of store-brand coffee. You know, sometimes coffee is just coffee.

I got the pot started and went to the door to get the paper. Frank, who had finally roused himself from his doggy dreams when I opened the cupboard, followed me. The moment I opened the front door and leaned down to pick up the newspaper, he barreled out barking, nearly knocking me off my feet.

"Quiet!" I said in a loud whisper, the kind I like to pretend is inaudible at 8 a.m. I looked up to find that Frank had a reason for barking.

Sarah's 1975 lemon yellow Firebird was crunching up the driveway. The car stopped short, spraying gravel against my garage door. She jumped out. "Get dressed. We're going over to the Harpers'."

"What—" I started, but Sarah already was herding me

and the sheepdog back into the house, practically nipping at our heels.

I swung around and grabbed both sides of the door jam as she tried to push me into my bedroom. "What in the world is going on?"

Sarah backed off and started pawing through her purse. Looking for a cigarette, I presumed. "Sam called me. David didn't come home last night." She finally met my eyes.

"Oh-oh."

"Yeah, oh-oh. Now get dressed."

We were out of the house in five minutes, but Sarah managed to finish one cigarette and light another in that time. She laid a patch on the road as we departed.

"What did Sam say? Are he and Courtney okay?" I asked.

Sarah gave me the look the question probably deserved. "Sam thinks his father took off because of what he told him about Patricia and Roger, of course. He's afraid he'll do something stupid."

We'd been worried about Sam and here Sam was worried about David. "Like killing himself?" I asked.

"Or Roger."

I hadn't thought of that. "Should we try to get hold of Roger? Make sure he's okay? Or call Gary?"

Sarah didn't answer me as the Firebird pealed around the last corner and she slammed on her brakes. Since the vintage car had no shoulder harnesses or air bags, I came *this* close to smashing my head on the dashboard.

"Hey," I squawked, straightening up, "You almost put me through the windshield. I said, shouldn't we—"

But Sarah wasn't paying any attention to me. I turned to follow her gaze. Four squad cars were parked in front of the

Harper house, two in the driveway and two on the street. The squads on the street were county sheriff's vehicles and still had their lights flashing. The cars in the driveway were town police and they were empty. I recognized one of the empty squads as Gary's.

"Looks like Sam has already taken care of that," Sarah muttered.

"We'd better go in."

Sarah left the car where it was and we made a dash for the front door. All around us, neighbors were sticking their heads out, wondering what was going on.

Sarah stomped up the front walk past a young sheriff's deputy who was talking to a neighbor. I scuttled dutifully behind her and we had almost reached the door when the deputy called out. Sarah didn't even turn around, just kept walking as she shouted something about being from the Harpers' church.

As the deputy tried to intercept us, a car door slammed. I had a sinking feeling before I even turned to look.

Rats. Pavlik.

And why was I surprised? Patricia's murder was his case. The disappearance of her husband would obviously concern him. I just hoped that Gary could keep Pavlik from scaring the hell out of Sam and Courtney.

Pavlik strode up the front walk even as Sarah was brow-beating the deputy at the door. "Step aside, deputy. Let the ladies in."

Despite his polite words, Pavlik looked grim. He ushered us in ahead of him and pointed to a couch in the living room on our right. Sarah tried to object, but Pavlik just shook his head and pointed again. Sarah sat. She did not speak, neither did she beg.

Pavlik said something to the deputy and went down the hall in the direction he indicated. I knew from previous visits that it led to the kitchen.

The Harper house was a large, well-appointed colonial, which looked like every other large, well-appointed colonial in town. Huge center foyer with a crystal chandelier, living room on the right, dining room on the left, kitchen straight back, family room next to it opening into the living room. Three bedrooms and a full central bath were crammed into one half of the upper level, the other half was taken up by a master bedroom suite, complete with walk-in closets, sitting area and whirlpool.

But no character, no soul. Not like my blue stucco.

Sour grapes? You betcha.

The couch where Sarah and I sat faced the foyer, which meant we could see only that and the dining room across the way. To get a right-angle view into the kitchen, I would have to go back into the foyer, where the young sheriff's deputy stood watch. I had no doubt that was by Pavlik's design.

The deputy was absently fingering the leather strap that snapped over the handle of his gun. Any second now, I expected him to take the gun out, twirl it and replace it in his holster. He looked up, catching me watching him, and glared. He was about twelve.

I couldn't stand the waiting. I needed to do something. Sarah was uncharacteristically quiet, so I left her undisturbed and disturbed the deputy instead.

"Listen," I began, "we don't want to cause any trouble, but we're concerned about the kids." I glanced into the kitchen, but the action was taking place out of sight around the corner. I could hear voices, but that was about it. "Their son called us—"

Pavlik came in from the dining room, blind-siding me. "What did he say?"

I swung around to face him. The sheriff looked like he hadn't shaved this morning.

"I'm not sure exactly. He called Sarah and told her his dad hadn't come home. But if Sam didn't call you, why are you here?"

He didn't answer, and that's when I got it. "You found David."

Pavlik rubbed at the stubble on his chin. "We found him. In Poplar Creek."

My heart was thudding loudly in my chest. "Is he dead?" No, Maggy. He was swimming.

Pavlik nodded wearily, not even taking the opportunity to poke fun. "Apparent drowning." He spoke softly.

I moved closer and gestured toward the kitchen. "Does Sam know?"

"No. He and his sister are upstairs. Donovan says the boy is practically incoherent. Do you know what happened between him and his…" He broke off. "Does Sam call Harper 'Dad' or 'David'?"

That was one question I could answer, at least. "He calls him Dad. I just—"

"Excuse me, is this a private club or can I join?" Sarah said in my ear.

I jumped. "Geez, I'm sorry, Sarah. The sheriff was just telling me…" I stopped and turned back to Pavlik, not wanting to get in trouble with him again. "Can I—"

Pavlik told her for me. "David Harper was found at 6:00 a.m. this morning by a man walking his dog. He was in Poplar Creek. Dead. Presumably drowned."

I thought of David floating in the muddy creek waters, a

bizarre counterpoint to Patricia in the pool of skim milk. I decided to stop thinking.

"Suicide?" I asked.

Pavlik answered with a question of his own for Sarah. "Why did the boy call you?"

I looked at Sarah. She looked at me.

Pavlik continued. "You're obviously concerned about him. What's going on?"

Sarah spoke up. "Sam called me this morning and said David hadn't come home last night. He was very worried."

"Why would he call you?"

Sarah bristled. "I've been a friend of his mother's since she moved here. Sam and I have gotten close."

"He repairs her car," I added helpfully. They both gave me dark looks.

"Let me get this straight," Pavlik started.

Danger, danger, Will Robinson.

"You're a friend of his mom and he repairs your car, right?" He looked at Sarah for an affirmative, which she gave him warily.

"So when his dad disappears, instead of calling a relative— a grandmother or grandfather, an aunt or an uncle, or even the police—he calls you out of the blue?"

Sarah's ears were flattened and her teeth bared.

I jumped in to save Pavlik. Just call me a softy. "He called Sarah because he felt guilty about something he'd said to David."

Pavlik eyed Sarah. "And you know what that was?"

Sarah sighed, apparently deciding to level with the sheriff, too. "Listen, the kid felt terrible." She pulled him over to the dining room, away from the deputy. "You know about Patricia's affair."

Pavlik nodded.

"Well, Sam did, too. But his father didn't, until yesterday."

"Sam told him?"

I picked up the thread. "David was telling him they should forgive Patricia's killer and Sam just exploded. He told David about Roger and Patricia and that he thought Roger killed his mom."

"How did Harper take it?"

Back to Sarah. "Sam said David acted like Sam had punched him in the gut. He asked Sam to leave him alone, that he wanted to pray."

"And then went and threw himself in the creek, instead," Pavlik muttered under his breath. He shook his head. "I need to tell the kids what happened. If you're so close to them," he nodded at Sarah, "it might be easier for them if you're there."

I had a hunch Sarah might be regretting that "close" comment, but she turned and followed Pavlik up the stairs, me trailing.

Gary was just coming out of one of the bedrooms. Pavlik eyed him. "Find anything in there?"

Gary shook his head.

"Okay, then your guys can take off. We'll take it from here." Pavlik turned and knocked on the door across the hall, the one with a "KEEP OUT!" sign on it. It had to be Sam's room. Eric's door had a similar sign on it when he was Sam's age. Except that his had a scribbled, "This means YOU, Mom," below the typed words.

Gary sketched a salute at Pavlik's back and trotted down the steps.

I turned my attention to the task at hand. Sam. Pavlik and Sarah were already in the room. Teenage boys' bedrooms all look alike. And they all smell alike. Eau d' Dirty Socks and Congealed Food.

Sam was sitting on the bed, holding a pillow in front of him. Pavlik had pulled up the desk chair and was sitting opposite Sam. Sarah was standing back a ways.

"Sam. I'm really sorry to have to tell you this." Pavlik sounded genuine, even empathetic. He looked like he was going to put his hand on Sam's shoulder, but then thought better of it. "Your stepfather is dead. He—"

Sam lost it right there. He started sobbing, great choking sobs, and rocking back and forth on the bed, still clutching the pillow. Sarah and I froze.

Pavlik took the boy's shoulders. "Sam, listen to me. Look at me."

Sam's sobbing quieted down a little and he seemed to finally see Pavlik's face in front of him.

Pavlik kept his hands on the boy's shoulders. "I want you to know something, Sam. Listen, I want to tell you something. Do you hear me?"

Sam nodded.

"I know you told your dad about your mom and Mr. Karsten."

Sam's gaze shifted toward Sarah and me.

Pavlik gave him a gentle little shake to make him look back at him. "I want you to know that I was going to tell your father today, Sam. Do you hear me?"

The boy nodded mutely.

"I was going to tell your father about your mom and Mr. Karsten. It was all going to come out, and it would have been even harder for him to hear it from me. But he had to be told, Sam."

"He…did he…"

Pavlik answered the unarticulated question honestly. "We don't know. He was found in Poplar Creek. The water's running fast at this time of year. Maybe he fell—"

Sam was shaking his head, starting to rock again. "No, it's my fault. He did it 'cause I said—"

"Sam!" Pavlik barked like a drill sergeant. A deputy in the hallway stuck his head in to see what was going on and hurriedly pulled back out. "Your father had to be told. Either by you or by me. Do you think it would have been better for him to find out from me? Do you?"

Sam shook his head no.

"Your father was an adult. Your mother was an adult. Whatever they did or didn't do is not your fault. You understand?"

Sam nodded again.

"Okay." Pavlik stood up. "I have to go in and talk to your sister. I think she'll need you there."

Sam looked down at his lap, struggling to get his breathing under control. Finally, he stood up, setting the pillow carefully aside on the bed.

"Thank you." Pavlik said. He put his arm around the boy's shoulders and they walked out of the room and down the hall. We heard another door open and close. Then a cry. Then gentle sobbing. Sarah and I finally moved, finally left Sam's room and went into the hall.

Pavlik was coming out of Courtney's room, his face drawn. As he closed the door gently behind him, I caught a glimpse of Sam, holding his sister while she cried.

"What's going to happen to them?" I whispered. "Who will take care of them?"

"I will, for now." Sarah spoke up.

Pavlik looked at her with new appreciation and nodded. "Good. We'll need some time to locate next of kin."

"David's parents are dead," Sarah said, "but he has a brother who moved away from Brookhills years ago. Not that it matters," she said grimly, "since David never got around to adopting Sam and Courtney. I *told* Patricia they should have—"

She interrupted herself. "Anyway, David's family would have no legal standing when it comes to the kids' custody."

"What about their real father's family?" I asked. "Or Patricia's?"

"Patricia's father died a couple of years ago and I don't think she's seen her mother for years. The old lady has been married a number of times, I gathered, and loses track of how many kids she has and from what marriage. I don't know anything about Sam and Courtney's biological father except he's dead."

Sarah started down the steps. "I'm going home to pack my things. I'll be back in a half hour and stay until you find someone." She stopped and looked back. "Sheriff Pavlik?"

Pavlik was already heading back down the hall. "Yes?"

"I don't know what kind of sheriff you're going to be and I don't really care. But the way you handled that boy up there? Well, you're a good man."

She turned and went down the steps toward the door. Pavlik, looking bemused and a little less weary, continued toward the master bedroom. Realizing I had arrived in Sarah's car, I ran down the stairs and followed her out the door.

Sarah was right, I thought as she and I drove back to her house. We had underestimated Pavlik. He'd handled Sam just right, trying to dispel his guilt, while directing his energy into helping Courtney deal with what had happened.

The enormity of the situation, especially for the kids, was just beginning to sink in. Sam and Courtney had lost three parents in their short lifetimes.

I turned toward Sarah who was hanging onto the steering wheel with both white-knuckled hands. "What can I do?" I asked. "How can I help?"

She pulled the car into her driveway and turned off the engine before answering me. When she turned, her face was ashen. "You can find out how David died, Maggy. Because if there's anything I would bet my life on, it's that David Harper did *not* commit suicide."

FIFTEEN

"YOU'RE SURE OF THAT?"

"David wasn't like you or me or so many other people these days. He didn't go to church and pick and choose which rules he would live by and which he wouldn't. God's laws were not subject to interpretation for him. Suicide is a sin."

"But, Sarah," I said gently, "his wife had been killed. He had just found out she had been seeing another man. Don't you think that in his grief and anger he might have—"

"No!" she exploded, and I backed off as far as the confines of the Firebird would let me.

Sarah sat silently for a moment, looking up at the ceiling of the car, shoulders drooping. She shook her head finally and turned back to me. "You don't understand. To David, suicide would have been the ultimate sin. The final sin, the one that would place him beyond God's mercy, with no chance of repentance or forgiveness."

"Maybe he didn't think he deserved forgiveness," I said softly, thinking about the possibility that David *had* killed Patricia.

"No! He didn't leave those two kids alone on purpose." She went to get out of the car. I did the same and our eyes met over the roof of the Firebird. "Maybe it was an accident. Maybe it was murder. But David did not commit suicide. I know it and those kids need to know it."

"What can I do?" I asked again, my voice sounding small to me.

"I told you. You can find out how he died." She had the keys out and was heading up the walk now.

"Are you—"

She turned at the door. "I have to be with Sam and Courtney. You'll have to do this." She unlocked the door and went in, closing it firmly behind her.

SINCE SARAH'S HOUSE was less than a mile from downtown Brookhills, I decided to walk into town. Not that I had much choice. My car was at home, which was another mile *past* downtown. Anyway, the walk would give me a chance to think.

Sarah was sure David hadn't committed suicide. I understood her logic, but maybe David had simply snapped. He certainly had reason. Maybe Sarah didn't know him—or his faith—as well as she thought.

As for my suspicion that David had killed Patricia, I decided to bury that along with David. Two sugar packets do not a theory make. Besides, it was obvious now that he hadn't known about his wife's affair, so what motive would he have had? Thank God I hadn't told Pavlik what I'd been thinking. The Harper kids didn't need any more pain.

The Harper kids. Funny how we all referred to them that way, even though Sarah had said David never adopted them. I wondered what their real father's last name was, and what names they would go by now.

I had reached the corner of Civic and Brookhill Road. I turned down Civic toward the police station.

Gary was working at the Department's aging PC when I got there. The computer had been donated and resembled Sarah's in brand name only.

He closed out of what he was doing. "You okay?" he asked.

"No. I'm sad, and I'm angry, and I'm confused. And," I added, "I'm ashamed for ever suspecting David of killing Patricia. I was playing detective. I don't know what got into me."

I had been sitting forward on my chair, elbows resting on the desk, hands clutching my hair. Now, I raised my head to rest my chin on my hands. "You didn't say anything to Pavlik about what I said, did you?"

I wasn't making a lot of sense, but Gary understood. "No, but—"

"Good, because I found out that David didn't know about Patricia and Roger until yesterday. He had no motive."

"Well, you—"

"Sam is a mess, you saw that. Besides both Patricia and David being dead, he feels responsible because he told David about the affair."

"I know, he told me."

I sat up a little straighter and brushed back my hair. "You know, Pavlik surprised me. He was really, really good with Sam. Said he wasn't responsible for anything David did."

"Pavlik doesn't seem the type to take time with a kid."

I shook my head. "I know. People surprise me. Sometimes for good, sometimes for bad." I thought about Caron and Roger, and about Bernie's reaction to the affair. You just never knew what human beings were capable of. And on that subject: "Sarah swears David would never have committed suicide."

"That's what everyone says when something like this happens, Maggy. 'So and so would never commit suicide for this reason or that.'" He shrugged. "People don't want to believe that a person they loved chose to die, chose to leave them."

"Couldn't it have been an accident?"

"Anything's possible, I guess. But it looks like he went off Poplar Bridge. That rail is at least three feet high. It would be pretty tough to accidentally fall over it into the creek."

The town storm sewers empty into Poplar Creek. Between that and run-off from the spring thaw, at this time of year the creek ran as deep and fast as a river. Eight to ten feet of muddy water and unpredictable currents, and a spring day didn't go by when Brookhills parents didn't warn their kids to stay away from it. And the kids didn't ignore them. I thought about what Eric has said about Poplar Creek and Sam being caught with a girl there.

But Gary was still talking. "…so, like it or not, Maggy, I'm going to have to tell him."

"Tell who? What?"

Gary was used to my lapses. "Tell Pavlik about your sugar packets," he repeated patiently.

My sugar packets. Sure, it was *our* bomb and our robbery, but when it came to my hare-brained sugar packet theory, I was on my own.

"But we've already decided it wasn't important," I protested. "Why bring it up now? It's not going to change anything. Patricia and David are dead."

Gary looked uncomfortable, but he persisted. "But we don't know why, and Pavlik won't stop until he knows that. Since they were apparently short on money, David might have needed Patricia's share of the store. Or maybe there's an insurance policy on her."

I was confused. "Wait. Who said Patricia and David were having money problems?"

"I just told you. Laurel Birmingham checked the records for me. The Harpers were in arrears on their property taxes. Two years in arrears."

Boy, I had missed a lot when I tuned out. The Harpers were broke? I thought about the beautiful house and cars.

"There's more."

Great. "What?"

"Patricia was going to see Gene Diaz."

"I heard. She probably wanted to talk about the election." I didn't mention my other theory.

He frowned. "Diaz and Patricia were friends. He said she called him and said she needed some advice. She was talking softly, seemed to be afraid someone would overhear."

"So?"

"So, she was calling from home and evidently didn't want David to hear. She wanted advice from a friend who is also an attorney. She was having an affair. What does that all add up to, Maggy?" He seemed to think I was being obtuse.

Maybe I was. "Divorce?"

"Bingo." He stood up. "I'm sorry, but I have to talk to Pavlik." He smiled wryly. "And believe me, that's the last thing I want to do."

I got up, too. "But Roger told me Patricia said she couldn't divorce David. And, like I said, what does it matter now? They're both dead. Wouldn't it be better if we just let everyone keep thinking—"

Gary shook his head sadly. "I'm sorry, Maggy. Pavlik won't, and I can't." He picked up his hat. "Do you know who's with the kids now?"

"Sarah. She's going to stay with them at their house."

"Good. I'm going over there now to see Pavlik. Maybe I can take them out to lunch or something."

I nodded and he left me standing there in his office, trying to think what to do next. Since I couldn't stop Gary or Pavlik, I supposed I should concentrate on Sarah's "assignment" to prove that David's death wasn't a suicide. Before I did anything this time, though, I had to be sure of my facts.

I checked my watch—nearly eleven-thirty. It seemed much later than that. I wasn't sure what time the services were held at Christ Christian, but maybe if I hurried, I could still catch Langdon. And since my house was on the way, I could pick up my van.

I needn't have worried about getting to church in time to see Langdon. According to the sign out front, he practically lived there. Christ Christian was "On God's Side," and had services at 7:30, 9:00 and 10:30 a.m. Sandwiched in between were Sunday School and Bible Study.

Can't make it on Sunday? Try Tuesday or Thursday night at 7:30 p.m. or Saturday at 6:00 p.m. Still not enough for you? The Salvation Women's Club meets following Tuesday's service and the Men's Good News Bible Study, after the Thursday service. I didn't know where Langdon got the energy.

He was shaking hands in the narthex of the church as I entered. I wasn't sure if he knew about David, so I hovered on the fringes of the faithful until Langdon noticed me and held up one long bony finger, signaling me to wait.

After assuring a woman whose name badge read "Hi! I'm Mrs. Cox" that he would speak to the organist to make sure no more New Age music crept into the selections played during the collection, he excused himself and swept over to me. His bony face and hands hanging out of the long black robe reminded me of The Ghost of Christmas Yet To Come.

Langdon took my hands in his. I shuddered and he mistook my reaction. "I know, I know, my dear. David is dead. What could be more tragic? We must keep our faith, though, that God has a plan. Something that we can't see, can't understand with our feeble human brains."

Personally, I was glad I couldn't see it. Chances are, it would scare the shit out of me.

But Langdon was still talking. "We mustn't question God's will."

I felt a pat coming on and extricated myself from his grasp.

He gave me a hurt look, but muddled on. "Maggy, we must now reach out to the children. Give them our support. Show them God's love in this difficult time."

I wasn't sure God's love would seem like much of a substitute for having a mom and dad right now. Too abstract. God can't tuck you in at night and make your lunches.

I touched Langdon's arm in an effort to stem the flow of platitudes. Mistake. He had my hand again and was patting in earnest.

I let him keep it. "The police think David committed suicide."

His vague eyes suddenly focused, giving me a little shock. They were sharp and intelligent behind his thick lenses. "That's not possible."

Just like that. "You're sure?"

Langdon Shepherd had changed before my eyes from a dithery old man to a man of conviction. He nodded firmly. "I have no doubt."

But he saw the doubt in my eyes. "Maggy, I know you're not one of our flock. For people like you," (read heathen), "it's hard to understand, but we believe that suicide is the one sin for which no absolution can be given. Any other sin, no matter how horrible, can be confessed and forgiven. With suicide there's no time, you see. No time for forgiveness."

"But—"

"No. David, of all people, would not have killed himself. He would not have left the children alone. He knew how that felt."

"How what felt?"

"How it feels to lose a parent in that way."

"David?"

Langdon nodded grimly. "It was kept very quiet, but David's father hung himself in the garage one Sunday morning. David and his brother found him when they came home from church. David was twelve."

Courtney's age. I felt sick. What a horrible, selfish thing to do. And in the garage, where his family was sure to find him. I thought about the small red-haired boy watching his father's body swing... Stop it. Stop it.

But maybe David's father had mental problems. If so, wasn't it possible that David did, too?

Langdon answered my question before I could ask it. "David's father had inoperable cancer. David understood why he had killed himself, but he hated his father for it all the same."

I thanked Langdon and went back out into the spring day. I shook my head to clear it. I knew there was logic to what Langdon was saying. Having suffered through his own father's suicide, would David have condemned Sam and Courtney to do the same? I didn't believe so.

Gary had gone to Patricia and David's house to tell Pavlik about the sugar packets and the Harpers' money problems. What would Pavlik say? This was the one time I'd be thrilled if the sheriff simply blew him off. I decided to go and find out.

By the time I got back to the Harper house, the police cars were gone. Everything looked normal on the quiet street, except for Sarah's screeching yellow Firebird in the driveway. And except for the parade of neighbors dropping off food at the Harpers' front door. The old tradition of taking a hot dish to neighbors in time of need was still observed in Brookhills. That some of those hot dishes carried labels from the best deli counters in town was beside the point.

Sarah led me into the kitchen, where she had been wrapping lasagnas, soups, casseroles and breads for freezing. She thrust the last one into the large chest freezer and closed the lid. "So. Did you go see Langdon?"

Now how did she know that? I looked around for the kids before I answered.

"Gary took them out to lunch," Sarah said. Geez, was the woman psychic? "Sam didn't want to go, but I made him. Now, tell me: I figured you would double-check with Langdon. What did he say?" She lighted a cigarette.

"The same thing you did. That David wouldn't have committed suicide. Did Gary talk to Pavlik before they went to lunch?"

Sarah was searching in the cupboards for an ashtray. "Yeah. Pavlik was out of here like a shot. What was that all about?"

I sank down at the table and confessed to telling Gary about the sugar packets in the wastebasket. "It's all my fault," I added miserably.

Sarah was totally supportive. "Are you nuts?"

I ducked my head. "I know. I know. But Gary is a friend and—"

"Gary is the police chief. You should have known he would tell Pavlik."

"But, at first—"

Sarah had taken a couple drags of her cigarette. It seemed to calm her. "Well, I can't see that even Pavlik could make something of this."

"I know. That's what I thought. Until Gary told me David and Patricia were having financial problems."

Sarah stared at me, her Virginia Slim Menthol hanging out of one corner of her mouth. "Where did he get *that* from?"

"They're two years behind on their taxes."

"Impossible. Look at this place." She swept her arm around the room. Gorgeous, from the granite countertops to the top-of-the-line appliances.

She sat down at the table with the delicate bone china saucer she'd chosen as an ashtray. "I would have known if they were having money problems."

"That's what I thought. And how would Patricia have come up with the money to invest in Uncommon Grounds? It doesn't make sense."

"No. It doesn't," Sarah said carefully. "I suppose Pavlik will think this gives David a motive."

"Who knows what Pavlik thinks? But with this and Patricia's affair—"

The doorbell rang and Sarah stood up. "You'll have to find out."

"Find out?"

Sarah was heading for the door. I followed her. "You'll have to find out what Pavlik thinks." She ushered me out the door to make room for what looked like a tuna noodle casserole.

SIXTEEN

SARAH WAS OBVIOUSLY not my Watson. She was Nero Wolfe sitting around issuing orders and I was her Archie. It didn't take me long, though, to fulfill my mission, even if I did so unintentionally.

Pavlik was waiting for me when I got home. Or more accurately, he was standing with one foot on the stoop, trying to peer in my front window. When he turned, he looked pretty damned pleased with himself.

"Why are you peeking in my window?" I asked.

"Playing hide-and-seek with Frank. Can I come in?" He smiled. So I let him in.

After the two friends, one furry and one infuriating, had greeted each other, I put Frank out and let Pavlik on the couch. I remained standing. "David didn't kill himself, you know."

Pavlik was skeptical. Wasn't that a surprise. "So how did he get from the bridge into the creek? It would be one hell of an accident."

"Patricia's death turned out to be murder and that seemed like an accident, too."

His dark eyebrows went up. "So you think that Harper was murdered, too?" He stood up again and strode across the room. Given the size of it, it didn't take long. When he reached the kitchen door, he turned. "So this is a plot, to what? Rid Brookhills of all the white Anglo-Saxon Protestants?"

I thought that was in particularly poor taste. "Don't be an idiot. All I know is that David Harper didn't kill himself."

"Why?"

"Because it's against his religion. And because his father committed suicide. Hung himself in the garage for David and his brother to find." I was angry all of a sudden. "David would not have done that to his own children."

"But they're not his children," Pavlik pointed out.

"It doesn't matter, he wouldn't…"

Geez, there I was again, with the tears thing. There was something seriously wrong with me. I turned away, but then Pavlik was there, letting me cry on the shoulder of his pretty gray topcoat. I cried for Sam and Courtney, for Patricia and David, and then, just a little bit at the end, for myself.

Slowly, the tears started to subside. As I g___ y emotions back under control, I gradually became aware o___ ___er things. I couldn't help but notice, for example, how good Pavlik smelled. No cologne, just good male scent, with a little soap and a hint of Mint Crest. I couldn't help but notice, too, how nice it was to feel a man's solid body against mine again. Or how well my head fit on his shoulder. I couldn't help but notice how his hair curled at the nape of his neck, and feel the warmth of his cheek as he rested it against my hair. I couldn't help but notice…the puddle of slobber I'd just left on his cashmere shoulder.

God, I was worse than the dog.

I attempted to wipe discreetly at the mess, at the same time trying to regain control of my raging hormones.

Damn. I was hot for the sheriff.

I lifted my head and tried to step back, but his arms were still around me. I looked up at him as he turned his head toward me. Our eyes met and I felt a tiny, almost imperceptible charge—a charge I hadn't felt since the day I met Ted. And we know how well that worked out. I stepped back. Pavlik dropped his arms and did likewise.

We just looked at each other.

"I'm sorry," I said. Then, "Thank you. I'm okay now."

Pavlik cleared his throat. "Good." He was messing with his tie. "Umm. I came here to ask you a few questions."

Of course. I waved him back to the couch and took the chair on the other side of the room, as far away as I could get. It wasn't far enough.

Pavlik reached inside his coat for his notebook. I cringed as he tried not to notice the slime on his shoulder. He flipped open the book. "First, did you know the Harpers were having financial difficulties?"

I shook my head. "No, I couldn't believe it when Gary told me."

His eyes went dark gray and ominous, suddenly. "Donovan told you that?"

Aww, geez—talk about walking on eggs. I tried to back-pedal gently. "Well, he didn't really say that. He just said they hadn't paid their taxes. I told him to forget what I'd said about the sugars yesterday, and—" Oh blast.

His eyes were almost black now. Black and boiling, like the clouds on the leading edge of a Wisconsin electrical storm. "Yesterday? Donovan knew about this sugar thing yesterday?"

Oh Lord, let me say the right thing to cover Gary's tail and defuse Pavlik before he goes off. "Not really. I mean, I just mentioned to him that I wondered why there were empty sugar wrappers in the basket when Patricia didn't use any sugar. And that David *does* take sugar. I was stupid to even bring it up."

He was just staring at me.

I continued to try to explain. "You were absolutely right. Those kids lost their mother and then their stepfather and there I was playing TV detective. All I cared about was getting the store open..."

Dang it, I was crying again. This time, though, Pavlik just watched. He sat impassively, arms crossed, on the other side of the room while I fought to get my breathing back to normal so I could talk. My throat felt like a rock the size of my fist was jammed down it—something I should have thought of doing when I opened my mouth in the first place.

What's worse, I had nothing to show for all this emoting. No sympathy, no cashmere shoulder, nothing. Except the slobber. Pavlik stood up finally and got me a paper towel from the kitchen. He practically radiated anger.

"You're right," he said standing over me. "It probably doesn't mean anything. But I needed to know about it. Me. Not your friend Donovan. Me. I'm the one in charge of this investigation. Don't forget it."

And he stomped out the door.

I remembered those pit bulls Pavlik had been talking about. Their trainers alternating between affection and mistreatment to make them fight. Pavlik seemed to be using the same technique on me, one moment he was asking me to dinner or giving me a shoulder to cry on, the next he attacked. It kept me off balance. Just another version of the good cop/bad cop thing?

How could I have been attracted to him, even for a second? A man like Pavlik could only be trouble. Some women found those brooding Heathcliff types attractive, but I'd seen too many of them turn abusive. And cops were probably control freaks to begin with.

Though that wasn't true of all of cops. Look at Gary.

Speaking of Gary, since I'd gotten him *into* trouble, the least I could do was warn him. I tried calling the office, but he wasn't back yet. On a hunch, I tried the Harpers and got him there.

He just laughed when I told him what had happened. "Don't worry Maggy. Pavlik can't do anything to me. I'm elected by the voters. The worst he can do is endorse the other candidate when election time rolls around. If there *is* another candidate. He's just making noises to scare you."

And it had worked. Again. But, more importantly, what was this change in attitude from Gary all of a sudden? "Where did you take the kids for lunch?" I asked.

"McDonald's down on the highway. They didn't want to see anyone they knew." We were both silent for a moment.

"Are they—"

"They're doing as well as you'd expect. I don't think either death has sunk in for Courtney yet. It's going to be tough going for them. I told Sarah I'd try to stop by again. Anyway, Maggy, I have to run now."

He sounded cheerier than I'd heard him in a long time. That made one of us.

THE NEXT DAY was Monday. That meant arriving at five-thirty to open in Patricia's place. Caron got there just before six-thirty, singing a happy song. Things must be okay with Bernie.

I asked her and she smiled. "It's wonderful, Maggy. I haven't felt this close to Bernie in years." She leaned over and whispered, "I get horny when I look at him." She giggled and started to fill the cash drawer.

Horny? I hadn't heard "horny" since the days when Caron

and I hung out at the bar across from the office and drank Tom Collins. "Horny, huh?"

She giggled again and I went to open the front door and flip the sign.

The day passed quickly. It was a cool, cloudy April Monday and business was brisk.

I served vats of Scandinavian, a smooth full bodied coffee, to commuters. People were bubbling over with the news of David's death, discussing it amongst themselves as they waited in line. Once they reached the front, though, the subject was dropped.

Rudy came in looking sour. I wondered why and asked Laurel when she stopped in a few minutes later. "What does he have to be upset about? The recount didn't change anything. He won."

Laurel laughed. "You're going to get a lot of old sourpusses today. Goddard's coffee brewer sprang a leak, so they're all coming over here." She waved her hand toward the tables that were normally empty in the early hours, when our main trade was commuters. The tables were filling up with older folk.

I groaned. Not that I didn't appreciate the business, but I was anticipating the clash between the senior crowd who would settle in for the long haul, and our tennis moms who would show up in their whites around ten, expecting to find their regular tables available. I could already hear the whining and gnashing of dentures.

Laurel looked around to see if anyone was listening. They were, of course. It didn't stop her. "What is going on around here? First Patricia, now David. The rumor is it was suicide." She shook her head sadly, made me promise to call her soon and took off.

After the drive-time crowd thinned, the drink of choice changed from regular coffee and plenty of it, to specialty drinks—more time consuming, but better profit margin. I was just twisting a portafilter off the espresso machine to knock out the old grounds when Kate McNamara walked in. I smacked the grounds out a little harder than I intended and sent them flying.

Kate, not one to stand in line, walked around the machine and watched as I tried to corral the wet grounds with a dry cloth. I gave up, filled the portafilter and brewed a shot while she stood there breathing down my neck. I poured the single shot into a cup, topped it off with an equal amount of steamed milk and froth and placed a tiny spoon on the saucer. I handed the single cappuccino to Caron to serve, and turned. "What?"

"What? You ask me what? You knew about David's drowning yesterday and you didn't call me. We had a deal." I could almost see the steam coming out of her ears. If the frother ever broke, I knew who to call.

I was exhausted, mentally and physically, and I'd had enough of Kate McNamara, even if she had a point. I pulled her into the office, leaving Caron to serve the tennis moms, who were making for the door after having played bumper cars in the parking lot with their SUVs. I didn't understand people who played three sets of tennis for exercise, but were unwilling to walk more than ten feet from a parking spot.

"Listen Kate," I said. "I spent yesterday over at the Harpers with Sarah. Do you have any idea what those kids are going through? Do you even care? There was no way I was going to excuse myself to call a reporter with an exclusive."

Kate's nose turned red.

"Besides," I continued, "you cover the police band on the radio. You know as much about it as I do."

"Did he leave a note?"

Everyone seemed sure David's death was a suicide. Maybe I could do some good here after all. "You're assuming that he jumped?" I asked. "Isn't that a little premature?"

Kate's eyes widened in surprise. "No one has suggested anything else. His wife was murdered, then he found out she had been cheating on him and, if that's not enough, they were going broke."

"Where did you hear the broke part?"

Kate went all mysterious. "I have other sources you know. Good thing, because you haven't been any help."

"Well, it's obvious you don't need my help. Although I think you're wrong. I don't believe David committed suicide."

"So what happened? He got careless and toppled over the bridge railing?"

I shook my head stubbornly. "I don't know what happened, but he didn't commit suicide." Now I was starting to sound like Sarah.

Kate's eyes narrowed. "Are you saying somebody pushed him?"

I'd been resting one knee on the desk chair, now I rolled the chair away and straightened up. "I'm not saying that Kate. I just think that before you print something, you had better check your facts."

I pushed past her and went back into the store. The tennis moms were starting to look good to me.

SEVENTEEN

By FIVE, MY LEGS and back were aching and I was anxious to get home. We had served ninety-two specialty drinks and who knows how much coffee. The battle between the seniors and the tennis moms had been averted when the seniors, realizing they only were entitled to a single free refill instead of the bottomless cup at Goddard's, stood *en masse* and stormed McDonald's.

I was hanging up my apron in the office when Bernie came in looking for Caron.

"She's putting the trash in the dumpsters. Monday is her day to close."

He rubbed his bald head. "Oops. I thought she opened on Monday and you closed. I guess last Monday threw me off because you all went in early. For the opening, you know." There was a moment of awkward silence.

Bernie cleared his throat, trying to make conversation. "But you're right, you know. Caron didn't get out of bed until after six this morning." The smile that crept onto his face made me think he had a reason to remember what time she'd left. Personally, I've never understood the appeal of sunrise sex myself. Morning breath and a full bladder. But maybe it was just me.

Caron came back in then and I was halfway out the door when the phone rang. Bernie, who had started to wash up the counters at Caron's direction, answered it. The call was for me. Bernie handed over the phone and snapped his towel at Caron's rear end. She giggled. I wanted to gag. I think I liked them better pre-Roger.

It was Sarah on the phone. Could I come over for dinner? My back and legs screamed, "Hell no!" The rest of me asked what I could bring.

"Just get your butt over here." She hung up.

I called my neighbor and asked him to let Frank out, said goodbye to Caron and Rodger, who barely noticed me, and went to my van. Pulling it around the corner I waited for the light to turn green so I could turn left out of the parking lot. At rush hour, the traffic lights favored the cars on Civic, meaning about a three-minute wait. I knew because I had timed it.

It only seemed like an eternity because the rest of the day the light would change almost immediately, stopping traffic on Civic so you could get right out. It made me wonder what strings Way had pulled to get a stoplight placed there solely for the convenience of his strip mall customers.

When I finally made it to the Harpers, I drove up the driveway and parked next to David's midnight blue Mercedes. As I got out, I noticed the left front fender and headlight of the Mercedes had been bashed in and the bumper was hanging.

When Sarah answered the door, I pointed to the car. "You weren't hurt, were you?"

She peered at me. "What?"

"David's car. The right front fender is smashed."

"Goddamn it! Sam!" She dashed out the door and rounded the car. Standing with both hands on her hips, Sarah surveyed the damage. "Sam!"

I shooshed her. "Keep it down. You want all the neighbors over here? What does Sam have to do with this?"

Now she was scrabbling around for something in her pockets. Her cigarettes, of course. When she finally came up with the pack, she knocked one out and stuck it in her mouth. Her hand shook as she lighted it.

She saw me looking. "Can't help it. I'm trying not to smoke in the house." She exhaled slowly, appreciatively. "Second-hand smoke isn't good for the kids."

I waved away a cloud. "Or for me. And first-hand smoke isn't good for you either, though it hasn't stopped you."

She was puffing furiously now as she walked around the car. "I knew this would happen. Sam!"

Why was she blaming this on Sam? "Wait a second, Sam doesn't even have a driver's license. He's fifteen."

She gestured with her cigarette, the ash from it barely missing my shoulder as it fell. "Exactly my point. But he said his father let him drive."

"So you believed him and let him drive the Mercedes. Have you lost your mind?"

The shakes seemed to be going away. "I know, I know. But we were out of milk this morning, and I…"

"…was too lazy to go yourself," I finished for her.

But Sarah was back in control. "Well, no use crying over spilled milk. Sam must be up in his room. I'll talk to him later."

I followed her into the house. She'd ordered in Chinese and Courtney was opening the cardboard boxes and inserting serving spoons. Sam was nowhere to be seen. "Is Sam in his room?" Sarah asked her.

"Yes." Courtney looked at us through Patricia's blue eyes. "He said he wasn't hungry."

I could understand that. The three of us sat down and picked at Sweet and Sour Chicken, Vegetable Fried Rice and Spicy Crispy Beef. I asked Courtney if she had gone to school today. She had, and that was all I got out of her. Finally, she politely excused herself and went to her room to watch television.

"Has she talked to you about her mom and David?" I asked.

"A little." Sarah shrugged. "Langdon was over to see both of them. I don't know how much to push. It seems like I'm always asking them how they feel. I don't think either of them knows how they feel yet."

"They're going to need professional counseling," I ventured, "and the sooner the better."

Sarah sighed and started to pull out the spoons and close the cardboard containers. "I know, I was talking to Gary about it, too. Did I tell you he stopped by this morning?" She held up a white box. "Do you think it pays to keep Sweet and Sour Chicken? It always looks like lumpy orange Jell-O the next day."

I ignored the change in subject. "Maybe Sam and Courtney's pediatrician can give you some names."

She set the box down. "I guess I don't want to make them talk to a stranger about what happened."

"Sometimes it's easier to talk to a stranger."

Sarah silently stacked the cartons and stuck them in the refrigerator. She turned when she closed the door. "You're right, I guess. Better they should talk to someone without all the emotional baggage we have. So what have you got for me?"

The abrupt change in subject signaled, I thought, the return of the old Sarah. Bossy, self-assured, obnoxious. I'd missed her. Sort of.

"Not much," I admitted. "Pavlik is mad because I told Gary about the sugar packets and not him."

"Pavlik thinks it's important?"

"I don't think it's so much that he thinks it's important, as that he thinks *he* walks on water. How could Gary not have told him? Why didn't I tell him? And on and on."

I was following Sarah into the family room with a Diet Coke in my hand, when the doorbell rang. Since I was closest, I set down my Coke and went to answer it. It rang again before I got there.

"I'm coming!" I swung open the door.

Pavlik. He seemed to be behind every door these days. The wind was cold and rain was falling beyond the porch where he stood. A spring rain in Brookhills often turns into sleet, freezing rain or snow as the temperature drops overnight. It looked like freezing rain for tonight.

Pavlik's coat collar was turned up and the porch light reflected in the droplets on his dark hair. My heart gave a little twitch. Or maybe it was another body part. Whatever, I compensated for the betrayal by inviting him in brusquely.

I tried to see his eyes in the dim entryway light, looking for some clue to his mood. They were neutral tonight, gun metal gray, which didn't help me much.

Sarah came into the foyer. "Sheriff. Is there something…" She trailed off.

"Could I speak with you?" He glanced over at me. "Both of you, I guess. Somewhere the children can't hear us."

This didn't sound good. And he didn't seem especially happy to see me there. If I thought he was omnipresent, he probably felt the same about me.

Sarah led the way into David's den and closed the door. We

all stood staring at the chair behind the desk and the two guest chairs. Where to sit, where to sit.

Pavlik made the decision for us. "Why don't you take the chairs, I'll stand."

Sarah and I sat, and Pavlik perched on the edge of David's desk apparently trying to put us at ease. He looked down at his tie before he spoke. "I don't know if this qualifies as good news or bad news."

He looked back up at us. "Frankly, I don't know if there can be good news in a case like this. But here goes. We think we've solved Mrs. Harper's murder."

"But?" I thought I knew what was coming. And it was all my fault.

He gave me a dirty look. "But—"

Sarah jumped up. "You think that David did it!"

Pavlik held up his hands, trying to calm Sarah. "Yes, but—"

"You think he killed her for money? For her part of Uncommon Grounds? That was half his anyway!"

But Pavlik was shaking his head. "I think he killed her because she was planning to divorce him."

Now I stood up. "That's pretty flimsy isn't it? Lots of people file for divorce and their spouses don't kill them." They just *wanted* to kill them.

Pavlik's face hardened. "About as flimsy as two sugar wrappers, I suppose. But put it together with other things…"

"Like what?" I demanded.

He stuck his face within inches of mine. "Like David Harper. He wasn't paying income taxes and he wasn't paying property taxes. And his wife was getting ready to turn him in." I could feel the damp heat coming off him.

"How do you know that?"

"Your friend Donovan," he snarled.

"What?" I whispered.

He pulled a sheath of folded papers out of his breast pocket. "Donovan. He finally did something right. He found these in Mrs. Harper's bedroom this morning. They're copies of the checks Harper received for his consulting work. There are also records of cash received. All income that Harper didn't declare. We think that's why Mrs. Harper was going to Diaz. She was preparing to turn him in."

He stuck the papers he'd been waving back in his pocket. "Or, she was just threatening to do it, so he wouldn't contest the divorce."

"So he killed her." We both swung around to look at Sarah, who had just spoken. She looked stunned.

"And what about David?" I asked after a moment.

Pavlik answered, speaking to Sarah. "I know you don't want to believe it, but he committed suicide. There's no evidence to support anything else."

Sarah was shaking her head.

I was still thinking about Patricia's murder. "But if he wanted to kill her, why the espresso machine? You said yourself, that it was just dumb luck on the killer's part that Patricia was killed instead of hurt."

"Even if it didn't kill her, it would have scared the hell out of her. Maybe that's all he wanted. To make her back down."

"No." It was Sarah again.

Pavlik started to answer, but Sarah went on, oblivious to what we had been talking about. "David did not commit suicide. Maybe he committed murder, justified it in some way in his mind, but he would not have killed himself."

Her thinking was a little convoluted even for me at this

point. Pavlik's scenario seemed logical, and if even Gary bought it… "But, Sarah, if he could murder his own wife, especially in that way, why couldn't he—"

"Because he just wouldn't!"

Pavlik took Sarah's hands. "I know what you believe. And what he believed. But maybe he just snapped. We'll never really know."

"*I* know." She pulled her hands away and turned to leave the room. We heard her climbing the stairs.

"There's something else." Pavlik's voice stopped Sarah halfway up. She didn't turn.

The sheriff waved one of the sheets of paper at her back. "In addition to the papers Mrs. Harper copied, there was a legal document that she probably pulled off the Internet and filled out."

Sarah swiveled her head.

"It names you the guardian of her minor children in the event of her death."

Sarah continued up the steps.

I DON'T KNOW WHERE Pavlik went, but I went home. I'd had enough for the day, for the year, for a lifetime.

I buried my head under the pillow and tried to sleep. My feet wouldn't cooperate, they kept moving. So did my brain. But neither got me very far. I finally sat up and threw my pillow across the room. Frank staggered over to the pillow on the floor, collapsed on it and went back to sleep. I stayed awake, mulling over what Pavlik had told us:

1.) David had killed Patricia.

It seemed to me that while David had a motive, the sheriff really had no evidence that David was there that morning except for the sugar packets, which might have another explanation. But if the killer wasn't there, how could he be sure Patricia used the machine first?

2.) David felt remorseful and killed himself.

"No!" Sarah shouted in my head.

"No!" agreed Langdon, although, of course, Langdon would never shout.

But why could they believe that David would kill Patricia, but not that he would kill himself?

"His faith, his faith, his faith…" The words echoed in my sleep-deprived brain.

The phone rang.

I awoke startled, feeling like I'd only fallen asleep minutes earlier. I probably had. It was 5:00 a.m. I rolled over and grabbed the phone as it started to ring a second time.

"Hello."

"Hell, how long does it take you to answer a phone?" It was Sarah. Big surprise.

"I got it on the second ring." I yawned.

"Only because you slept through the first three. I thought your machine was going to pick up."

"Five rings, it picks up after five rings. I take it you had trouble sleeping, too."

I could hear Sarah suck in some nicotine. Geez, how could anybody smoke this early? I'd smoked for a few years, but even then the first cigarette had always made me nauseated. Didn't stop me though, because I was cool. Yes, I was.

She exhaled. "I figured you would be up early. I wanted to catch you before you went in."

Went in. I checked the clock again. 5:05. Caron was opening, so I didn't need to be at the store for over an hour. I tried to settle back into the pillow, but it wasn't there. "What did you tell the kids?"

"Nothing. I told them nothing."

I sat up and crossed my legs Indian style, trying to phrase this right. "But Sarah, people will be talking. Pavlik's not going to keep this quiet. He thinks he solved the case, or both cases."

"He hasn't," she said quietly.

"What about the custody papers?" I asked. "Patricia obviously was afraid something was going to happen to her and wanted to make sure the kids were taken care of. And not by David. How do you explain that?"

"I can't," she said. "Not yet."

She was quiet.

That morning somewhere between wakefulness and sleep, I'd realized I still wasn't satisfied either. I just couldn't explain why. I didn't have the conviction of faith that Sarah did, but I didn't think David had killed himself, and I also had my questions about Patricia's murder.

"Okay, but how do we prove it?"

Sarah let out her breath in a sigh of relief. "Thank God. I was afraid you believed that goddamn sheriff."

Not for the first time, I wondered how Sarah reconciled her strong faith in God with her love of taking his name in vain. "I think this is a nice tidy resolution for two very messy cases for Pavlik and let's face it, Sarah. With the will and the papers she copied, it is the most logical explanation. Gary obviously believes it, he found the copies in Patricia's room. I thought you said he came to see the kids. Did he search the house while he was there?"

I had to wait for an answer while Sarah lighted another cigarette. "Where are you?" I asked. "I thought you don't smoke in the house."

"I'm in the screen porch."

I pictured Sarah huddled under a blanket in the chill air, trying to light the cigarette without setting herself on fire.

She finally got it and exhaled. "Gary did come to see the kids. Actually, he brought doughnuts. But he was honest— said he needed to take one last look around Patricia's room."

"Did he tell you anything when he left?"

"Nope. Just that he had to run." Another puff. "That's your first stop, Maggy. Talk to Gary. See what he actually found."

"And then?" I was already out of bed, pulling up the covers. I didn't make the bed every day. It seemed like a silly waste of time, considering no one ever saw it. More's the pity.

"Then we'll talk. Now I have to go." Sarah hung up.

I looked at the phone. Why did she keep doing that to me? And what could Sarah possibly have to do at five in the morning? I'd wanted to ask her how she felt about being named Sam and Courtney's guardian.

Well, that would have to wait. I hung up the phone and dragged myself off to the bathroom. Might as well take a shower and go help Caron open.

EIGHTEEN

SARAH'S DEMAND THAT I talk to Gary immediately aside, I had a business to run.

At least for now. The morning was disturbingly slower than yesterday. Either Goddard's coffee urn was repaired or the seniors had been converted to the Golden Arches on the highway.

During our noon lull—which was pretty much a continuation of the morning lull and a prelude to the afternoon lull—Kate McNamara came in. She surprised me by ordering a tall Monkey Mocha, the coffee of the day, premium chocolate and a touch of banana syrup, topped with whipped cream and cocoa dust. It resembles coffee about as much as a Cosmopolitan resembles a martini. Kate carried her drink over to the counter by the window, pulled out her laptop computer and started typing away.

After about five minutes, I couldn't stand it any longer. I walked over ostensibly to wipe off the condiment cart and tried to read over her left shoulder.

"Don't tell me I could be writing anything you don't already know, Maggy." She swung around and her green eyes glittered. "You're the one with all the information. I'm sure you already know the case is essentially closed. Patricia Harper was killed by person or persons unknown, officially. But we all know who the police think that person was. And David Harper's death is a suicide."

"I don't think—" I blurted.

Kate closed out her document and snapped down the lid of her laptop. "Save it, Maggy. A truck driver saw a man matching David's description walking along Ridge Road toward Poplar Bridge last night. That was just before eleven."

She stood up. "I don't know what your issues are, but I'm reporting what the police have told me." She looked me up and down. "You should be happy. This gets your friend Caron off the hook. And now this place is only split two ways."

"Patricia's interest will go to the kids, unless we buy them out," I said automatically.

Kate zipped her computer into its case. "Good. Then maybe those kids will have something." She tucked her notes into the outside pocket and was gone.

"Why did she come in at all?" Caron asked, moving over to bus the spot where Kate had been sitting. "Just to be unpleasant?"

"Sounds like Kate," I said, taking the dirty mug from her and putting it into the dishwasher.

"At least they're not coming right out and saying David killed Patricia."

I'd given Caron the bare bones of what Pavlik had told us and Sarah's reaction to it. "Yeah, but they can make their suppositions pretty clear," I muttered.

"So *is* Patricia's murder investigation closed?" she asked, hopefully.

I shrugged. "For all practical purposes. I mean, if no one is investigating it, how can it be solved?" I closed the front of the dishwasher. "Hey, I'd really like to go see Gary. Do you think you can hold down the fort alone?"

She surveyed the empty store. "I think I can handle it," she said dryly.

I pulled off my apron and threw it on the desk in the office. "Great. I should be back in half an hour." I started out the door.

"Maggy?" Caron's voice stopped me. "Maybe we *should* buy out Patricia's share. It would at least give the kids something."

It was probably a good idea, assuming I could come up with the money. I just wondered who we would buy it from. Did Patricia's share go to David—and then on to his family— or to Sam and Courtney?

Thinking about it made my head hurt.

GARY WAS IN his office when I got there, double and triple-clicking the mouse on his computer.

"Can I interrupt?"

He wheeled around and sighed. "Might as well. I'm not getting anywhere fast. Modem problems. I'm going to have to take this home anyway."

Gary had a computer system identical to mine at his house. The difference was he—like Sarah—knew how to use his.

"Well, at least the Harper case is solved," I offered. It was the verbal equivalent of sticking my toe in to test the water.

Gary shrugged. "The photocopies pretty well sewed things up. I'm sorry Maggy. I know it's not what you or Sarah wanted to hear."

"What exactly did you find?"

"Folded photocopies stuck in a library book. That's how we missed them the first time through."

"Those must have been the copies she made at the library on Saturday," I said thoughtfully. "Pavlik said they were copies of checks or—"

"Some checks, but also David's personal records of cash paid for services rendered."

"Income he didn't report?" I asked.

Gary nodded. "According to the IRS, he hadn't filed taxes for years."

And I'd felt guilty when I forgot to report $8.25 in interest on one of the savings accounts I'd set up when Eric was born. "How could he get away with that?"

"It's a big country, Maggy. Lots of taxpayers. But if the wheels of the IRS turn slowly, they turn surely. They would have gotten to him eventually."

"But don't companies have to file forms when they pay a consultant?" I remembered very clearly getting into trouble with our Vouchers Payable department at First National when I didn't get a social security number from a freelancer I had hired.

"People don't like to pay taxes. If they can get away with it, they don't. And these apparently were very small companies. Either that or David used bogus names when he listed them. I doubt we'll ever find most of them."

"So David wasn't declaring his income." I remembered Mary telling me that David prepared his own tax returns. Or not. "But why would Patricia turn him in? After all, she had to have known about it."

Gary shrugged. "Maybe. Even probably. But now she wanted a divorce. Those copies gave her leverage over David."

"Do you know for a fact that Patricia wanted a divorce? I thought Diaz didn't know what she wanted when she set up the appointment."

"We finally tracked down her mother in Florida, living there with her fourth husband." Gary's expression told me how he felt about a woman having four—count 'em, four—husbands. I knew Gary's wife had died young and he had never remarried.

"Patricia called her out of the blue," he continued. "Told her she was filing for divorce and asked if she and the kids could come stay with them in Florida if necessary."

"What did her mother say?"

Gary picked up a pencil from his desk. "Her mother said that would be an awful inconvenience and Patricia should solve her own problems."

"Nice woman. No wonder Patricia gave Sarah custody."

"Sam and Courtney are good kids. They deserve to be with someone who will love them like Sarah." Gary stood up. "I have a meeting at Town Hall."

He escorted me to the door, then waved goodbye and headed across the parking lot.

Hmm. Did I detect a warm spot for Sarah? From Gary? Sarah and Gary, together? I tried to picture offspring combining Sarah's unusually long face with Gary's uncommonly wide jaw. Came out looking a lot like Mr. Potato Head.

I walked back to Uncommon Grounds, stopping at the traffic signal on Civic. I had my finger on the button you push in order to get a walk sign to cross Civic, when I remembered Pete, my moving man.

He'd told me he had been stopped at the signal on Civic at about five-fifteen last Monday morning, the day Patricia was killed. That he had been able to see into the store because the backlights were on.

I looked across the street towards Uncommon Grounds. Sure enough, I could see the side window of the store. Although the reflection off the glass made it difficult to see in at this time of day, in the dark it would have been no problem. That wasn't what was bothering me.

I started across the street. Pete said he'd been *stopped* on

Civic at the light. That light didn't change—and traffic on Civic didn't stop—unless a car was coming out of the parking lot and tripped the sensor. That meant, unless I had misunderstood Pete, that a car had been leaving our parking lot at five-fifteen that morning. Knowing who was driving that car seemed very important suddenly.

Trapped in the store for the rest of the day, I kept watch for Pete's moving van, knowing full well he could be anywhere. I even tried calling the company, Move It!, but only got a recording for my efforts. Maybe I could catch him if I went in early tomorrow morning and turned on the lights. I'd bait him with coffee.

I called Sarah when I got home that night and filled her in on my conversation with Gary. I didn't mention Pete. I wanted to see what he had to say before I raised her hopes.

"So Patricia's mother wants nothing to do with the kids," she said, when I was done. "Doesn't surprise me. Patricia never even talked about her."

"So why do you think she called her now?"

I could feel Sarah shrug. "Maybe she was desperate. Maybe she figured no one could find her there. Especially David, if the shit hit the fan."

Which it had.

"And the old witch said no," Sarah continued.

"Maybe she had a reason." And here comes the other side of the story. I couldn't help myself. "Patricia certainly hadn't stayed in contact with her. Maybe—"

"Oh, cut the crap, Maggy. You don't even know the woman, why are you defending her? She's on her fourth husband and she doesn't give a damn about her grandchildren, or at least *these* grandchildren. God knows how many of them she has out there."

Sarah had a point. "I'll give you the woman's a bitch, okay? So what are you going to do?"

"What do you mean, what am I going to do?"

"About the kids. What are you going to do?"

"I don't know."

"Do you care about them?"

"Yes."

"Do you want them shuffled off to a foster home or shoved down the grandmother's throat?"

"No."

"Patricia wanted you to raise Sam and Courtney and the paper she signed gives you that right. It seems pretty black and white to me. Good night, Sarah."

I hung up the phone and smiled at Frank, who smiled back.

VERY EARLY the next morning the phone rang just as I was walking out the door.

"What Sarah?"

"You really think I can do this?"

"Of course," I said. Could Sarah raise two kids? Sure. Would they all live through it? Who knew? But I didn't see a better solution for two kids who needed to be loved and cared for, than a woman who—despite the front she put up—seemed to need the same. "Gary was really impressed with how much the kids care about you and how comfortable they seem with you."

"He was?"

I was getting out my keys. "Um-hum. Did David have insurance? Will it pay, even if the death is ruled a suicide?"

"He didn't have insurance. Neither did Patricia."

I shouldn't have been surprised. Does a guy who doesn't

pay taxes pay his insurance premiums? "So what happens? There will be funeral costs when they finally release the body."

"I'm talking to Pavlik this morning to see when that will be," Sarah said. "I wonder if I can get access to any accounts David and Patricia had. They must have money somewhere, though most of it probably will be taken in back taxes."

"But you don't have any legal standing. Patricia's mother is probably the only person who has. Is there a will?"

"Not that I've heard of." Sarah sounded thoughtful. "Maybe I should call her. Do you think Gary would give me her number?"

"I think you can count on it," I said, and rang off.

It was about 5:10 when I flipped on the lights in Uncommon Grounds. I hoped I wasn't too late. I went in the office to get an apron and, sure enough, the words "Move It!" were framed in my display window when I came back out. I went to the door and let Pete, who had just climbed out of his rig, in.

His smile was broad. "Opening early, huh? Guess your boss took my advice."

These days the thought of having a boss again—besides Sarah—was looking pretty good. "Come on in and sit down. I don't have anything brewed yet, but I'll make you a custom cup. Is Guatemalan okay?"

He nodded, staying put at the cash register. He watched me as I ground the beans and ran the hot water into the filter. "That's pretty cool," he said. "You mean I don't need my Mr. Coffee?"

I added a little more water. "All you need is hot water, a filter and grounds. Mr. Coffee just puts it all together for you."

I set aside the cup and leaned on the counter. "Listen, Pete, didn't you tell me you went past here last Monday?"

He nodded, probably wondering why I wasn't handing over his coffee.

"You said that you were stopped at the stoplight on Civic at about five-fifteen."

He started to look wary. Like he thought I was going to slap handcuffs on him and read him his rights. Or, worse yet, not give him his coffee.

I went on. "So, if you were stopped at the light, that means somebody was coming out of the parking lot, right?"

The light bulb went on and he saw what I was getting at. "I'll be darned. You're right, somebody *was* at the light."

Thank God. Finally, something concrete. "Did you happen to see what the car looked like? Model? Color?" Please. Pretty please.

Pete was smiling now. "That wasn't just a car."

Even better. "What was it? A truck. A van?"

"No, ma'am, that was a classic. They don't make Mercedes like that anymore. Early nineteen eighties, I'd say. Looked like it was in mint condition. Dark color, probably blue or black. Prettiest car I've seen in a long time." He reached past me to grab his coffee and was gone.

I trudged back to the office and collapsed with my head on the desk. Old Mercedes. Blue or black. Mint condition-at least until a couple days ago. It all added up to David. David leaving the store about five-fifteen, right around the time Patricia had died.

SARAH CALLED ME later and I broke the news. There was silence on the other end of the line. Then, "So it's true."

I let my breath out. I'd expected her to argue. "I honestly can't see any way around it."

"Yeah."

There didn't seem to be too much to say after that, even

for Sarah. We talked about David's funeral, which she said couldn't be held until at least Monday, since the police weren't releasing the body before Friday or Saturday.

"Sunday's good," I said. The store would be closed and both Caron and I could attend without a problem. Attending funerals was getting to feel like a habit. I asked Sarah if she had spoken to Patricia's mother.

"No. I haven't gotten hold of Gary yet. I'll call over to the station later."

I agreed that was a good idea and hung up to get a little old lady a caramel latte. I'd noticed a few seniors defecting from Goddard's and McDonald's over the last couple of days. Taking a walk on the wild side.

BEING WEDNESDAY, it was my turn to close. As I vacuumed, I saw an unmarked gray sheriff's car pull into the parking lot. It hovered for a second and then turned and tucked itself neatly into a parking space. The driver got out. It was Pavlik. It was *always* Pavlik.

I turned off the vacuum and went to the door. As Pavlik stepped in, I noticed he'd had his coat cleaned. I locked the door behind him, then changed my mind and unlocked it again.

He stood with his coat open, hands in the pockets. "Now that the case is over, I wanted to apologize."

I didn't have the energy anymore to fight with him over whether or not David had committed suicide. David was a murderer. Whichever sin he rotted in hell for was okay by me. "What are you apologizing for?"

He gestured, hands still in his pockets. "Losing my temper when you told me you had talked to Donovan and he didn't come to me."

I shrugged. "That was my fault. I asked him not to. I told Gary as my friend, not the police chief."

He took a step closer and pulled his hands out of his pockets. "That wasn't fair to him. He's a cop, foremost, and you put him in the position of having to decide whether to pass on information you had given him as a friend."

I looked away. "I know. I guess I just didn't want to accuse David then…" I trailed off.

Pavlik tilted his head sideways. "Are you okay? You seem…down," he ended lamely.

Down? Was I down? Damn right I was down. I sighed. "Okay. I have something to tell you. Something I just found out this morning."

Pavlik waited.

"Pete—he's a mover who comes in here—told me last week that he was stopped at the light on Civic at about five-fifteen last Monday."

"Last week? You're saying he saw something?" Pavlik was getting out that blasted notebook again and looking irritated.

"Oh stuff it." I'd had enough of bruised egos. "He said the backlights were on, but he didn't see anybody inside. You knew Patricia was here about that time. What difference did it make?"

Pavlik started to answer, but I waved him down. "Anyway, that's not the point. I realized last night that if Pete was stopped at that light, it meant someone was coming out of this parking lot."

Pavlik's mouth was hanging open.

"You see, that light stays green on Civic unless a car from the parking lot trips the signal. So there had to be a car coming out."

Pavlik had closed his mouth and was writing again. He looked up. "Did he see the car?"

I nodded. I hated to tell him because I knew it would only confirm his theory. "A dark-colored Mercedes, an old one in mint condition, he said."

"Harper. That fits. You say this guy's name is Pete? What moving company?"

I told him and he wrote it down, then flipped closed his notebook. "Well, I have to get back to the office. I just wanted to apologize and say goodbye. Thanks for the information." He held out his hand.

I took it. It was warm and firm. Mine was cold and clammy. What was it about this guy that made me leak? "Goodbye."

He let go of my hand and, to his credit, didn't wipe his on his coat. He turned when he reached the door. "That information you put together about the traffic signal? That was a good catch. I'd missed it. I'm only sorry it didn't turn out like you hoped."

Yeah. Me, too.

NINETEEN

BY THE TIME I finished closing, I was totally depressed. I went home, changed into sweats and took Frank out for a run. I hadn't run for years and the look of astonishment on Frank's face as I broke into a gentle trot made me laugh. "You and I, young sheepdog, must get in shape."

We didn't run far, maybe a mile, but I imagined we both felt better for it. When we got in, Frank went for his water dish and I headed for the shower.

After we were both watered, we settled down in front of the television for some of that mindless entertainment I love. I was determined not to think about Pavlik or the store or Patricia or David or anything tonight. By the time the Ten O'Clock News rolled around, I already was nodding off.

"New tonight," the announcer said. "Attempted robbery at First National Bank averted as the perpetrator is killed by his own bomb."

See? They said "perpetrator," I thought sleepily.

"According to Brook County Sheriff Jacob Pavlik, the lone bank robber was apparently the same man who robbed Midwest Bank and attempted to rob First National recently."

Jacob?

The picture switched to Pavlik. "We believe the bomber, identified as Ed Groschek, was a member of a Chicago militia group that is also mounting tax protests in the area and has been tied to other anti-government activities," Pavlik was saying.

Back to the anchorman. "The suspect, seen here in security footage from the earlier First National robbery attempt, was evidently killed as he fled with an undisclosed amount of money and attempted to deposit a pipe bomb in the alley adjacent to the bank. In the earlier attempt at First National, a bomb identical to today's was planted, but was not detonated."

I was wide-awake now, watching the grainy video from the First National robbery. The man on the tape wore a stocking cap and had a bushy black beard, as Gary had said. I moved closer to the TV. As the robber gestured at the teller, he glanced toward the camera and then I was sure.

Ed.

Our L'Cafe technician.

The man who had installed the espresso machine that killed Patricia was also a bank robber. Perhaps L'Cafe should do better background checks, but beyond that, who better to booby trap our espresso machine than the man who installed it in the first place?

But when? And why? What connection could there possibly be between suburbanite Patricia Harper and Ed the Tech Guy who, according to Pavlik, was involved in a militia.

When had the first robbery attempt on First National been made? I went into the kitchen and pulled out my recycling bin. Luckily, I'd been too lazy to take out last week's newspapers. Digging down to the bottom of the pile, I finally found what I was looking for.

There it was, the Saturday before Patricia's death. The headline blared, "Attempted Robbery at First National Bank, Pipe Bomb Left." The still photo that accompanied the story was taken from a frame of the surveillance tape and was tough to make out. The article said the robbery had taken place Friday afternoon.

I grabbed the phone and dialed. "Caron? I'm sorry to— Yes, but it's only ten—

"Yes, of course I know what time you have to be up tomorrow. Listen, that Friday night when we were at Patricia and David's, you said they were having a fight about the television, right? Okay. Yes. All right, go back to sleep. Thanks."

I hung up the phone. Caron thought that Patricia was angry about the television being *on*. But maybe she was mad about something *on* the television. Could Patricia have seen the tape from the robbery on the news and recognized Ed? But why would that have caused a fight between Patricia and David?

I got out pen and paper and sat down at the table. What did we know about David and Patricia?

• Patricia was having an affair
• Patricia was filing for divorce
• They had a beautiful house in the suburbs
• David was a marketing consultant
• They didn't pay their property taxes
• They didn't pay income taxes
• They didn't have any insurance
• David's car had been seen leaving Uncommon Grounds the morning of the murder

I thought for a second and added:

• Their son says they let him drive without a driver's license

I picked up the phone again. This time to call Sarah, who likely wouldn't bite my head off for calling at ten-thirty at night.

"Sarah, listen to me. Could David and Patricia been involved in some kind of anti-government group? A militia or something?"

There was silence at the other end.

"Sarah?"

"I'm here."

"Did you hear me? Is it possible?"

"I heard you, Maggy," she said in no-nonsense tones. "I'm trying to figure out if you're serious."

"Listen Sarah, you've read the papers, you know about these groups. The don't pay their taxes, refuse to get social security numbers, *drive without driver's licenses.*"

"Oh come on. Just because Sam—"

"Do you think he lied? Or do you think David really let him drive the car?"

Silence again. "I don't think he lied."

"So you think it's possible?"

"Anything's possible, I guess." I could almost hear her shrug. "This is a very conservative town, Maggy. There are probably a dozen Republicans for every Democrat."

"I'm not talking about Republicans. I'm talking about the far right fringe. People who distrust the government, protest taxes and bomb banks."

"We all protest taxes… My God. Are you talking about the bank bombing this morning?"

I was getting cold all of a sudden. In fact, I could scarcely keep my teeth from chattering. I recognized the symptoms from the last crisis in my life, the day Ted had left. Nerves, shock, whatever. "Listen, I have to go. I'll call you in the morning when I've had a chance to think." And stop shaking.

I hung up the phone, went into my room and crawled under the covers. I thought and shook, shook and thought. A militia in Brookhills? Impossible. Besides, militias were sort of old hat. We had terrorists to worry about these days.

Pulling my old chenille bedspread off the bed, I wrapped it around my shoulders. "C'mon Frank, let's make sure the house is locked up." I tangled my hand in the thick fur at his neck and we made a tour of the house, my making comforting sounds like "eek!" and the occasional "oh-my-God" to keep Frank calm.

When we were done, I allowed him up on the bed and wedged myself under what was left of the covers. A hundred pounds of smelly sheepdog practically on top of me, I tried to organize my thoughts.

So what was I thinking here?

I was thinking that David might somehow have been involved with Ed. That maybe Patricia had recognized Ed in the news footage and confronted David. Maybe *that's* why she decided to divorce him. After all, according to Roger, Patricia had no intention of leaving David before that. And when David found out what she had planned, he… He what? Killed her? Or had Ed kill her? Or both of them had killed her?

No matter what, Pavlik's theory still held up. David was the killer. Or one of the killers.

I went around and round all night. I wished I knew more about militias. Weren't they wild-eyed fanatics who accused the government of bugging their homes and their dentists of bugging their teeth? Guys wearing fatigues and carrying Uzis in the north woods staging protests and chaining themselves to cars in Chicago? Could they possibly be the nice family down the street?

ANOTHER SLEEPLESS NIGHT. I jumped every time I heard a noise and Frank barely moved, which created friction between us as you might imagine.

About the time the sun was coming up, I made a decision. I would call Pavlik. I'd prefer to talk to Gary, but I wasn't about to incur Pavlik's wrath again and jeopardize Gary's career. Besides, I had to admit I wanted to see Pavlik again.

I was separated, not dead.

When I called the sheriff's number from the store later that morning, I asked his voice mail to meet me at home at seven tonight. The day dragged and so did I, from both nerves and lack of sleep. About three Henry came in, walking a little slower and stiffer than usual.

I cleared a table for him and brought over a big piece of coffee cake, cinnamon butter streusel. "Coffee or a cappuccino today, Henry?"

He folded his creaky body into the chair. "Espresso, please. A double."

"Need a little caffeine today?"

Henry took off his hat and set in on the chair next to him. "I'm still having trouble sleeping nights."

Aren't we all?

Wait a second, hold that thought.

I made the double espresso and brought it to him. Then I moved his hat, a gray felt job with a red feather, and sat down. "You told me before that the kids playing 'Cowboys and Indians' at Poplar Creek were disturbing you. Have you ever actually seen them or have you just heard them?"

Henry looked surprised. "Please join me."

Since I already had, I just thanked him and repeated the question.

He ducked his head to take a sip from the tiny espresso cup before he answered. "It's not always them yahoos that keep me up every night, sometimes it's the runs."

Lovely. I tried again. "But when they *are* down there, is it kids?"

He sighed. "Suppose so. It's too dark to see much and I have some night blindness from the war. But one thing," he raised a gnarled finger, "if it's kids, it's big ones. Not the little ones. It's ones old enough to know they shouldn't be out raising a ruckus and shooting firecrackers at eleven o'clock at night."

Kids with firecrackers?

Or a militia with guns on night maneuvers? Seemed nuts, but then there was a lot of that going around.

The bell above the door tinkled. I wasn't done with Henry, but Caron was in the back so I had to get up to wait on the newcomer. I rang up the sale and finally the customer was gone. Henry was getting up to leave, too.

"Henry," I called.

He stopped.

"The last time you told me the kids were making noise down there—do you remember what night that was?"

"Certainly," he said as he carefully placed his hat on his head. "Thursday night. It's always Thursday night."

And today was Thursday.

FINALLY, FIVE ARRIVED. I pulled off my apron, pulled on my coat and sped home. I was too tired to think about what I was doing. I just hoped it was the right thing. Or at the very least, not the wrong thing.

There was a message from Sarah on voice mail commanding me to call the moment I got home to give her an update. I ignored it for once.

I hadn't forgotten Pavlik was coming by, but I hoped to have him in and out in an hour so I could prepare for the rest of my evening. While I waited, I dug through a box of mittens and scarves in the basement and in triumph pulled out a red-trimmed navy ski mask. It would do.

The doorbell rang a little before seven and I went to the front window and peeked out. Sure enough, it was Pavlik. I must have caught him on his day off. He had on jeans with a blue sweater and a buttery leather jacket.

I dropped the ski mask on the table by the window and went to the door. I had no intention of mentioning night maneuvers to Pavlik. His eyes were a clear cool gray tonight. A good sign, I thought, and I hoped to keep them that way.

I invited him in and asked him to sit down. Frank lumbered in and settled at his feet, not even treating him like a visitor any longer. I wished I was as calm.

Pavlik gave him a scratch. "You said you needed to talk to me?" He was talking to me, presumably, even if he was paying more attention to Frank.

"I saw the film of the First National Bank robber on the news last night and I recognized him."

"I'm not surprised. He was your L'Cafe technician."

I must have gaped, because he went on. "Oh, I didn't put it together until I looked back at the tape from the first robbery again. Then I finally realized I'd seen him before."

Do you think he might have mentioned it to me? "Ed was installing the loaner when you came to the store the second time," I remembered.

Pavlik nodded. "Remember, he didn't have plates on his

truck? These guys don't believe they have to license their cars. After all, the Constitution doesn't say so. Of course, the fact that cars didn't exist at the time the Constitution was written doesn't affect their God-given right to drive one."

"Of course," I said, "and he asked for cash instead of a check."

"Cash can't be traced, obviously, or taxed."

Like the Harpers' income. My mind was racing. "So you're sure he was tied to one of these anti-government groups?"

"Domestic terrorist, really. And yes, I'm sure. The Feds had been watching him and they found plans for pipe bombs and nerve gas in his apartment printed right off the Internet. He'd been hanging out at some of the survivalist home pages on the net."

Okay, now to take it the next step. "And David and Patricia?"

Pavlik stood up and walked to the front window. "I don't know, but it's certainly possible they're part of the group. Mrs. Harper is from Chicago where the group is based."

As is Pavlik, I thought.

"And the tax evasion points to it obviously." He picked up the ski mask and dangled it off one finger. "I know this is Wisconsin, but isn't it a little warm for this?"

"It's my son's," I said, snatching it. "He's away at school and I'm sorting through the things he left behind. I must have carried it from the closet when I came over to see who was at the door."

Pavlik was just staring at me.

"When you rang the bell," I added, knowing full well I was explaining way more than what a ski mask, even in April, called for. "Now where did I put those matching gloves?" I said, looking around in an addled housewife kind of way. I figured Pavlik would buy that, given his opinion of me. I tossed the cap at the couch and turned back to him. "Oh, well, I'll find them later."

"Sure you will," Pavlik said. He looked like he was trying not to laugh.

I'd fix that. "So Ed killed Patricia."

"How do you figure that?"

"He obviously had the know-how."

"But you used the machine after he installed it," he pointed out.

"He could have come back."

"When? How would he have gotten in?"

I had been thinking about that when I wasn't babbling about ski masks. "It must have been Sunday."

Pavlik was looking at me like I was nuts, but then I was used to that.

"Tony Bruno, the dentist next door?"

He nodded.

"He spoke to Ed the day he installed the loaner. Kidded him about being back so soon."

"So? He saw him on Friday when he installed the first machine."

"No," I insisted. "He didn't. Tony's office is closed on Fridays, so he and his family can go up north. They come back before mass on Sunday. He must have seen him then."

Pavlik shook his head and pulled out his notebook. "Okay, so I'll talk to Dr. Bruno. But even if Groschek was there, it doesn't get Harper off the hook. Somebody had to let him in, and it's possible Harper was up to his ears in this stuff. *And* somebody had to get Mrs. Harper to use the machine. That could only be her husband—with or without Ed. Besides, we know Mr. Harper was there. Your friend Pete saw his car."

But I was thinking about David and Patricia's argument on Friday night. I filled Pavlik in.

"So?"

"So that was the night the first robbery took place and the surveillance video was shown on the news. Maybe Patricia recognized Ed."

"Did she give any indication that she knew him when he installed the machine?"

That stopped me short. "No. No, she didn't. Although she certainly wasn't very friendly. I just chalked it up to Patricia being a snob." Oops, speaking ill of the dead again.

Pavlik grinned.

I felt myself flush. He laughed and shoved his dang notebook and pen back in his jacket pocket. "I have to meet someone. Is there anything else?"

Yeah. Who are you meeting? But I didn't ask. After all, I had plans for tonight, too. I just said no, and walked him to the door.

As I opened it, he hesitated and looked down at me. "You stay out of this—I'll check it out. But I want to make sure you understand that implicating Groschek in Mrs. Harper's murder doesn't exonerate Mr. Harper. And," he touched my nose with his index finger, "it also doesn't mean that he didn't commit suicide."

He turned and walked down the sidewalk to a motorcycle waiting at the curb. He pulled on his helmet and roared off on his big black Harley hog. Hot damn.

TWENTY

So, DOES ONE take one's handbag when one goes surveilling?

I was willing to bet Miss Manners didn't have an answer for that one. I opted to leave the handbag at home and slid my drivers license into my pocket. That way they could identify the body.

I waited in the minivan in the driveway, ski mask in hand, and sure enough, at 11:00 p.m. the parade commenced down Poplar Creek Drive just as it had last Thursday.

Four…five…six cars, each with more than one person in it, best as I could tell. I let the last car get well past before I backed out and followed.

We were all heading downstream toward Brookhill Road. If my hunch was right, the cars would pull in….

Sure enough, the first car took a right just past Brookhill, turning off Poplar Creek Drive onto a service road. The rest of the cars followed, but I continued on, turning right at the next driveway, which led to Brookhills Senior Manor. Poplar Creek ran directly behind the Manor's back parking lot, separated by a barbed wire fence.

I slid my ignition key under the mat so I wouldn't lose it and got out of the van to look around. All was quiet. I didn't even see Henry. Pulling apart the two strands of barbed wire, I ducked through and skittered down the muddy hill toward the creek. Although I couldn't see in the dark, it sounded like it was still running high and fast.

I planted myself behind a wild honeysuckle bush and tried to pull down my ski mask. That's when I remembered I'd left it in the van. Damn. Maybe this was like lying. You got better at it, the more you did it.

I was sort of hoping I wouldn't get the chance.

I settled in to wait. And wait. Geez, how long does it take to get out of cars and walk a block or two? What were they doing? Handing out name badges? Assigning seats for the ride back? It was probably all of fifteen minutes, but it seemed a lot longer sitting there on the ground imagining field mice crawling up my pants leg. Not that I would notice, since my legs were asleep. And my butt was frozen.

Maybe this wasn't such a great idea. In fact, maybe this was really stupid.

But something was going on down here and whatever it was, I knew David had participated last Thursday because his car had passed my house. Of course, it also could have been Sam driving the Mercedes since, according to Eric, he had spent quality time at Poplar Creek, too.

But somehow I doubted kids carpooled to makeout spots. Then again, these days…

I heard a noise downstream. The wind carried the sound of underbrush crackling, of people walking towards me. Having seen enough TV shoot-em-ups to know that the good guy should never stick his head up or somebody will try to blow it off, I tried to peer through the shrub. Since the honeysuckle hadn't leafed out yet, it was fairly easy to see through. That might work both ways, I supposed.

I could barely make out several small spots of light, flashlights, maybe. And voices. Henry was right. They were awfully noisy. Either they didn't realize their voices carried, or they didn't care. I thought I recognized a couple of them—maybe Rudy's or Way's—but that was likely wishful thinking. The sounds just seemed to tumble over each other on the wind.

When the lights stopped moving, I crept out from behind the honeysuckle and made for a tree, ten yards ahead. From there, I crawled forward on my belly until I was less than a half a football field away from the group.

I had to admit I was feeling pretty cool. Like when I played army in the backyard with Danny Danielli when we were eight. I could still only see an occasional figure in the moonlight, and I strained to see what they were wearing.

After all, militias wear fatigues right? Teenagers wear…just about anything. I crept a little closer into the moon shadow of another tree. Something about the way the figures were moving made me think they were adults—and older adults at that.

Yeah, Maggy. Brookhills' senior community was out for maneuvers. Still I was certain now that these weren't kids, but men, and that they were carrying—

Pop! A splinter of wood exploded from the tree trunk next to me. Had that been a gunshot? In Danny Danielli's backyard the guns went "bang" not—

Pop!

Still, "pop" worked just fine.

Damn, someone was shooting at me. I attempted to become one with the earth—but not in the Zen kind of way—and scutter away like a crab. A hand grabbed my leg.

I almost peed in my pants. I turned and another hand went over my mouth and a body covered mine, flattening me even further into the grass and mud. I pulled at the thumb of the hand over my mouth like Gary had shown me in self-defense class, trying to break the hold. I wasn't having much success, so I sunk my nails in and tried again.

Bingo—the hand loosened and I sucked in air to scream.

My attacker shoved my face into the mud to stop me and that was when I smelled it. Mint Crest. And the arm holding me down was encased in what had been buttery leather, but was now buttery leather covered in mud.

"Will you shut up?" Pavlik snarled in my ear. I nodded the best I could and he let go of the back of my head. He didn't get off me, though.

"What the—" I started.

"Not a word," he said, and a finger waved in front of my face. I nodded again. "Just follow me. You got it?"

His face was next to mine, but I couldn't see his eyes in the dark. I was kind of glad about that.

Pavlik slid off my back and slipped behind the trunk of the tree. I followed, trying not to get panicky just because I couldn't get a lungful of air into my squished chest.

Another "pop!" or maybe it was a ping. Either way, I looked at Pavlik. Maybe *he* wasn't going to hurt me, except for my feelings, but the fact remained that somebody was shooting at us.

A ping, a definite ping, closely followed by a pop. I dove onto Pavlik, practically climbing him. Could a bullet go through both of us?

"They're going to kill us," I whimpered from somewhere in his jacket. I felt rather than saw him shake his head.

No? They weren't going to kill us? Then why bother shooting at us? Seemed sort of silly, didn't it?

I pulled back and looked at him and his eyes shifted to the tree in front of us. There was a round cardboard disk on the side away from us, the side closest to the shooters.

"What…" Pop! and the disk spun wildly. It was a target. I'd stumbled into a firing range.

Pavlik crooked his finger at me and crawled away.

I followed. When we got to the fence he separated the strands of wire and let me crawl through first, then he followed.

When he straightened up on the other side, he was pretty ticked. "What the hell did you think you were doing out there? I *knew* you were up to something when I saw that stupid ski mask."

He walked as he ranted. "Silly me, I hoped, I *hoped* that it was something as simple as a train heist. But noooo…."

I trailed after him. "I heard that people were hanging out at the creek on Thursday nights," I tried to explain, "and last week I saw a bunch of cars heading in this direction. What with all the militia talk…"

He turned and I nearly ran into him. "Didn't we just talk about this? Didn't I just tell you to let me handle it? If you had an idea, scatterbrained though it might be, you should have—"

Scatterbrained, huh? "Why would I *ever* tell you *anything,* when I know you're going to make me feel like a fool?"

Pavlik looked hurt. "I listened to your traffic light thing. And even about the possibility of Groschek sabotaging the espresso machine."

"Sure," I said as we reached my car. Pavlik's Harley was parked next to it. "But only after I had the facts to back them up. Look at the sugar packets. You said Gary and I should have told you, but *you* know," I poked him in the chest, "you would have pooh-poohed it."

He looked at his coat and then at my finger. "Pooh-poohed it?"

"Of course. Gary's a good cop, but you even have him spooked."

Maybe poking Pavlik hadn't been such a good idea. He'd noticed the mud that caked his sleeves. Lucky for him, my body had protected the rest of him.

He brushed at the mud. "Listen I'm not going to discuss this with you. Donovan's a big boy, he doesn't need someone to protect him. As for you, I'm starting to wonder."

I had pulled open my car door and was searching under the mat for my ignition key. "Wonder about what?"

"About whether you should be put away for your own protection. One minute you're a ditz, the next minute, you're coming up with something that actually makes sense."

Ditz? I was a ditz? I opened my mouth and then slapped it shut. Maybe he had a point. I had to admit I certainly wasn't operating on all cylinders these days.

"You could have been killed out there," Pavlik was saying. "These people are dangerous."

"Then why don't you arrest them?" One of my rare moments of lucidity, apparently. "They're shooting guns out there and you're the sheriff."

And they almost shot the sheriff. But they did not shoot the deputy. I giggled to myself. So much for lucidity.

Pavlik reached under the mat and came up with the key. "There's an on-going federal investigation."

I moved to take the key, but he didn't let go. "I'm not involved in it, and you're not involved in it, so let's say we just let the Feds do their jobs."

"So they must be after them for something more than gun charges, right?"

"That's all I'm going to say," Pavlik said flatly. "And truthfully, I don't know much more."

"Not that you would tell me if you did," I said, plucking my key out of his hand.

"You're damn right about that," he said, pulling on his helmet and straddling his bike. "But what I will tell you is not to say a word about this."

He shook that finger in my face again. "Not what you saw tonight, not what I told you about the investigation. Nothing. Or I will not hesitate to tell the Feds you need to be put in protective custody. And then where will your business be?"

Good question.

"One other thing," he said as he started his bike. "Next time you try to disguise yourself, you might want to change clothes. You smell like a coffee pot."

Oh.

TWENTY-ONE

THE NEXT MORNING, Sarah called me at the store in a panic. "Langdon says we can't bury David in hallowed ground, because everyone thinks it's a suicide." The Brookhills *Observer* had come out yesterday, making it exceedingly clear in its convoluted way that the authorities were considering David's death a suicide.

"But if Langdon is so sure David didn't—"

Sarah cut me off. "The man doesn't have any balls. He won't stand up to the elders. Maggy, you have to do something!"

I had to do something. I told her about my first conversation with Pavlik about Ed Groschek. I *didn't* tell her about my midnight foray into the world of espionage, marksmanship and stupidity. I didn't want to jeopardize a federal investigation or my own freedom, and I wouldn't put it past Pavlik to mess with the second if I messed with the first.

"Would it be so horrible for David to be buried somewhere else?" I asked Sarah. "After all, it looks like he was a murderer."

The sounds from the other end of the phone made it clear that it would be. I promised her I would do my best and hung up.

Pavlik notwithstanding, the first thing I had wanted to do today was to confirm my suspicions about Ed Groschek being involved in Patricia's death. Unfortunately, it was Friday and the dental office was closed, so talking to Tony Bruno about exactly when and where he had seen Ed would have to wait until Monday. I'd seen Pavlik's deputies pass by our windows earlier en route to Tony's darkened office, so I figured they had been stymied on that front, too.

So what did I do now? I didn't know, so I occupied myself with alternately serving coffee and drinking enough of it to keep me awake. I hadn't been gotten much sleep last night again.

At about eleven, Mary came in waving my tax papers. "Okay, they're done. Sign and send these in. Keep this set for your records. And if you ever wait this long again I'll let you swing in the wind."

Her voice dropped. "Can you believe it? First Patricia, then David? Who would have thought it?"

Not me, that's for sure.

"And all over that jerk Roger?" She lowered her voice even further when she saw Caron. "Honestly, the man can't keep it in his pants?"

I didn't want to think about what was in Roger's pants, but Mary saved me from answering by asking three more questions in quick succession, ending with an "I'm late—gotta run?" before rushing out the door. I hadn't had a chance to utter a single word.

Whether it was because of all the coffee I served or all the coffee I drank, by noon I felt like I was going to crawl out of my skin. Fresh air seemed to be in order, so I asked Caron to mind the store and walked toward Town Hall.

Gary was getting into a squad car in the parking lot. "I'm going over to Harpers', want to ride along?"

I said sure and hopped in. I could walk back from the house if I needed to. I'd done it before. "Going to see the kids?"

Gary turned red. "Taking Sarah the phone number for Patricia's mother."

I guess calling her with the number wasn't an option. "Maybe you should treat her to lunch as long as you're there."

Gary gave me a sidelong look, and then grinned. "Okay, it's just an excuse. So?"

I settled back into the seat happily. "So, nothing. I think it's great. *Sarah's* great."

"Yeah, well, don't start getting ideas."

"Who, me?" I shut up though. Gary and Sarah both struck me as the skittish type and I sure didn't want to spook them. We were passing Christ Christian and I occupied myself with this week's laundry list of activities on their signboard.

That's when it struck me: Christ Christian's Men's Bible Study met on Thursday night—last night—and Langdon had said that David was in charge. Could the Men's Bible Study be a cover for the group at Poplar Creek?

That sure would explain the 11:00 p.m. caravan. Church from 7:30 to 8:30. Bible Study following, probably from 9:00 until 10:30 or so. By the time you organized who was riding with who, got the name badges and the guns… Yup, it would all add up.

I looked over at Gary as he pulled into the Harper driveway and turned off the ignition. "I saw Pavlik on the news about the First National robbery," I said. "They've linked it to an anti-government group?" Pavlik couldn't fault me for that perfectly innocent question, could he?

Gary sighed and went to get out of the car. "Pastorini's not saying much. I probably pushed him too far when I asked him about the money."

"What money? From the last robbery?" I was starting to

use The Mary the Librarian Method of Conversation and Interrogation. "Wasn't it destroyed in the explosion?"

"Paper usually blows all over in an explosion. It doesn't just vaporize."

Good point, I thought, getting out of the car, too. "So what do you think happened to it?"

Gary slammed the car door. "What do I think? I think there was an accomplice they're not telling us about. I think he or she has the money and is still out there someplace."

Or maybe there was a whole churchful of accomplices. Gary started for the front door. "Hey listen," I called to his back, "I think I'll leave you to your lunch and walk back. Tell Sarah I said hello."

Gary grinned. "You're transparent, Maggy, you know that?"

"Actually, I think of myself as 'opaque'—lends just a touch of mystery. Have a good lunch." I waved goodbye and headed back down the driveway.

As I walked, I wondered whether we would ever know who had been at the creek last night or who Groschek's accomplice might be. Rudy? Langdon? Way? Roger? Would Pavlik and his "Feds" find out?

I wasn't sure I could live amongst these people without knowing for sure.

TWENTY-TWO

IT WAS SATURDAY NIGHT when Pavlik next appeared at my door. I'd just stepped out of the shower after a run when he rang my bell. Feeling fairly mellow thanks to the run, I threw on a pair of sweats and opened the door.

He was looking official with his gray car, gray suit and gray eyes. I peered past him towards the street. "What, no Harley?"

He sniffed. "What, no coffee?"

I waved him into the room, discreetly kicking my discarded running clothes under the couch. "Just sweat. We were out running."

"You and Frank?" He laughed and sat down, reaching over to pat the dog and then pulling back. "Whoa. I hope you smell better than he does."

I plopped down in the chair across from Pavlik. "I took the first shower, he's waiting for the water to heat up again. So what have you found out? Is there a connection between David and the militia?"

Pavlik held up his hands. "I thought you were going to keep quiet about that."

I looked around the room. "Unless Frank is going to squeal, I think we're safe talking here."

Pavlik didn't answer. "Listen," I said, "I have to talk to someone about this or explode. Given your little rules, like it or not, that someone has to be you." Or else why the heck are you here?

"I do need to ask you some questions."

Ah. I had a hunch he meant to ask me those questions and then escape quickly before I could get any answers myself. I had some experience in that field.

"Okay," I said agreeably, "but let me get something to drink first. I'm dying of thirst. Can I bring you something?" I stood and ticked off the options on my fingers. It was a short list. "Coke, Jolt, Diet Coke and Mountain Dew."

"Interesting selection."

"If it doesn't have caffeine, I don't own it. So what'll it be?"

Pavlik chose Coke and I went into the kitchen to get it and a can of Diet Coke for myself. As I crossed from the refrigerator to the cupboard to find glasses, a tennis ball came bouncing through, followed by a sheepdog moving at warp speed.

Pavlik was obliging Frank in his favorite game, "chase the slimy tennis ball." Frank ran headfirst into the cabinet. I gave up on the glasses and returned to the living room, almost getting flattened by him on the return trip.

"Wouldn't you just like to take him home with you?" I asked, handing Pavlik his Coke.

He tossed Frank his ball and wiped his hands off on a handkerchief. "Nah. I don't think Muffin would handle it very well."

I laughed. "Your pit bull is named Muffin?"

"Yeah, well, my daughter named her."

Now here was new information. "You have a daughter? How old?"

Pavlik pulled out his wallet. "She's ten." He showed me a picture of a serious dark-haired girl with big gray eyes.

"She has your eyes." I didn't ask what she had inherited from her mother. Or where her mother was. Then again, I didn't have to. I already knew it all from the Internet.

He tucked the picture away and returned the wallet to his back pocket. "Tracey lives with her mother most of the time, even though we have joint placement. I don't exactly keep regular hours."

"Maybe it's best that she's in one place. She's so little." It was tough for a kid to keep track of two sets of friends, two sets of clothes, two sets of toys and, often, two sets of parents.

"She has a much more stable life with Susan than I could give her. I don't even have weekends free most times. I'd just be shipping her off to baby-sitters."

"Do they live in Chicago?"

"No, Susan got a job in Milwaukee. That's why I moved up here. I couldn't ask her not to take the job and I couldn't let them move two hours away. So I came, too."

So the Chicago address for Susan had been outdated, too. I felt a twinge. "That was a big sacrifice for you, wasn't it? I mean leaving the Chicago police force to come here?"

"I thought so at the time, but it was probably the best decision of my life. I didn't realize until I got away, what my job was doing to me. Not a night went by when there weren't multiple murders, drug deals going down, gang fights, kids getting shot in the street. I just thought that was the way life was. Until I came here."

"Where we have militias," I said wryly.

"Believe me, we had that and more down there. Which brings me to my question." He set down his Coke. "We caught a break. Groschek was a computer hacker. He communicated with other members by e-mail. He trashed the messages, but some were still in his cache file. We have a list of screen names we're sifting through."

He pulled a sheet of paper out of his breast pocket and handed it to me. "Does this one mean anything to you?"

I looked at the paper: ngdseyed

"Just a bunch of letters," I said, passing it back to him. "Can't you trace it through the Internet provider? I read about some kid they tracked down through AOL, because he was making on-line threats."

Pavlik set the list on the table. "Groschek was using a remailer. Remailers are—"

"I've heard of them," I said, remembering my Internet adventure with Sarah. "But I thought you said you caught a break."

"It turns out that Groschek also enjoyed creating new computer viruses."

"That's good?"

"In a way, because it fits the profile. It seems you may have been right about him tampering with the espresso machine after all."

I didn't get it. "What does creating viruses have to do with hotwiring espresso machines?"

"Different crimes are committed by different kinds of criminals. Some are very personal crimes. You've heard, probably, that if someone is stabbed in the head and face, we look for someone they know."

I nodded.

"A bomber is on the other end of the spectrum. Bombing is a long-distance crime. He sets it and leaves. The damage is done when he's gone. Same thing with the computer viruses and, in this case, re-wiring the espresso machine."

I opened my mouth and closed it. Pavlik wasn't done.

"But, that doesn't mean David Harper wasn't involved. In fact, I'm sure he was, after talking to your friend Pete. I just don't know how deeply."

Speaking of who might be involved in what, I filled him in on my Bible Study theory.

He smiled and his eyes lit blue. "Not bad, but don't go getting paranoid. Even if people at Christ Christian are involved, most of them are probably harmless. This is just a lark for them. But any movement attracts loners who are looking for a place to belong. Somewhere to be important. Those are the people who can go off."

"Like that guy who killed those people at the abortion clinic," I said slowly. "The legitimate pro-lifers condemned the killings."

We sat for a second. Finally, Pavlik set down his Coke can and got up. "Well, thanks for the caffeine. I'll let you know if we come up with anything else."

I wondered why he was being so obliging. Frank and I dogged him to the door. "Thanks. I appreciate that." See? I could be nice, too.

Pavlik opened the door to leave. "So don't worry about anything. Just keep your mouth shut and don't do any more nosing around. These groups are like bees. Leave them alone and they'll likely leave you alone. Let the Feds get to the bottom of this."

I watched him walk down the sidewalk to his car.

Had I just been finessed? Thursday night, Pavlik said the Feds were involved and threatened me with "protective custody" if I got in the way. Then today, he took great pains to assure me the militia—if it existed at all in Brookhills—was harmless.

Then he warned me not to mess with them.

I unlocked the front door I had just locked behind Pavlik and let Frank out for his evening constitutional. I was thinking about Henry and *his* constitutional. And the militia and their constitutionally-inspired constitutional.

I wandered into the living room. What in the world was going on in Brookhills? I absently picked up the Coke can Pavlik had been drinking from and the damp paper beneath it.

As I started to crumple up the paper, I realized it was the screen name Pavlik had shown me. I tossed the can into the recycling bin in the kitchen and sat down at the desk with the paper. Summoning a Word document on my computer, I typed:

ngdseyed

I sat back and stared at it.

It was starting to seem familiar somehow, though I had no idea why. Maybe I really had seen it before, or it was reminding me subliminally of some other word. Or I'd just been staring at it for ten minutes.

I typed it again, putting a space between each letter.

n g d s e y e d

Saturday night and this is what I had been reduced to, I thought. Word puzzles. Maybe after this, I could crochet something.

Okay, stop feeling sorry for yourself. Let's try sounding it out:

"n-geds-eyed"

"n-geds"

No, how about "gods," that would make more sense with this group.

"nogged sighed"

"n-Gods-eyed"

"In Gods eyed."

"*On* God's eyed…"

I sat back in my chair. On God's side. Of course. Everybody thought God was on his or her side. Even the bad guys.

But where did deciphering the e-mail address get me? I still didn't know who it belonged to. But I was certain now that I had heard or seen "On God's Side" very recently. Maybe it really was an e-mail address I'd sent to without even realizing.

I opened my e-mail program and hit "Write" for a blank e-mail. If I'd ever sent anything to ngdseyed, I could type in the first letters and my program would automatically complete the rest, right?

I typed "n" and got my nephew Nathaniel's e-mail address. I added "g" and got…nothing.

Dang. Maybe it was case sensitive. I'd try all caps. I held down the "Shift" key and hit "Return" to go to the next line.

The e-mail disappeared.

In its place was a box that read: "Your message has been sent."

"Nooooo…" I jumped out of the chair, staring in horror at the screen. Outside, Frank picked up on my wail and started to howl in chorus. I ran to the door to let him in.

"Oh, my God," I told him, as he pushed past me to get to his water dish, "you wouldn't believe what I just did."

He turned to look at me, gave a toss of his fur and went to get his drink.

I returned to the computer. What had I done? And how had I done it? I'd switched to all caps and then hit the return key to get to the next line. The combination of the two apparently had sent the e-mail. Or had it?

I needed to check my mailbox, but I managed to accidentally hit "Stock Quote," "Doppler Radar" and "People.com" before I finally clicked "Sent Mail" dead on.

And there it was:

Sent
Date: April 13
Subject: No subject specified
E-mail Address: ngdseyed

Damn, damn, damn. Could I recall the sent message somehow? Eureka, there was an "Unsend" button. I clicked on it and was rewarded with a "You can not unsend Internet mail."

So why did they have a frickin' "Unsend" button? Talk about raising one's hopes and then—

"Mail!"

I jumped about a foot and looked at my computer screen. Sure enough. Mail.

I reached out for the mouse, and then pulled back like the thing was going to bite me. What was I afraid of? It was probably a message from Eric or maybe Sarah or, most likely, a Viagra supplier or porn-site. Any one of them would look mighty good to me right now, because—except for Eric, Sarah and the omniscient spammers—no one else had my new e-mail address, except...

I double-clicked, and there it was:

New Message
Date: April 13
Subject: No subject specified
E-mail Address: ngdseyed

It was from one of them.

"Well, so what?" I said out loud, and Frank came running from his water dish. He put his big wet muzzle on my knee, and for once I was grateful for the combination of water, drool and dog hair. "After all, they don't know who I am, any more than I know who they are."

Frank tilted his head up at me and smiled. Taking strength from his quiet courage, I double-clicked the e-mail to open it.

The message was simple:

"Who is this?"

TWENTY-THREE

AS SHOULD COME as no surprise, I didn't sleep well that night. When I woke up groggy, the clock said nine-thirty.

There was a ten-thirty service at Christ Christian. Instead of hiding in my house for the rest of my life, tempting as that had seemed at 2:00 a.m., I was going to church to confirm something and to talk to Langdon.

I invited Sarah to come with me for both cover and protection, but she had a date for brunch with Gary. Between Sarah and Gary, and Caron and Bernie, love was in the air in Brookhills. Along with bullets.

I had to admit Langdon's service was inspiring, with lots of heartfelt singing and testaments of faith from the enthusiastic crowd. During the collection Langdon reminded the congregation that God required us to tithe. For those who didn't know what "tithing" was, he explained that God expected ten percent off the top. I wondered what God did with it up there.

After the service, I hung back so I'd be the last one out of church. When I reached the door where Langdon was shaking hands, I asked if I could speak to him. He looked around like he was searching for a reason to say no, then said yes. We stood off to one side of Fellowship Hall, where church members were wolfing down doughnuts.

"Coffee?" Langdon offered, looking hopefully toward the doughnut table.

"No, thank you. Langdon, did David talk to you about Patricia's death?"

His thin lips got even thinner. "Maggy, you know I can't tell you anything that David said to me in confidence."

"Then he *did* talk to you." People turned to look at us.

Langdon held up his hands. "No, no, he didn't talk to me."

I didn't believe him and he knew it.

"Maggy." He pulled me further into the corner and looked around. "We don't hear confessions in this church. At Patricia's funeral, David simply asked to speak with me privately. We were going to meet today after church. But…" He held out his hands.

"But David died before you could."

The minister was shaking his head sadly. "He wanted to see me earlier, but my schedule just wouldn't allow it. What with six services a week, weddings, funerals. There just wasn't time." The eyes behind the thick glasses filled with tears. "Maybe if we had spoken, he wouldn't have done it."

"So, now you believe he committed suicide?" I wished everyone would make up their minds.

Langdon was ringing his hands. "Oh dear, oh dear, I don't know what to believe. The paper essentially said it was suicide." He lowered his voice to a whisper. "We can't bury him in sacred ground, you know, if he committed this horrible sin."

"Which you now believe he committed?" I asked again.

He folded his hands over his black-robed stomach. "My dear, I'm just a simple man of God. I don't have any answers."

Well, he had at least one answer, I thought, as I walked down the front drive to my car parked on the street.

David had wanted to talk. Though I hadn't realized it at the time, I'd actually heard him set up the appointment. David was speaking to Langdon just as I reached the front of the receiving line at the funeral. He didn't get a chance to keep that appointment. Why? Maybe because someone, maybe Groschek, had killed him.

And I had another answer, too.

I crossed onto the lawn, my heels sinking into the grass like they had when I'd chased down Roger at Patricia's funeral, and circled around to the front of the wooden sign.

"Christ Christian Church," I read.

And below it:

"On God's Side."

BACK HOME, I let myself into the house and went right to the kitchen, where I dug the red can of coffee out. It was nearly noon, I had a monster caffeine-deprivation headache and I really, really needed to use my head right now.

I dumped the pale, dried-out ground coffee into the filter basket, slopped in the water, pressed "on" and sat down to think.

Obviously, Christ Christian was involved. That was proven by the fact their slogan—did churches have slogans?—matched the e-mail address Groschek had been communicating with. And how stupid was *that?* Wouldn't you think that people who had masterminded at least one, and maybe two, murders could have done better?

And what *about* that second murder? David had told Langdon he needed to talk to him, and then died before he had a chance. Because Langdon or someone else in the church wanted to shut him up? But then why would Langdon have told me about the conversation at all?

Maybe David truly had killed himself, simply deciding not to wait to talk to Langdon, perhaps thinking there would be no forgiveness pending for his crime anyway.

Or was Langdon's revelation of David's attempted "pre-deathbed confession" an effort to support the theory that David was filled with remorse and therefore had simply jumped the gun—or in this case, the creek.

I felt like I was trying to think through cotton, my head one dull ache. The coffee was brewing, so I got up and took a mug from the cupboard and pulled the pot off the burner, replacing it with the mug, so the auto drip would filter directly into it. I waited until it was half full, switched the cup and pot back, and took a sip.

Awful. Not just because the coffee grounds was very old and dried out, but because the first coffee thr   the filter is always the strongest. I opened the fridge and, no big surprise, had no cream. But then why would I, when I didn't even keep good coffee at home? I pulled out a quart of skim milk, blew the dried stuff stuck to the neck of the bottle off and poured the milk into the cup.

I took another swig and grimaced. Better, but not much. I started to put the milk back into the fridge, but then checked the date: April 6. No wonder it tasted so bad. And it didn't help that it was skim. Even whole milk would be better, I thought as I poured the milk down the drain. But who drank whole milk anymore?

In fact, I'd just had to dump the entire gallon I'd bought to replace the one that had been out on the counter when Patricia had died, because it already was past its freshness date, and…

I sat down at the table.

If it weren't hurting so much, I'd wonder where my head

was. The gallon of milk on the counter the morning Patricia died was whole milk.

But Patricia drank skim lattes. David drank skim lattes. And Pavlik had said the milk spilled on the floor that morning had been skim, too. So why was the gallon of whole milk out? The only person I knew who used whole milk was...

Gary.

I thought back to his office as he dumped half a carton of whole milk into his coffee. And then added sugar.

I thought of the pot of coffee on the heating element of the brewer the morning Patricia died. Why would she have brewed coffee already, nearly an hour and a half before we opened, when we didn't keep coffee longer than a half hour max?

Because she had brewed it for someone else. Someone who drank whole milk in it and used sugar, which explained the sugar wrappers that had mistakenly led me to David. But it wasn't David.

It was Gary. But why?

I didn't know, but it was the same question David had asked that morning.

"Why, Why?" David had asked Gary as he knelt next to Patricia's body. I'd thought the question was rhetorical. A "Why would someone do this? Why would God let this happen?" kind of question. Now I wondered whether it was a very non-rhetorical, "Why did you kill her?" directed at Gary.

Maybe that was why Gary had sent Caron and me home and kept David there that morning. So he could talk him down.

I took another sip of sludge and shuddered, but not because of the coffee.

My God, what was I saying? That one of my closest friends, not to mention the town police chief, had killed Patricia?

I thought I was saying that.

So did that also mean that Gary was "ngdseyed"? I went over to the computer and checked my e-mail. Nothing but spam and, for once, I was grateful for it. But "ngdseyed" *had* e-mailed me back once and, if it was Gary, he'd find out sooner or later that it had come from my screen name, either by using his official status to check with my service provider or because someone told him.

But only Ted, Eric and Sarah knew my new e-mail address and right now—I checked the clock—right now...

Gary was having brunch with Sarah.

Sarah, who also was a member of Christ Christian.

Sarah, my Pancho.

Oh, Cisco. I had more suspicions than I knew what to do with. And who could I trust with them, except Pavlik? I picked up my phone and heard an uninterrupted dial tone, meaning Pavlik hadn't returned my earlier calls and been bounced to voice mail.

Damn. I had already left two panicky messages, one last night and one this morning. Now here I was with yet another theory. The guy was going to think I was nuts, and I wasn't so sure he was wrong.

I checked the clock yet again. Twelve-thirty. Sarah had said she and Gary were having brunch at the Country Club at noon. That meant Gary's house was empty. And I had a key, the key I kept to water his plants when he was out of town.

So why did I want to go to Gary's house? Because if Gary was "ngdseyed," he had e-mailed me from there last night. And if he had, his computer, which was identical to mine, would auto-confirm that for me.

I'M NOT A *COMPLETE* FOOL, I did leave Pavlik yet another message before I left the house, telling him where I was going. Better that he think I'm nuts, than that he knows I'm dead.

Gary's house is on Elm, a side street off the far end of Brookhill Road. The street was quiet as I parked a few houses down. I strolled up the sidewalk like I was visiting and stopped in front of the door, pretending to ring the bell just in case a neighbor was watching. Then I let myself in with the key.

Gary's computer was in the spare bedroom, so I crossed the living room into the kitchen, where he kept the jungle of plants I'd watered. The two bedrooms and bathroom were lined up along a short hallway just off the kitchen.

The computer wasn't on so I booted it up, hoping there wasn't some gadget on it that tells you the last time it was turned on. I'd never seen one, but God knows there were all sorts of things I didn't know about computers.

I looked around nervously as I waited for the computer to finish its gyrations and show me the main screen. Gary's office looked like...well, an office. Papers on the desk, bills next to the computer, books on the bookcase. No makings for bombs, or rewiring of espresso machines.

The main menu came up and I double-clicked on Gary's e-mail icon. The "Sign-on" screen came up. It asked for both screen name and password. I clicked on the arrow next to "Screen Name" and it showed me just one name: GDONOVAN.

I had expected that. I mean you wouldn't route your message through a labyrinth of remailers to hide your identity only to have it show up with your real screen name, right?

So I was prepared for "ngdseyed" not to be on the list. What I had forgotten about was that I needed a password to get into Gary's e-mail and I, obviously, didn't have one.

Although maybe…

I typed "ngdseyed" in the password square and sat back as the welcome screen came up. Well, that hadn't been real smart of him. Then again, people were creatures of habit. I still used my wedding date as my password, and that was stupid on a lot of fronts, too.

Even though I already had the confirmation I needed that Gary was "ngdseyed," I clicked on "Sent M

The message he sent back to me wasn't there. Nor was my original message under "Old Mail." In fact, there was no mail saved at all.

Hmm. I opened up a blank e-mail and typed "N" and then "O."

TED filled in.

"No Ted." Gary was standing in the doorway. "I didn't get it at first when Sarah told me. Clever, Maggy."

"Too clever" were going to be his next words, I just knew it. Probably followed by a diabolical laugh. "You're supposed to be at brunch," I said, standing up.

"I thought I saw your van and couldn't help but wonder what you were doing on the wrong end of Brookhill Road. Sarah's waiting in the car."

He smiled and shook his head. "You're a trusting fool, Maggy."

Tell me something I didn't know. "And you're a murderer, Gary." I was sure I sounded more confident than I felt, since the alternative wasn't possible.

"Only when I have no other choice." He looked rueful, but it was only surface rueful. There was no depth behind his eyes at all. No real emotion, and I didn't know why I had never noticed that before.

As for me, I was feeling all sorts of emotion: Fear. Anger. Incredible irritation at my own stupidity. And a smidgeon of hope that Pavlik would get my voice mail messages, actually listen to all of them, and get there in time. "Pavlik knows I'm here."

Gary shrugged. "Then we'd better hurry." He reached out and grabbed my arm, twisting it behind my back and forcing me to walk in front of him. I stumbled and almost fell, but he propelled me forward, out of the bedroom and down the hall.

"Sorry, boys," he said, as we entered the plant-lined kitchen, "but I can't take you with me. Maybe Sarah will water you, now that Maggy won't be able to."

The man speaks to plants. And that didn't tip me off?

"You killed Patricia with an espresso machine," I said. "What do you have in mind for me? The blender?" Sure, Maggy, give him ideas.

He laughed and I could feel him shake his head. "Don't be silly. You and I are taking a little trip."

I had a feeling my trip was going to be "littler" than his. I looked around frantically, playing for time. "Don't you need to pack? Or at least take your computer?"

"Nah, there's nothing on it that matters anymore." He pushed me across the kitchen toward the back hallway. "I'll just disappear, and I have everything I need to do that packed and waiting for me in the shed out back."

Always prepared. "Still playing the Eagle Scout, huh Gary? What a fraud you are." I imagined a duffel bag stuffed with canteen, compass, cook stove, notebook computer and Swiss army knife. It was the last one that worried me. Along with the fact he'd switched from "we" to "I."

My voice was cracking now, but I kept talking. "Pavlik was right. He said you were a lousy cop and you were. I thought it was because you were being compromised by our friendship, that I was putting you in a bad position. But you were purposely mucking things up."

He gave my arm a tug. "I couldn't very well arrest myself, could I?"

A chill ran up my spine. "Why did Patricia let you into Uncommon Grounds that morning?"

"I was driving David's car. She saw me pull into the lot and unlocked the door for me thinking I was David. Not that it would have mattered. She trusted me. I'm the police chief, as you say, and also the head of our little group at Christ Christian."

"So she made you a cup of coffee? Then what did you do, tell her to make a latte for herself?"

I felt him shrug. "I told her we needed to get ourselves something to drink and sit down and talk. Both the group and the church are patriarchal organizations, so she was used to taking direction from men. The problems only started to arise when she got ideas about running things herself. Being town chairman. Opening your little coffee place. She changed."

"And that's why you killed her?" I couldn't believe it. This wasn't Stepford, it was Salem. "You killed her for not knowing her place?"

"That was actually an accident. I only meant to scare her. A little shock therapy—"

He laughed at his own sick pun and I wanted to throw up.

"—so she would come to her senses and stay with David."

I twisted to try to see him. "She was going to divorce him?"

He gave my arm a twist in return. I gave a yipe and faced forward. "Not divorce, exactly, but she was threatening to leave him. I think she really did care for Roger Karsten, believe it or not, and when she saw Groschek on the surveillance tape, she decided she wanted out. Despite the fact that we had financed her life over the last four years, as well as her little investment in Uncommon Grounds."

The bank robberies. "You planned the First National robberies. Who better to rob a bank than the man who designed the security system?"

"No one better," Gary admitted. "Though Pastorini was making it more difficult by clamming up. I think the Feds had something to do with that."

"Pastorini was in on it?" Gary's replacement at First National had seemed a real straight arrow. But then, so had Gary.

"Nah, but he liked to talk over beers. Kept me in the loop." I felt Gary shrug. "I knew enough about the security system that when the money from the first robbery ran out, I decided it was time to hit First National again."

"But you botched the attempt when Groschek was caught on tape." I was rewarded with another arm twist.

"The first robbery—not counting our robbery, the one while I was still at First National—was a practice run. Midwest Bank, a diversion. The third was the real payoff."

"Except Groschek was killed, just like the bomber in 'our' robbery. How successful could it have been?"

"As successful as that one. After all those years of protecting other people. Protecting their money. Now I have the money," Gary said cheerfully, "and one fewer person to share it with—or to talk."

"Is that why you killed David?" The wall clock next to a Boston ivy said one. Where was Pavlik? Didn't he *ever* check his voice mail?

Gary started to push me toward the back door and the tool

shed. "David wasn't too bright," Gary was saying, "but after Patricia's death, he finally put two and two together. Even accused me of getting rid of his brother."

I dug in my heels and stopped our forward movement. "Wait. His brother? Who is David's brother?"

Gary stopped shoving and I got the feeling he actually wanted to tell me this part. "The man killed in the original First National robbery, of course. Patricia's husband."

I wanted to get this straight. "Patricia's first husband was the unidentified robber who was killed? So she turned around and married his brother, who she then wanted to divorce? For Roger?" And I thought I had a headache before. But it explained why Sam and Courtney were always referred to as "the Harper kids," didn't it? Their last name *was* Harper, since their stepfather was also their uncle.

"Patricia and David couldn't get a divorce." Gary was propelling me forward again, and my go-to-church high-heels were sliding on the wood floor of the back hallway. "They were never married. I just brought Patricia and the kids here to live, so David could take care of them." He laughed. "I have to say it worked out great, though."

Yeah, until you killed them. "So Christ Christian is part of all this?"

"Langdon Shepherd's flock? They mean well, but they're a bunch of fools toying at being subversives by evading taxes and playing in the woods." We hit an area rug and Gary gave me a hard shove, succeeding only in getting my heels more tangled up in it.

I thought I had the picture now, for all the good it would do me. "But they provided good cover for you, didn't they?"

He pulled me back away from the rug. "A lot of cash passes

through that church, Maggy. More than you would think. It made laundering—"

As he leaned down to untangle the rug, I raised my knee sharply and caught him square in the nose. Then I stepped back and stomped my heel into the top of his instep, just like he'd taught me in self-defense.

When he let go, yowling in pain, I made for the door. Slipping off the chain lock, I yanked it open.

Behind it stood, not Pavlik this time, but Sarah.

And she had a gun.

"I told you never to trust anyone, Maggy," she said as she raised it.

TWENTY-FOUR

SARAH. OF COURSE.

She was a member of Christ Christian.

Even had a collection of guns in her house.

"Don't move," she said, waving one of them.

"Listen, Sarah," I said, raising my hands. "Don't do anything stupid."

"Stupid?" Her face crinkled up in a grimace, leaving just her teeth hanging out. "*I'm* not supposed to do anything stupid? I told you, you can't trust anyone but yourself."

And sometimes not even that. My instincts obviously sucked bigtime. We were more Superman and Lex Luther than we were Pancho and Cisco, or Archie and Nero. "But I…"

"Don't move!"

I glanced at each of my hands. Yup, still in the air. "Umm, I didn't move."

She waved the gun again. "I'm talking to him, you idiot."

I turned to see Gary about three feet behind me, hands raised in the air, too, like he was my shadow. I was just in time to see his face change from the "Reassuring Gary," he'd probably hoped to bluff Sarah with, to "Really Scary Gary," and then back again. All in the blink of an eye. And I'd thought *Pavlik* was schizophrenic.

"You're talking to him?" I asked Sarah, just to make sure.

She rolled her eyes. "Will you *please* snap out of it and call 911?"

Shades of Caron and me when we found Patricia's body, except this time *I* was the one who was being dense. Maybe I should have cut Caron more slack.

"Now!" Sarah demanded.

Yeah, I definitely should have cut her more slack.

THREE WEEKS LATER on a Friday, I testified at the preliminary hearing. Gary sat at the defense table, wearing a tweed sports coat, white shirt and tie. I'm sure he looked perfectly normal to everyone else. I could feel his eyes on me the whole time, but I didn't look at him. I couldn't.

He reminded me of one of those figure/foreground optical illusions from Psych 101. The one that looks like two pretty ladies in feathers until, literally in the blink of the eye, you realize it's a picture of an old hag.

And after you've seen the hag, it's almost impossible to turn the picture back to what it was, to see the pretty ladies again. I didn't know that I could ever look at Gary and see the man I used to see.

Sarah also had testified and we drove back to her house together afterwards. She, Sam and Courtney had moved back there when the bank started foreclosure on the Harpers' house. There were legal issues to address, but for now it looked like the kids were going to be able to stay with Sarah.

I drove and she stared out the window. "Are Sam and Courtney okay?" I asked.

"I'm getting them that counseling you suggested," she said absently. "They've been living a lie for so long." She shook her head.

Sam and Courtney had apparently known that David was their uncle, not their father, but had been told to keep it a secret or the government would take them away from Patricia. No wonder Eric had said Sam was quiet.

"And are *you* okay?" I asked next.

She didn't answer right away and we both sat silently as we passed by Christ Christian. Since Gary's arrest had hit the papers, the militia had either fallen apart or gone underground. We'd probably never know exactly who they all were and I really didn't care. They had been duped by Gary, just like I had. And like Sarah had. And Patricia. And David.

I rolled down the window and stuck my arm out. We were passing Christ Christian's cemetery. David had finally been buried there next to Patricia. When Eric was small, he swore if you didn't hold your breath when you passed a graveyard, the spirits of the dead people could enter you. Ted would slow down in front of cemeteries just to tease him.

I sucked in the spring air and let it out. "I appreciate what you did, Sarah." I glanced over. "Though I have to admit, I still don't understand why you took a gun to brunch."

She shrugged. "I was responsible for two kids whose parents both had been killed. I figured carrying a gun in my purse was only…" she hesitated, looking for the right word, "prudent."

I sure wasn't going to second-guess her instincts. I tried to imagine her scrabbling through the purse, pushing aside her cigarettes and lighter before finally coming up with the gun and circling around to the back door. "Did you suspect Gary from the beginning?" I asked.

She didn't look at me. "I had no idea he was involved until we saw you driving toward his house on our way to brunch.

You should have seen the look on his face. It was as if his mask had slipped."

Like my optical illusion. Neither Sarah nor I would ever see the "old Gary" again. "Listen," I said, "I know you were starting to care about—"

She laughed. "C'mon, Maggy. We both know he was sniffing around me in order to keep track of us and make sure the kids stayed in line. When I think of all the deceptions— even the little ones, like stealing the ballot to throw Pavlik off, and trying to pin Patricia's murder on poor David with those papers he 'found.'"

"Not to mention the big stuff," I added, "like killing Patricia in the first place and luring David to Poplar Creek when he realized he might talk. Even Groschek," I mused. "Gary took the loot from the robbery and then left him to plant a bomb that was set to go off a full minute earlier than Groschek thought it was."

"What a bottom feeder." Sarah shook her head. "I just thank God I didn't sleep with the man."

Sarah's mind worked in mysterious ways. "Were you thinking of…"

"None of your goddamn business." She lighted a cigarette. "So what about you? I know Gary was a good friend."

I turned the corner. "Gary was a fraud."

Sarah wisely left it at that. "I was thinking. Since Patricia wasn't married to David, she and Roger weren't really having an affair."

I looked over. "You're right. They were dating."

She smiled, her big ol' teeth hanging out. "So have you seen Pavlik outside the courtroom?"

I sighed. "I saw him at a meeting in his office. That's it."

"A goddamned shame." She knocked an ash off on the side mirror of my van. "I thought you two had something going there."

"Then you thought wrong."

Pavlik had finally picked up my voice mails and shown up at Gary's just after Sarah. He'd seemed more than a little irritated with me and, once I had agreed to testify, had turned me over to the assistant DA and washed his hands of me.

Sad? Yeah. Bitter? Maybe. Stupid? You bet.

I'd taken to running as a substitute for sex, which apparently was another thing Ted had gotten custody of. I was up to four miles a day and Frank was a lean, mean sheepdog machine.

I DROPPED SARAH OFF and was home a little after five. After letting Frank out, I sat down at the kitchen table.

Gary would go to trial on murder charges. I didn't know if the DA could prove he'd killed David, but with my testimony and independent evidence—including the contents of both his computer and the tool shed behind his house— they certainly had him on Patricia's murder, as well as Groschek's.

For my part, I felt betrayed. And stupid. Why hadn't I seen it coming?

I got up to turn on the kitchen lights and let Frank in the back door. There was a knock at the front. My heart thudded, as had been its habit the last three weeks. I moved the curtain and saw a big black Harley on the street. And there was a Pavlik at my door.

I opened it. He had on jeans and his soft leather jacket. He grabbed my hand. "Come for a ride with me."

You betcha. Then I hesitated, looking down at my long jacket and short skirt. "Let me change."

He tugged on my hand again. "No, now." His eyes seemed brilliant blue, the bluest I'd ever seen them.

I nodded, mesmerized.

He pulled the door closed and handed me a helmet.

"Do you think—" I started.

He stepped in close, his body almost touching mine, and put his finger on my lips. "Let's just take a ride."

He swung onto the bike. I got on behind him and wrapped my arms around his waist. Luckily, the long jacket covered the fact my skirt was practically around *my* waist. We were off, the roar of the Harley throbbing around us, obliterating everything else. I buried my face in the buttery leather of his jacket and just hung on.

Eventually we stopped. I lifted my head. We were on a hill outside town. To one side of us were the lightly sprinkled lights of little Brookhills, to the other, the dense lights of the city. We got off the bike and walked to the city side.

"Brookhills isn't the only place to live, Maggy," Pavlik said softly. "There are lots of wonderful places out there."

He turned to face me. "Donovan is going to trial and I know it's not going to be easy on you."

I shivered and Pavlik put his arm around me, drawing me in close to him.

I liked it.

My hair made whish-whish sounds on his jacket as I nodded. "I know. But, my friends are here. My business is here." Or what was left of either of them.

He pulled me in tighter. "I don't think you're in any physical danger. It's just going to be the talk, the media."

I pushed back a little and smiled up at him. "I think I can handle Kate McNamara. Is that what you brought me up here to talk about, Sheriff?"

He laughed. "The name is Jake. And no, that's not what I brought you up here for."

Praise the Lord, and pass the ammunition.